# THE BLUE OCEAN'S PEACE

ISBN: 978-0-9821223-0-3
Library of Congress Control Number: 2009929135
Published by Global Authors Publications

*Filling the GAP in publishing*

Edited by Barbara Sachs Sloan
Interior Design by KathleenWalls
Cover Design by Kathleen Walls

Printed in USA for Global Authors Publications

# THE BLUE OCEAN'S PEACE

WALTER P. HONSINGER

AKNOWLEDGEMENT:

Thanks to Esther Kachel who encourages me to write.

## WALID

Walid Hattab sat with Orman Negev, a nuclear physicist. "Orman you could build a nuclear bomb, couldn't you?" Walid asked.

"It's possible, but I need to know the purpose."

"Suppose by terrifying the Americans, we freed Mecca so our Imams could rule the world?"

"It depends on what you want," Orman said.

"A nuclear bomb," Walid said.

"Yes, a nuclear bomb, but does the size and type matter? If you want to terrorize the Americans, then the bomb can be as small as a book and would have the Americans shaking in their boots," Orman said.

"The destruction?" Walid asked.

"Massive. It would kill, or terribly sicken, everyone in a complex of buildings or a localized area. The press reports of a nuclear bomb being detonated will cause fear unlike anyone has ever seen … mass panic."

"Could you build such a bomb?" Walid asked.

"The Russians, Africans, Iranians and Koreans all have what we would need. It's really just a question of money, technology and …," Orman said.

"What?" Walid asked.

"Time."

## THE FLIGHT

A group of Russian college girls waited in the Moscow Airport for their plane to arrive. Hotels in Ocean City, Maryland had hired the girls for the summer. The charter flight was delayed due to bad weather. Liana Yeglov sat off to the side.

"Can someone help me with my luggage?" Margrite asked, struggling with three suitcases. Liana got up, lifted her heavy suitcase, and carried it to the counter.

"You're stronger than you look!" Margrite said. "Liana you're the tiniest one here. I wish I had your pixie figure. Do you practice ballet?"

"No."

"With your blond hair and blue eyes, boys will be chasing you up and down the beach!" Margrite said.

"I'll outrun them," Liana said.

"I won't even try to!" she explained.

Liana remembered Margrite being hired before her. The hotel flyer explained that the pay was excellent and room and board was included.

"Candidates must be fluent in English, have good grades and be willing to work for four months," the flyer stated. It didn't mention that the hotels chose the prettiest girls. She, and hundreds of other college girls, had waited to be interviewed. They called Margrite first.

"Liana Yeglov?" a man called a few minutes later. They escorted her to an interview room. A man sat at a desk, and his assistant sat nearby.

"Your resume says you're fluent in English," the man said.

"Yes," she replied. "Also Polish, German …."

"Your grades are excellent, but we need strong girls who can carry and lift things," the assistant said.

"I could lift and carry you if I wished," she teased the assistant.

"She is not only fluent in English but strong. Hire her," the supervisor instructed.

Now she waited in the airport for her flight to arrive.

"VTO flight 1716, Moscow to Baltimore, Maryland, is now loading at Gate 72A," a voice called.

"Liana, we're really going," Margrite said.

"I dread flying," Liana said. "I usually keep my eyes shut until we land."

"It's a long flight, so you may as well sleep," Margrite said.

Twelve hours later Liana woke up to chatter in the plane.

"We will be landing in Baltimore in a few moments. Return to your seats and fasten your safety belts," the pilot called over the intercom. She gritted her teeth when the plane touched down.

*I'm finally on the ground again.*

Liana worked as a hotel maid. She found the hotels also hired Belarus, Polish and Ukrainian crews. Being fluent in many languages, she often translated among the groups.

After work one evening she decided to take a stroll on the boardwalk. The cries of seagulls filled the air as children threw french fries to them. The smell of the salt water and the aroma of food cooking filled her senses. What she enjoyed most of all was seeing so many children laughing, playing and building sand castles. She sat down at a bench and stared out at the deep blue ocean. She did not notice that a boy had come up to her.

"Are you doing anything tonight?" he asked.

"I am sorry, I do not understand."

"Are you doing anything tonight?"

"I am watching the ocean...."

"Would you like to go to a movie?"

"Are you asking me out on a date?"

"Yes."

She stared at the boy for a moment. He was probably in his second or third year of college. He seemed nice enough and was cute, but she couldn't believe he had been forward enough to ask her out.

"No, I don't go out on dates."

"Do you mind if I sit down?"

"Go ahead, but please be quiet, I'm trying to relax." The two sat in silence watching the activity on the beach. She went to leave and the boy stood up.

"Can I see you again?"

"No!" she said and walked off into the crowd. Liana had few encounters with Americans and realized that she knew nothing of the culture. The exchange had not gone well, and she needed to do better. She found him about a hundred feet down the boardwalk.

"I go to the library on Thursdays. Do you like books?" she asked.

"I love to read. What's your name?"

"Liana," she answered and disappeared into the crowd.

***

It had been a long day and she fell asleep while reading. She began having a nightmare, calling out and thrashing around in her chair.

"Liana! Liana! Are you all right?" she heard Margrite call through the door. She awoke, straightened her robe, and opened the door.

"I heard you screaming! Are you okay?" Margrite asked.

"I am fine. I had a nightmare," Liana explained.

"You scared me silly!" Margrite explained.

"I'm sorry," Liana said.

"Have you been sleeping okay? You look exhausted?" Margrite asked.

"It was just a nightmare."

"Liana, any time you want to talk I'm here, okay?" Margrite asked.

"No, I'm okay," Liana explained, shutting the door.

*Talk to her and tell her that I somehow survived endless years of combat where everyone else died? Tell her I shot and killed Russian boys just like those at school? Tell her I was reliving hiding in a rock crevice during an artillery barrage?*

*What do I tell Margrite? Do I explain that I'm not a Russian Christian but a Chechen Muslim, a pawn in a cruel and deadly game? To her and the rest of the world I'm a terrorist! What could I possibly tell her?*

## LIANA

Liana, a Chechen Muslim, grew up in southern Russia and lived with her mother, Sarena, and her grandfather, Aslan. Her father, Aslan's son, was dead. Her grandfather, a hero of the Red Army, was a sniper in the battle of Stalingrad. Sarena worked as a nurse at the local hospital but also tutored students in her free time.

Liana learned Russian culture, not strict Muslim teaching. Family gatherings included dancing and singing, which many Muslim cultures would consider forbidden. Sarena taught her all the languages she knew from birth, including Arabic.

"You need to know Arabic to correctly understand the Koran," her mother explained. "Always remember we are a kind and loving people. We have always sheltered everyone around us, even if it meant our death. We will have to decide soon whether to help our relatives in Chechnya."

"We do not need to get involved in it!" Aslan warned.

"Chechnya is going to break away from the Soviet Union. We're Chechens. We must go help," Sarena insisted. "I pray it will become an independent nation."

"There will certainly be war and fighting, and you cannot imagine how terrible it might be. I remember the hopelessness, the hunger, death...," Aslan said.

"At Stalingrad you and a small group of men held off eighty thousand Nazis and won. You could help the fighters in Chechnya."

"Sarena, I'm seventy-two years old and you want me to lead men into battle?"

"You could train them to be great fighters!" Sarena felt troubled about going to Chechnya, but considered it her duty. They sold their home, gathered what money they could, and left Russia. They moved to a small cottage north of Grozny, the capital.

"Liana, I have raised you in a Russian culture and I am proud of all you have learned, but please never forget that in your heart you are Chechen," Sarena said.

"Momma, the girls here don't like me, and the boys won't even talk to me."

"Liana, I think fighting will break out soon, and you must realize you are Chechen, not Russian. Your grandfather has trained the local militia in the methods the Red Army uses in battle."

"I know Momma. I rub his back and feet at night. He's too old for this...."

"Since your grandfather's a hero of the Red Army, he is also trying to negotiate with the Russians, but it's not going well."

*Momma doesn't know that I've been training along with Grandpa's men. He taught me how to shoot as a child, and now I know how to hide, shoot and think like a sniper.*

Two weeks later talks broke down completely, and the Russians sent troops into Chechnya to stop the independence movement. Everyone prepared for a long brutal war.

"I will now be fighting against an army I loved, containing the sons of men I fought shoulder to shoulder with!" Aslan cried to Sarena.

"We're Chechen. We must protect our own people," she said. "The Russian troops are raw recruits and conscripts pardoned from prison. They will run when you attack them."

"Yes, they will run, and many will be slaughtered, theirs and ours, but in the end they will attack with might!" Aslan warned.

A bloody war of hit-and-run tactics began with Chechen militia attacking Russian convoys and surprise retaliatory raids by the Russians.

"Liana your skill with a rifle is unbelievable," a militia officer stated one day. "Could you join us tomorrow?"

"Yes, I'll pull fatigues over my school uniform after I leave home," she explained. Accurate up to six hundred meters, she shot Russian soldiers with abandon.

*Every Russian soldier that dies is one less that could kill Grandpa. He taught me to shoot and scoot. I need to find a vantage point and a route to flee. By the time the sound of my seventh shot reaches the Russians, I will be gone and they will find nothing.*

Liana kept up her schoolwork during this time and seemed to be living a normal life. One day, while reading, the door of her home burst open and three Russian soldiers entered.

"We know you've been firing on our men, and we're going to find your rifle!"

Sarena, struck with a rifle butt, arose with blood dripping from her head. The Russians tore the cottage apart but found nothing.

"Test her hands. We will find if you've been firing a gun or not!" The soldiers swabbed Sarena's hands with a solution. If the solution turned red, it meant that she had recently fired a rifle. The solution did not change color. One of the soldiers struck her very hard, and they left.

"Momma, are you okay?" Liana screamed, running forward. "It's me they wanted. I'm the one who's been killing them. I've been using my rifle, it's hidden in the woods."

"Liana, you're Chechen. You should help your own people," Sarena explained.

"Momma, the Russian boys I shoot look exactly like those I danced with in grade school!" Liana said.

"I know it is hard, but they are here to kill us, and we must endure," Sarena explained.

By autumn burned-out Russian tanks and military vehicles clogged the roads. The Russian conscripts were demoralized. They retreated toward Russia.

"Aslan, they are beaten. Now you can help negotiate a great peace."

"Sarena, they gave up too quickly. Russian pride does not give way that easily."

"Aslan, we've won, you should be proud."

"Sarena, Chechnya has oil reserves, the devils dung. They will be back to claim it, and we have little time left. When they attack again they will do so with vengeance as their pride is hurt."

"No one in Russia wishes to fight us. They will not return. You need to rest and not worry."

## THE LIBRARY

On Thursday Liana went to the local library. "Liana, how are you!" She looked up to see the boy she had met on the boardwalk.

"By the way, my name is Tim." She stared at the boy for a moment, unsure of what to do or say.

"I am fine. Did I say that correctly?"

"Yes," he said.

"Get a book then," she said, and he began searching the racks. He settled upon Dafoe's "Robinson Crusoe," since she was reading "Moby Dick."

*I feel so strange having Tim sitting next to me! Why couldn't I have grown up like any other girl? What do I do? And I'm sitting next to an American boy? I must be careful.*

"Liana, just relax and let things flow. I don't bite," Tim said.

"I do," she said, not really thinking. The thought that she might actually bite him amused her; she started giggling and then quietly laughing.

"Miss, you must be quiet in the library or I'll have to ask you to leave," the librarian said. Liana relaxed and found herself quietly reading elbow to elbow with Tim.

She finished three chapters of her book and had to be at work soon. She closed her book and went to leave.

"Liana, are you leaving?" Tim asked. "At least let me walk you home."

*Why does he need to walk me home? I know the way, and I feel safe.*

"No, I'm fine," Liana said. *Why does he look hurt? I should know what to do! Why did I have to miss this part of my life?* "Okay," she said quietly, "please tell me about yourself as we walk."

"I'm in my third year at Temple University, and I'm studying business," Tim said. "I spend the summers here. Tell me about where you grew up?"

"Russia is so different from here that I really can't explain; let's just say I am happy to be here." She was at her hotel now and went to walk in.

"Liana?" As she turned, Tim plastered a kiss on her lips. Stunned, she stared at him.

"Why did you do that? Is this expected?"

"Expected?" he asked.

"Is this normal?"

"I usually kiss all my friends goodbye." She wasn't sure he was being honest with her.

"All?"

"What do you do when you leave someone?" he asked. Liana thought a moment because she still wasn't sure if she should trust Tim or just run.

"We do this only for those we love and care for. Please don't do that again."

"Liana, when can I see you again?"

"The library on Tuesday, and do not forget your manners this time." Tim went to walk away and seemed dejected.

*I need to know how to do this; I'm handling this badly!*

"Tim, if I meet a relative or respected friend, the greeting I would give them is this." She gave him a quick hug and kiss with her cheek pressed against his. He seemed to brighten up and left.

*Tim could mean trouble but I need American friends to acclimate into their society. I can't let him dig too deep into my past. I have beds to make. I better get to work.*

"Liana, we saw your boyfriend. He is so cute!" Margrite said.

"He's not my boyfriend. We just met at the library and he walked me home."

"If he's not your boyfriend, then send him my way!" another girl called, and they all began giggling. Liana didn't know what to make of the girl's comments, as she had not really thought of him as a possible boyfriend.

*If I do not date Tim, will the other girls take him?* She concentrated on her work even though they were still giggling.

***

Liana's days fell into a pattern of working ten-hour shifts, walking on the boardwalk, and going to the library.

*I love going to the boardwalk and watching the children play on the beach. Seeing children building sandcastles and playing in the surf is so nice. I love watching the families spend time together.*

Liana returned to the library on Tuesday, and Tim was waiting for her when she came in.

"Liana, how are you?"

"I am fine," she replied.

"Would you like to go to the Smithsonian with me sometime?"

*I've dreamed of visiting the Smithsonian museum since I was a child, and now it could be possible.*

"I have work to do," she said.

"You have days off."

*This is moving too fast.*

"Tim, how about if I say yes, but not now?"

"Okay."

*I like having the warmth of Tim next to me. It reminds me of sitting next to Momma.*

They quietly read for almost two hours.

"Will you have lunch with me?" Tim asked.

"I don't eat American food."

"American food? What do you eat?"

"I eat fruit, vegetables, soup…."

"What do you think I eat?"

"Candy, fudge, pizza, pretzels … buckets of french fries," she said.

"Why would you think I would eat those?"

"The boardwalk …," she said.

"The boardwalk?" *The only American food she knows is from the boardwalk.* "Liana, let's go to the supermarket. I'll drive."

"Supermarket?" she asked.

"Where I shop for food?" he said.

*On TV they show what happens to girls when they get into cars here, but I need a laptop computer with wireless Internet ….*

"I really do not bite," he said.

They got into his car, an older Volkswagen.

"Tim, is there a shop where I could buy a used laptop computer, one with wireless Internet?" she asked.

"I know a pawn shop that sells them," he said. "We'll stop on the way."

He took her into the shop, and a disheveled looking man came from in back.

"Can I help you?" he asked, looking her up and down.

"She was interested in an inexpensive laptop, one with wireless?" Tim said.

The man produced one from under the counter.

"You can have this one, today only, for a hundred dollars," the man said.

"The modem picks up wireless Internet?" Liana asked.

"I'll show you the signal strength I have in the store," the man said. She bought the laptop, and they walked back to Tim's car.

"What did he mean by 'today only'?" she asked.

"I think he meant the computer was stolen," Tim said. "Let's not worry about it." He drove out of town and ended up at a Food Lion, the first supermarket Liana ever entered.

"This is a market?" she asked incredulously.

When they entered the produce section, Liana stopped in her tracks. *So much fresh produce ….*

"A pineapple!" she said picking up the fruit. "I've seen pictures of them but never had one."

"We'll buy one then," Tim said putting it in his cart.

"Beets! We could make borscht," she said. I *remember making borscht for the Russian troops as my mother was ....*

"Liana, are you okay?"

"I am fine. Please move on." They walked through canyons of canned goods. She passed refrigerated sections of every type of meat and displays of dairy items. She saw young mothers pushing shopping carts filled with groceries.

*I remember Momma and me waiting forever in line at the state-run market. We would finally enter, and the shelves would be almost bare ....*

"Tim, instead of borscht I could make a tomato and cucumber soup for you at my hotel."

"Please, can't we make it at my apartment?" he asked. She thought for a moment.

"Tim, not yet, okay?"

"Okay."

Later they entered the small kitchen the employees used.

"Tim, help me slice the cucumbers and tomatoes?" He did so, and then they sat to eat.

"I love this soup! It's light but very flavorful," Tim said. "It's different from anything else I've tasted."

"I must start work soon," Liana told him.

*Should I try to kiss her good-bye or just leave?*

"Can I kiss you goodbye?" he asked.

"No!" He looked hurt.

"Tim, you did better the last time. You just did it."

"You asked me not to do it again ...." She looked at him, giggled and walked away.

*I think I'm learning how this works. At least I feel at ease with Tim now.*

***

Liana woke up in the middle of the night and felt like a total fool. I*'m beginning to fall in love with that boy. How stupid can I get? I'm on a mission and must do as I'm told!*

She got up, found her laptop computer, and got dressed. She rode on a bus a few miles north to the Delaware beaches. She noticed a hotel with a bench out front. She opened her laptop computer and saw, as she expected, that the hotel had wireless Internet. She felt safe here and brought up a Polish gaming site.

*No messages from Walid. I wonder if my computer is working right? Perhaps a guest at the hotel would know how to fix it?*

As Liana sat outside the hotel, several carloads of boys stopped to ask if she needed a ride.

"Leave me alone. I do not need a ride," she stated. *Another car's stopped. How many times do I have to explain to these boys that I don't need a ride!*

*Great, I crossed the street to wait for the next bus back into Maryland and the boys in the car are coming back! When will the bus get here?*

They drove past her, stopped and turned around.

*I better get to close to a hotel! Here they come again!* The car sped up. Liana saw other boys approaching her on foot. *Great! Now the idiots are between the hotel and me. I'm not afraid of these fools; I'll deal with them as they come at me.* She turned to face them.

*Now what? Someone is blasting a car's horn!* She heard a scuffle behind her, followed by cursing and shouts. A moment later a car cut her off and Tim appeared.

"Liana, get in!" She jumped into his car and saw he had a bloody nose and a goose egg forming on his forehead. He took off driving south toward Maryland.

"Are you okay? I was driving home from a party, and I found a group of guys chasing you!" he said.

"Tim, you're bleeding!"

"Those guys were chasing you! What were you doing in Delaware?"

"I was waiting for the bus, and the boys began bothering me. Stop at that store, and let me get some ice," Liana said. He pulled over to a convenience store, and she got a cup of ice from the soda fountain. She wrapped the ice in a paper napkin and held it against his forehead. She used the damp towel to wash off his face. A few minutes later they were back in Ocean City.

"Will you come back to my apartment for breakfast?"

"I must get some sleep. I start work at noon. I just need to rest until I start work." She got out of his car and went to leave, and he got out of the car to say good-bye. As he got close she held up her hand.

"Liana, I was going to stop by anyway. I'm flying out to Las Vegas to meet some friends. I'll be gone a week."

"Friends?"

"A bunch of computer geeks. We get together occasionally to trade software and play games. I just wanted a kiss good-bye."

"Tim, not now …." He turned and walked back to his car. She ran back to his car, slid in and wrapped her arms around him. Liana hugged Tim tightly for a minute and then kissed him.

"Tim, thank you." She went into her hotel.

*He thought I was afraid of the boys in the car? He really doesn't even know what fear is ... the killing, the artillery blasts, the soldiers interrogating the wounded ....*

She drifted off to sleep and relived the second Chechen invasion.

## THE SECOND CHECHEN INVASION

"Grandpa, I heard attack helicopters flying overhead. The Russians have come back!" Liana said, as she woke him up.

Aslan was seventy-six years old and still fit enough to lead men, but did not relish the task. He heard the explosion of bombs and the feeble return fire of a few AK-47s. He gathered his things and stopped to say good-bye to Sarena.

"If we can hold Grozny, perhaps we can get the Russians to return to peace talks," Aslan said.

"You held Stalingrad against eighty thousand Nazis, I think you can hold Grozny against the Russians. I hope to see you soon," Sarena explained.

"I don't think I'm coming back. I think the Russians are serious this time."

"Aslan, there are burnt-out Russian tanks on the road. They have been here before and left. They will leave again."

He hugged her goodbye and quickly left.

"Momma, he will be alone and I won't be there for him!" Liana said. She noticed her mother brushing her long brown hair, contemplating what to do. *My mother is the most beautiful woman I have ever known ....*

Sarena was a woman of inner strength. Always optimistic, she believed better days were ahead. She always tried to instill confidence and hope in Liana.

"Liana, we must flee the village before the Russians arrive," Sarena called out. The clothes Liana had been wearing were on the floor, but she was gone.

A few miles from their cottage lay the road into Grozny, and a convoy of Russian vehicles was approaching. Liana lay hidden in a small hole.

*I must slow down the convoy so Grandpa can gather his men. Who are all these fighters in the woods? What groups are they with? Chechnya is full of militias, some pro Russian, some fighting for an independent Chechnya. I've got to stop shaking; I'll never be able to shoot.*

A Russian convoy of ten vehicles came up the road, and an attack helicopter flew overhead. The second vehicle in the convoy exploded, causing the remaining vehicles to swerve off the road.

Liana, still hidden, was badly jolted when the first Russian vehicle exploded. The next moment the trees around her exploded as the hidden men opened fire.

*I need to find a target. That truck radiator five hundred meters away, I'll shoot at each vehicle and then flee like Grandpa taught me.*

She fired, and antifreeze spewed out of the radiator. She quickly shot off six more rounds into the engines and radiators of the Russian military vehicles. In between her fifth and sixth shot she saw the attack helicopter swerve and fire missiles into the woods around her. The militia forces in the woods began screaming as shrapnel struck them.

*The helicopter is spraying the woods with machine gun fire, and it seems as thick as rain. I need to crawl deeper into the crevice and pull a rock over the opening. Please make it stop. Get me out of this. Please let me get out of this! The helicopter's coming back again! Why aren't the Russians retreating like they always did! What was it that Grandpa said, "I think they're serious this time ...." This is the real Red Army, not conscripts like before. Please don't let them catch me! Let me die quickly!*

Liana heard soldiers talking as they walked through the woods shooting wounded Chechen militia and dragging off others for interrogation. She lay hidden and twice-heard footsteps at her head as Russian soldiers walked past. She lay in the hole and heard the screams of wounded Chechen militiamen being interrogated.

*If the Russians come close again, I'll shoot myself.*

Very late that evening she slipped out of the hole and headed home. When she crossed the ridge, she smelled smoke and saw that her village was on fire. She found four dead men and a woman weeping near them.

"What happened?" Liana asked.

"Russian Special Forces came for Aslan, but no one would say where he was. They hung one man after another, but no one would talk. They left about two hours ago."

She ran down to her cottage looking for her mother. She found her sitting outside, staring at the ground.

"Liana, you're safe! We've been praying that you weren't taken away with the other girls!"

"The other girls?"

"The Russians forced all them all into trucks!"

*The girls will be used worse than prostitutes.*

Liana could not believe what had happened to her village, as all seemed lost.

"We must flee before the Russians return!" Sarena said.

"Where will we go?"

"We will have to sneak into Grozny and somehow find Aslan and his men."

*If I hadn't fought today, I'd be on the trucks with the other girls ... the will of Allah.*

"Please, Momma, let's leave now."

## CATHLEEN HALE

Cathleen worked as an analyst at the CIA and spent her days translating Arabic documents. She lived in Georgetown, Maryland, and enjoyed the shows and events.

Several years ago James Burrett, a friend of Cathleen's, had suggested Cathleen use her skills at the CIA, where he worked. He promised he'd assist her at the agency, as her first few years would be difficult.

"Jim, every day I get an endless supply of documents and telephone messages to translate. Didn't anyone else study Arabic in college? I hope what I'm doing is helping, but it seems anything I translate is simply sent upstairs. It seems ironic that the higher you rise in this building, the higher your importance," she said.

"What you're doing is important," he replied.

On Tuesday Jim invited Cathleen out to lunch at a local Subway, and each ordered sandwiches.

"How's everything going?" he asked.

"It's becoming more frustrating because I never know if anything I'm doing is helping at all."

"I'm sure your work is held in high regard, or someone would have complained by now. If you feel overwhelmed, you'll come and talk, won't you?" he asked.

"Yes, I'll call."

***

Cathleen transcribed a phone call made by a known terrorist sympathizer. During the phone call, she heard a non-Islamic name mentioned that intrigued her. The name mentioned was "Hesus," and she vaguely remembered it coming up before. During the phone call the man also made a joke about the meeting at "The Mouse."

*I'll crosscheck my work for the name Hesus and Jesus ... great, three hundred mentions of the word Jesus. Well, that's not strange; there are Christian Arabs as well as Muslim Arabs that use the word. An Arab college professor in Tampa mentioned Hesus twice. We have a record of a Hesus Rodriguez. He collected cash and forwarded it to a group suspected of being a front for terrorists.*

She crosschecked her files for the college professor. This revealed a document that included the phrase "Prepare to meet Hesus," and a reference to "616."

*Let me check his credit card records. What's this payment for an airline ticket? A flight is scheduled for someone named Karen on June 16th.*

She gathered all the documents, files and transcripts, and wrote a lengthy report detailing what she had found and what she suspected.

"If someone tails the professor I think he'll lead them a meeting on June 16th in Orlando, Florida," Cathleen explained to Mark Haskings, her supervisor. He seemed unimpressed and threw it on his desk.

*Great, he blew me off as usual! I really think this is something big. I think "The mouse" meant a meeting in Orlando. Why did he blow me off again? I can't stand this any longer.*

Cathleen went home, took her medication, and tried to calm down. The next day she resumed the tedious task of interpreting documents.

"Did anything come up with the data I gave you," she asked Mark.

"No, I looked it over and sent it upstairs," he replied. She spent the afternoon reading letters written in Arabic.

Two weeks later she joined a co-worker at Burger King.

"What's the hubbub on the TV?" she asked.

"They're announcing the discovery of a terror ring in Orlando, Florida, and praising Mark for having cracked the case." The names mentioned included the college professor and a shadowy Saudi man named Kareem. No mention was made of her at all.

*That bastard did me in again! I'm heading back to work and raising holy hell. If I don't have a reception committee waiting, I'm going postal!*

Cathleen walked down the hall and entered her area. Everything sat exactly as she had left it; no one was waiting to congratulate her.

"Wendy, I'm leaving for the day," Cathleen explained to the secretary.

"I have a phone call for you," the secretary said. "It's Jim."

"Cathleen, how are you?" Jim asked.

"I can't take it anymore; I'm going upstairs and raising hell!"

"Look, get it together! I'll be right down. Don't do anything stupid."

He arrived a few moments later and found her crying, make-up running down her face.

"Jim, I cracked this case and wrote a road map to follow, and I've been shut out of it again! I've been sitting down here four years acting as a stepping-stone for one person after another. I hate it! When will I get my turn? I'm on the first floor, and that's as low as it gets."

"The work you're doing is needed. Many here understand that you cracked this case. There is the official recognition and the unofficial, and many know the work that you've accomplished. Cathleen, the CIA is a series of boats that you can only rock if you have a larger boat. You have a rubber raft, and people are sailing past you in cabin cruisers. Follow me."

He swiped a card into a security device, and a door opened. They went to an elevator she had never entered. The elevator did not descend one floor but many before he stopped it. They stepped off and walked through room after room of employees who monitored radio broadcasts, clipped articles from overseas newspapers, and performed other boring tasks. The whole area smelled like a locker room.

"You mean people work in the basement?" Cathleen asked.

"There is floor after floor below us. These people made waves and are now stationed down here." Cathleen finally understood Jim's message.

"How you doing with your new guy?" Jim asked trying to break the tension. "What's it been, six months?"

"His name's Bob, Bob Winslow. He works for Senator Wright."

"The West Virginia senator?" he asked. "Where did you meet him?"

"At church, another Catholic boy. Graduated from Villanova, not Brown like us," she said.

"We're not all so bad," he said.

"On Friday he took me to the Kennedy center, a black tie event. You know all the senators and congressmen were there? They make me so mad; I'd just like to strangle them!"

"After a while you'll get used to it."

"Bob's the only decent guy I've met since coming to Washington. All the rest are married. He asked me to come and spend a weekend at his parents."

"Sounds serious," Jim said.

"Maybe it is. Jim thanks for talking to me. I just needed to calm down. I think I'll head home and try to breathe a little, though."

"Take your time. Relax a little," Jim said.

***

Two months passed in Cathleen's life. She now jogged each morning. She'd recently changed her diet and now ate fruit for breakfast and soup for lunch. She lost fifteen pounds and was able to get into clothes she had not worn in years.

Other than the situation at work, she felt that she was well on her way to getting her life back on track. On her way into work this morning she did something she had not done in a long time, she stopped by church.

*Morning mass starts at seven a.m., but I only want to go in, pray for a few moments and leave. What was it Dad said to me at graduation: "Now you can serve both God and country."*

Later Cathleen translated a phone call, and it troubled her.

*This call makes no sense. I'm sure it's some kind of code, but I have to translate it as spoken. It's mornings like this that drive me nuts!*

At eleven-thirty a.m. her phone rang.

"Cathleen, come upstairs to the conference room immediately," the voice said.

*That weird phone call, I'm going to be chewed out over that translation. I better prepare myself. Why don't I just walk out the door!*

As she entered the room she saw her supervisor, Mark Haskings, sitting at a table. Across from Mark sat two men she knew as Brooks and Stewart. An agency lawyer sat also.

*Brooks and Stewart are hatchet men; I'm surprised that a hangman's noose isn't waiting!*

"Miss Hale, we wanted to talk to you about your work and issues that have come up," Brooks said.

"I translated that phone call correctly. I think it was a code. It's not my fault. I can show you in my dict ...."

"Shut Up!"

"I mean it, I …."

"I told you to shut up!" Brooks demanded.

"Miss Hale, Haskings is resigning his post, aren't you Haskings?" Mark nodded yes.

"The work has become too stressful for him, and he has asked for other work. You have been assigned to be his replacement."

"I ...."

"That's all!"

"When do I begin?"

"You just have!" Brooks answered and slid out the door.

"I have some documents stating that you have asked for this position and that your request has been approved," the lawyer stated. "This position is an increase of three pay grades, and you will take over effective this morning."

"I don't understand," she said.

"The truth usually wins out, especially when you have people looking out for you."

"Jim?" she asked.

"I wouldn't know," the lawyer said with a sly grin on his face.

## THE NEVADA DESERT

Tim flew to Las Vegas to meet his friends Bill, Mark and Ken. They gathered together occasionally to spend the weekend playing games on their computers and socializing.

"Why did you pick Vegas?" Tim asked Mark.

"The Hackers' convention is in town, and we're going down to it," Mark replied.

"The Hackers' convention," Bill said, "draws every government agency on the planet, the FBI, CIA, KGB and probably even MOSSAD will be there."

"Oh come on, live a little. It's time to embrace the horror," Ken said.

"Hey I can understand playing games and hitting the slots but the Hacker's convention, that's you guys not me," Tim said. The three left Tim and got ready to go down and meet with fellow hackers from around the world.

Two days later Bill and Ken seemed bored. They walked down to the casino and watched everyone blowing money on the slot machines, black jack tables, and roulette wheel.

"Doesn't everyone know that the way to win in Vegas is not to play?" Bill asked.

"Out of all the games, black jack has the best odds if you can count the cards," Ken said.

"The only real odds are if you could dummy the slot machines or somehow time the roulette tables," Bill said.

"Mike!" Ken said, and they both ran upstairs.

"You want me to do what?" Mike said a few moments later.

"Write a calculation so we can time the roulette wheel."

"And that would get you what?" Mike asked.

"It would determine where it would stop," Bill said.

"You would need precise calculations, estimates of speed, instantaneous communications …," Mike said raising his hands.

"All of which we could send over our cell phones as you sat at your laptop," Ken said.

Two days later the guys were up a couple of grand each on the roulette wheel.

"We should have tried to make some big scores," Tim said. "Betting a hundred here and a hundred there makes no sense."

"We had to keep the bets low or casino security would have been on us in a minute," Bill explained.

"Yeah, but I would have loved to drive a new Porsche home to Ocean City," Tim said.

"We ran the odds out and came up on top. Let's be happy we weren't caught," Mark said.

"It's nearly one in the morning. We should be getting down to the Hackers' convention," Bill said.

***

Walid Hattab needed to quietly send cash to Las Vegas. He had a contact who could deliver cash, diamonds, or if need be, gold, anywhere in the world for a fee. The man's name was Hesus Rodriguez.

Walid contacted Hesus, and the two men met in Somalia. Walid transferred AK-47 rifles to Somalia and was paid in conflict diamonds. Hesus promised to sell the diamonds anywhere except Israel, as Walid refused to do business with the Israelis. Hesus knew that the bulk of the world's diamonds passed through Israel and, without Walid's knowledge, sold the diamonds to an Israeli dealer.

"Hesus, I need to send cash to Las Vegas."

"Okay, how much?"

"For now, one million, delivered in person."

"Las Vegas is full of federal agents, sifting through records looking for cash and tracing serial numbers ...."

Walid knew the price would be steep but no one else could accomplish the task.

*I remember what happened in Afghanistan. I had a deal with the Taliban to sell rifles for opium. An argument broke out among the Taliban commanders. One moment I was talking and smiling with them and a moment later I was shot, robbed and left for dead. I spent six days in a filthy hospital in Afghanistan before I was able to leave.*

*Hesus has survived every imaginable thing! He began flying piper cubs from Florida to Columbia to pick up marijuana and then went onto cocaine. When he accumulated enough cash, he left the deadly cocaine business and began transporting money and goods across the world. He now launders drug money for others; finances arm sales to every war-torn region of the world, and lives to tell about it!*

Walid agreed with Hesus's terms.

"Hesus, in the future I will also need to transfer cash to Washington, D.C., and Toronto, Canada; I hope you can be of assistance."

"I have contacts all over the world, and I can deliver anything of value, anywhere in the world."

Hesus flew into Las Vegas and delivered the cash and a letter to Orman. Orman, and three other men, had been quietly gathering information and data on the U.S. nuclear program.

"Walid wants to know if we've made progress on the bomb," Orman told his men. "He thinks the problem is building a tiny nuclear bomb, but the problem is knowing how to detonate it. It's very complicated." He left his crew in Las Vegas and quietly traveled to California. Here he, a nuclear physicist for the University of Toronto, could quietly discuss nuclear theory with professors in the area. A break came in an unexpected way. A professor from UCLA gave him an idea.

"You should talk with Dr Levin; he worked at Rocky Flats until he retired some years back. The poor man has Alzheimer's and drifts in and out of reality, but on some days he is as sharp as ever."

"Where is he living?"

"He has a villa in the desert because of his allergies."

*I met three times with Dr Levin, but I was unsure of the validity of anything he told me. He sometimes mistook me for his father and would go on and on about some childhood event. At other times he mistook me for his superiors and openly talked shop. It was the fifth meeting that Dr Levin described part of the equation I needed.*

Orman returned to Las Vegas and rejoined his crew.

"We found a math genius at the Hackers' convention," one of his men described to him.

"A math genius?" Orman asked.

"Yes, most of the universities pleaded with him to come and study, but he refused. He wants to study history instead. His abilities in calculus are considered to be off the chart."

"You could introduce us tonight at the Hackers' convention."

"Yes."

At around one in the morning, Bill and Mark sat explaining a sniffer program to a Pakistani hacker.

"The program is designed to sniff out passwords used by programmers to access their gaming sites," Bill explained. "It's not that we mind buying the games. It's that we want to play them before they're released."

The older Pakistani man approached Mark.

"You're the math genius?" he asked

"What ya' got?" Mark replied. Orman showed Mark an equation he had on his computer.

"Nuclear theory?" Mark said. "I really don't get into that much, but the equation you have is flawed. It's incorrect."

"Incorrect?" Orman asked. Mark took Orman's laptop computer and modified the equation.

"That," Mark said, "would be correct." Orman walked away, stunned.

***

At the end of five sleepless nights, Mark, Ken, Bill and Tim packed their bags to return home.

"Mark, did you purge that roulette wheel program from your laptop?" Bill asked. "With everyone in town, I wouldn't be surprised if we get hassled at the airport."

"Cleaned it to DOD standards," Mark said.

"And I pitched the dummy phone," Ken said.

"Okay. Where's Tim?" Bill asked.

"He went downstairs already," Mark explained.

They descended the stairs and saw Tim standing by the roulette table. He pulled some chips from his pocket and placed them on red nine.

"Look, security's surrounding him. What do we do?" Mark asked.

"Grab a cab and run for the airport," Ken explained.

Security escorted Tim into a back room.

"We know you're communicating by cell phone with someone upstairs," the security officer said, grabbing Tim's phone. "We sent officers upstairs to search your room." A moment later another security guard entered the room.

"Did you find who he was transmitting data to?" the guard asked.

"He only made one call on this phone all week, and it was to Ocean City, Maryland."

"And the room?" he asked.

"Empty."

They drove Tim to the airport and warned him to never return. He found the guys waiting for their flight.

"I told you we ran the odds too long!" Mark said. "A few minutes more and they would have had us."

"I'm going to be glad to get back to Maryland," Tim said.

"Maybe Bill and I can come and visit you sometime?" Mark asked.

## THE ISRAELIES

John Kline grew up in Chicago and when he turned fifteen his family returned to Israel. At the age of eighteen he enlisted in the Israeli army and served four years. During his enlistment he met other former Americans and got to know them well. He married a woman who was born in California. Sarah and John had a little girl who was born in Israel.

John felt his life was unfulfilled, but he had a radical idea. He wanted to form a group of former Americans, now living in Israel, that could travel to the U.S. and destroy the terrorist groups in America. The men and women, all U.S. born, would fit in perfectly and not be noticed.

John talked to MOSSAD, the Israeli security agency, and he described his idea.

"The idea is insane, traveling to America, to what, assassinate terrorists!" The man left him sitting and walked out of the room. After a half hour wait another man walked into the room.

"John, we cannot condone what you want to do, but we really have no way of preventing you from doing it either. If you wish to renounce your Israeli citizenship and travel to America to kill terrorists, we can't stop you." John sat, unsure of what he was hearing.

"What if we did?"

"I suppose we could denounce your actions if you are caught, and I don't see the harm in informing you of terror organizations in the U.S. for you to check out," the man explained to John.

"And when I am through?"

"I suppose if you wish to immigrate back to Israel, your citizenship could be restored. Remember this, though: You do not work for us, we do not finance you, and to us you are a traitor who renounced his Israeli citizenship and went home!" John nodded that he understood.

The group formed in Israel, renounced their citizenship, and returned to America. The members named their group the Danite's after the army of Dan that protected Israel.

"How will we raise enough money to pay for all of this?" Sarah asked. "Our jobs in America will barely pay our living expenses."

"We could rob banks," John said. "We all understand Uzi's and body armor from being in the Army. The robberies will go off with military precision, and we will all have perfect alibis. We will travel as couples, stay in resort areas and keep a low profile. I will provide fake ID's and credit cards linked to the fake ID's."

The first bank robbery went off like clockwork; the take was three hundred thousand dollars. They had enough cash to begin their work in America.

"We will form teams to track down and kill the three terrorists on our list. We need to use 9 mm pistols, which gang members use here, and make the killings look like robberies," John explained.

The third killing went bad. One of his men walked up to a suspected terrorist in Tampa, Fla., and was about to shoot him. The terrorist, suspicious of what was happening, pulled a pistol from under his coat. One of the back-up men saw the pistol being drawn and unloaded on the terrorist with his Uzi.

"We screwed up this time," John lamented. "We must do better, but we need cash and that means hitting banks. We'll head to Florida, stay in tourist areas, and look like vacationing couples. If things go bad during the robberies, everyone must be willing to shoot their comrades if they are facing capture."

The bank robberies went well. The group robbed banks in Daytona Beach, Palm Beach, Miami, Jacksonville and Tampa. The police had no clue as to who was robbing the banks, or why.

"If we hit one more bank then we'll have enough cash to pursue terrorists for years. The last heist will be in Kissimmee," John explained.

The robbery at the Kissimmee bank went perfectly, and the escape van followed John's rental car as planned. He drove through a yellow light and noticed a police cruiser entering the intersection with its lights on. The escape van struck the police cruiser. He left the scene to the sound of automatic weapons fire.

"Please John, don't leave, stay. They still have a chance!" his wife asked. Against his training he decided to stay and parked his car about one hundred yards from the scene. To his amazement Mara, one of the bank robbers, appeared without her body armor, carrying the sack of money.

"They laid down a diversionary fire so I could escape; I guess no one expected a woman because the police guided me away from the area around the van." John overheard on a police radio that both of his men lay dead on the street.

"Let me go and see," Sarah said. She walked close enough to the scene to verify what he'd heard.

John and his team of Danite's laid low for six months and then reunited at a Chicago Cubs game to talk.

"We need to begin our mission again. We need to protect Israel," John explained. "We will form three teams to go on scouting missions to locate terror cells. We will supply you all with fake identification, credit cards, airline tickets and reservations; all teams will be traveling as couples. Study the identification I have given you and make sure you know it by heart. Each team will leave as soon as you can arrange time off at work. Just before leaving I will inform you of your destination and mission. Sarah and I will have our own mission, and we will leave soon. Good luck."

John decided to travel to Toronto since terrorists operated in the area. He paid a small fortune for his wife's and his own fake ID'S. His wife and he now had time to read the ID'S and memorize them.

"We're going to Canada?" Sarah asked him.

"Yes."

"What do we need to find in Canada?"

"Men loyal to Walid Hattab work there. We will be staying at Niagara Falls, as if we are honeymooners."

"I like the idea. Does it include champagne and roses?"

He drove into Niagara Falls and rented a room overlooking the falls. They spent their first evening in a restaurant at the falls. He ordered lamb for dinner and she had pasta.

The next morning John headed north to meet Kevin, a private investigator, at a McDonald's. Kevin slid a thick manila folder across the table at breakfast.

"The man you're looking for is an enforcer for Walid Hattab; he goes by the name Ali. Ali is known to have killed at least three people in Toronto alone, the last one a Saudi lad. If Walid says 'kill someone,' then Ali kills him, no questions asked. The man is an expert in intelligence. If you're hunting him, he is already hunting your people. Be very careful," Kevin stated. "There are other men in town working for Walid also."

"Do you know who they are?" John asked.

"Yes, they are Pakistani, and they are working on something big."

"How do you know?" Normally Kevin would not have given up his sources, but this time it did not matter.

"A hooker ...," Kevin said.

"A hooker?"

"You'd be shocked how often hookers get the news first; a hooker had the kid as a client. The kid told her he was stuck underground working on a project, kept him in a chamber for three months at a time."

"And you believed her?"

"I would have put it at fifty-fifty, but as soon as she told me, her and the kid disappeared and have not been seen or heard of since." The story troubled him and he promised to pay Kevin more money to look into it.

"I need a hundred thou. Lots of risk in this," Kevin said.

"I can only pay seventy-five, take it or leave it. My wife and I will be in town on Sunday. We'll meet at the eleven a.m. mass at the Catholic cathedral," John said.

On Sunday, John and Sarah drove to Toronto to meet with his private investigator.

"John, what do you do in a Catholic Cathedral?" Sarah asked.

"We will just sit, keep quiet, and wait for Kevin to arrive."

"I'm having a really bad feeling in here. It seems really spooky," Sarah said.

"Just relax, and don't get nervous." They sat in the back of the church and tried to follow the service as people got up, knelt, stood and sang hymns. Kevin never showed up. They left and went to a restaurant for lunch.

"Do you think Kevin took the money and fled?"

"I hope not." John began reading a local paper while waiting for their lunch to arrive. On page two of the local section, there was a photograph and the caption read, "Local man dies in drug deal gone sour." The man in the photograph was Kevin. When the police searched Kevin's car they found drugs and money.

John grabbed Sarah's hand and pulled her out of the booth.

"What's up? My lunch!" He pulled her toward the car and once inside they sped away. He showed her the newspaper article as they drove.

"The man sold drugs, and you gave him seventy-five thousand dollars?"

"The man didn't sell drugs; they killed him and made it look like a drug deal gone bad! He told me he was tracking this guy named Ali, and that he was dangerous. The guy killed a hooker and a Saudi kid, and now Kevin's dead." They checked out of their motel at Niagara Falls and headed home.

Upon arriving home John received a coded e-mail message. His crew terminated members of terror cells in San Francisco and Mexico City. He also received a message from the Israelis.

"Sarah, I believe our mission is back on track, but I just found out I'm to report immediately to Washington," John explained. He kissed Sarah good-bye and wondered if he would ever return.

## THE DANITE'S

Thomas Eberly worked at the FBI office in Washington. On a Tuesday morning his phone rang.

"Tom a disturbing series of bank robberies has taken place in Florida, and they assigned the case to us," Shawn said. "The perp's wear head-to-toe body armor, carry Uzi's and use stolen vans."

"I think I've read about this case," Tom said.

"At the last robbery the perp's collided with a police cruiser. Upon sliding out of the cruiser, the officers found themselves under automatic weapons fire. Both police officers, former Marines, quickly recognized that they had three subjects wearing full body armor. The call for help brought the cavalry down on the site. The bank robbers brazenly walked around the van, shooting at police. A sharpshooter shot one of the bank robbers in the neck, killing him. The second bank robber shot himself in the head."

"Sounds like we're looking for a bunch of loonies," Tom said.

"The police made a massive search for the third bank robber, a woman, without success. The bank robber who shot himself didn't die immediately. He scrawled a name into the dirt. The name written seemed to be Daniel or Danielle, but was difficult to read or interpret."

"Start a search on the name and see if a Daniel or Danielle comes up on any other robberies," Tom said.

The following week Shawn stopped by Tom's office with a request. A college professor from Utah believed that the FBI misinterpreted what the dying bank robber scribbled. Shawn asked if he could meet with the college professor.

*Shawn's a bright enough guy and I like him, but he irritates me at times. It's his offhand manner, his overconfidence that drives me nuts. He dives into things recklessly. Now he's standing in here stating that the agency's misread the scribble a bank robber left in the dirt.*

"The college professor saw our photographs of the scene?" Tom asked.

"Yes, the crime lab asked for his help because he studies that kind of thing."

"Why don't we ask the professor to come here, at our expense, to explain himself?"

Four days later the college professor arrived.

*I'm getting too old for this!*

He expected some grizzled old professor from Utah State, but the professor standing in front of him was a young, attractive woman. The woman brought a stack of information with her that she towed on a cart. The woman's name was Dr. Sharon Fuller.

"Dr. Fuller, what is your theory on this scribbling?"

"I understand that your crime lab thought the writing read Daniel or Danielle, but I'm interpreting the writing differently."

"Sharon, how do you interpret the writing?" Shawn asked, to Tom's disapproval.

"Well, what you interpret as an e drawn in the soil, at least as far as I can determine, could also be t and be followed by an e. This is the pattern that would normally be left by a right-handed man lying on the dirt," she stated.

To explain what she was saying she laid on the floor with her hand now lying on a small chalkboard and scribbled as if she was writing the note.

"I'm sorry, Dr. Fuller, I'm not disputing your knowledge. I'm asking what you think the word means. What did the man write as he was dying?"

"I believe he was writing the word Danite, not Daniel or Danielle."

"Danite, what like dynamite?" Shawn blurted out.

*Shawn is starting to upset me. First he referred to Dr. Fuller as Sharon, and now he's making light of the woman's remarks.*

"Dr. Fuller, does the word Danite mean anything to you? It means nothing to me," Tom said.

"Outside the LDS community it would mean little, but inside the LDS community it reflects on a time that many would rather forget."

"The LSD community? You mean an LSD cult? Do you think this has something to do with drugs?" Shawn asked.

"Shawn, shut up and listen for a change!" Tom said bluntly. "Look, I'm sorry. I didn't sleep very well. Dr. Fuller is referring to the Church of the Latter Day Saints, the Mormon community." Dr. Fuller nodded.

"The word Danite or Danite's referred to militias and individual groups that swore an oath to protect the church, right or wrong," she stated. She spread her documents across the table and explained in detail what she had brought. Examining the documents took the rest of the afternoon.

"Dr. Fuller, do you think this group of bank robbers could be related to the Church of the Latter Day Saints or some splinter group of them?"

"It doesn't fit into any group within the church that I have ever heard of. If you had a splinter group of LDS members, the last person they would take on a mission with them would be a woman. They just wouldn't do it."

"Who do you think we should be looking for?" he asked.

"I would be looking for a militia group or perhaps members of the

Christian Identity Movement. The real interpretation of the Danite's referred to the army of Dan that protected Israel," Dr. Fuller explained.

"Shawn, do a complete search on the word Danite and find anything you can on them. Find any recent discussion of the group."

"Do you really think the bank robber was referring to Danite when he scribbled in the dirt?" Shawn asked.

"Yes, it would make much more sense that we are dealing with a militia group than with individuals, and …."

"And what?" Shawn asked.

"They have a million and a half dollars to finance their operations."

## TORONTO

Orman met with Walid Hattab in the Sudan.

"What did you find in Nevada?" Walid asked.

"I discovered a great deal. I believe I know how to trigger the bomb. I also discovered that one of our equations was incorrect."

"How did you find the correct equation?"

"You wouldn't believe me if I told you! Do you have the funding?" Orman asked.

"I have made arrangements to supply all the cash you need."

"I have three skilled, devoted men that I have selected," Orman said.

"And the location is in Toronto?" Walid asked.

"I have modified the underground shelter of a business, and it's is not shown on any maps. No one knows it exists."

"How can that be?" Walid asked.

"During the Atom bomb scares of the sixties, many men built secret bomb shelters to protect themselves against a nuclear attack. This was one such structure. A wealthy, eccentric millionaire built it, and he has long since passed away. I own the building now. A building constructed to protect someone from a nuclear bomb will now be used to build one," Orman said smiling.

"What about radiation from the bomb construction? Wouldn't sensors pick up the radiation?" Walid asked.

"The room was sealed to protect the people from radiation; I have a back-up plan in case any radiation does escape, a huge water fountain, very beautiful, made of granite."

"The water will absorb the radiation leakage?" Walid asked.

"No, Granite gives off radiation constantly; anyone who would investigate the radiation would come upon the granite fountain and assume the granite was giving off the radiation."

"I see."

"And the enriched uranium that we need?" Orman asked.

"It has been purchased from a very unhappy Russian general who believes the Soviet Union was given away to the Americans. It will arrive in Toronto, shielded as you have instructed," Walid explained. "And things are progressing?"

"Yes. I'm continuing to work at the University. It provides a cover for much of what I do. I bought a small business some time back selling office supplies to local companies. Unknown to anyone except my three faithful workers, the bomb shelter lays under the building my supply business is in."

"I don't want to deceive you any longer Orman, I know about the bomb shelter," Walid said.

"You do?"

"Of course. I assign my own men to monitor operations like this. I sent Ali to protect you," Walid explained.

"Ali? I've never met him."

"Pray you never do. He kills…ruthlessly. He discovered a security leak in your operation and dealt with it."

"A security leak? Walid, what happened?"

"A disappointment occurred, and we cannot stand for disappointments. It was Ahmed."

"Ahmed's off for a month."

"Ahmed is dead!"

"Why … who killed him?"

"I had him killed because of a breach of trust."

"Ahmed was my friend! You killed him … why?" he screamed.

"He hired a prostitute; Ali, my security officer, discovered this."

"And you killed him for it?" Orman asked.

"He was not killed for hiring a prostitute. He was killed because of what he could have told her. A man will tell a woman many things," Walid said.

Orman calmed down. What he was saying was the truth; Ahmed had broken the trust and could have put the entire project in jeopardy.

"Do we know what he told the prostitute?" he asked.

"I have no reason to believe he told her anything," Walid said.

"Are you sure?" Orman now wondered if all was lost.

"My men interrogated him for days, and we are sure he told her nothing."

"And the harlot?" Orman asked.

"She has been interrogated and disposed of also," Walid said. "Orman, be sure your men understand that this cannot happen again."

"The semester at the University is almost over. I will notify the school that I will be traveling. I will remain in the bunker myself, with my men, until the project is completed."

"Then we understand each other," Walid said.

"Yes, we understand."

## THE MEETING

Cathleen Hale married the attorney she had been seeing, Bob Winslow. The wedding, set up by her mother, had been a large extravagant affair. James Burrett acted as best man, and his wife as matron of honor. Cathleen decided to keep her maiden name of Hale.

After her honeymoon Cathleen returned to work at the CIA.

"What's this?" she asked holding up a list of names.

"Someone's knocking off men with known terrorist ties. No one knows who's doing it or why. Almost all have died from 9 mm pistols at close range. The bullets recovered from their bodies don't match any other, so we can't find a link," an analyst explained.

"Did you check with the FBI?" she asked.

"No."

"I'll check with them myself," she said.

***

At the FBI, Tom Eberly and Shawn searched all references for any mention of the word "Danite." They finally settled upon the Aryan Nation as having members who were capable of the robberies.

Shawn flew to Idaho and met with law enforcement officials. No one knew anything of bank robberies committed by the Aryan Nation.

"To be honest with you," a local FBI agent explained, "I think they're all but finished as a group. What I don't get is why Florida, I mean Florida is not militia central. You might expect a drug gang or a Cuban fringe group doing something like this, but not a militia." Shawn flew home empty-handed.

Two weeks went by, and Tom felt the case slipping away. A break in the case came from an unlikely source, the CIA. Cathleen Hale called the FBI asking for information on the shoot-out in central Florida. Tom returned her call.

"Ms. Hale, I'm handling the shoot-out. What can I do for you?"

"I understand you confiscated three Uzis at the shoot-out."

"Yes?"

"Did you test fire the weapons?" she asked.

"No, why?"

"I received photographs of the bullet you retrieved, and your Uzis may match the bullets we took out of an Arab professor from Tampa. I need to examine your bullets to make an exact match," she said.

*An Arab professor dead from an Uzi used in a bank robbery? Where the hell is this going to lead?*

Tom acquired the Uzis and went to meet with Cathleen Hale. The CIA tested the bullets and the Uzi and found an exact match.

"Do you have any clue why the same Uzi would be used to commit a bank robbery and an assassination?" she asked.

"Is there anything special about the professor?" he asked.

"The professor raised large sums of cash in the U.S. and sent it to Hamas," Cathleen explained.

"Terrorists? Maybe that's why these guys robbed banks, to send the cash to terrorists overseas," Tom said.

"If they robbed banks to send money overseas, then why kill off a Hamas leader? The men killed in the shoot-out, did you send their descriptions or fingerprints to Interpol?" Cathleen asked.

"No."

"We need to do so. Send them to me and I'll forward them. One other thing, Arabs don't like to use Uzis. They consider them to be made by Jews, and they almost always use something else," Cathleen explained.

Cathleen sent the photographs and fingerprints of the men to Interpol, and all requests came back negative. She called Tom and Shawn down to go over their files.

"Cathleen, we had one positive report back that was later corrected," an analyst explained to her.

"From who?" she asked.

"The Israelis."

"They usually don't make mistakes," she said.

"I know. First they said they had a hit on the fingerprints, and then said they did not."

Tom opened his files and laid the pages on the table.

Cathleen looked over the photographs of the men killed in the shoot-out. At first she believed the men to be light-skinned Arabs.

"I guess I'm no expert, but it's difficult to tell a Palestinian from an Israeli…." She almost bit her tongue, and Tom noticed.

"Could the dead shooters be Israelis?" Tom asked. It began to make sense to them. An Israeli group, killing Arab terrorists.

"Then why the bank robberies?" Cathleen asked.

"A rogue group without ties to any country, the Danite's …," Tom offered.

"The Danite's?" she asked.

"The army of Dan was constructed to protect the nation of Israel," he said. The pieces of the puzzle were falling together.

"Cathleen, if this is the work of a rogue group of Israelis, then where are they now, and how do we find them?"

"Tom, I'll have to get back to you on this," Cathleen said. *Please don't let this be Israelis; most of the information we get is from Israel. I hope the bank robbery doesn't cause discord between us.*

## THE MARYLAND SHORE

Tim returned to the beach and took Liana out to dinner.

"How was your trip to Las Vegas?" she asked.

"Oh, we played computer games, shared files, stayed up all night a couple of times."

"And the casinos?" she asked.

"Oh, I didn't win any money."

"But they are beautiful?"

"Oh, unreal, gaudy…."

Tim returned to his apartment and got a call from Bill.

"There's not much goin' on up here," Bill said. "Can we come down?"

"Who's coming?" Tim asked.

"Me, Mike, Cindy and Lisa. They'd probably like to meet this new girl. What did you say her name was?"

"Liana. We just sort of started hanging out together, no big thing."

The next afternoon they all gathered at a Pizza Hut in Ocean City.

"Tim, tell me about your Russian girlfriend," Lisa said.

"Liana?"

"Do you have more than one?"

"No," he said blushing.

"Yes, then Liana, invite her over!" Lisa said. "You never let us meet anyone you date."

"She's shy, but since everyone's here she might stop by," Tim said. He called Liana and she shocked him when she said yes. Tim picked her up after work and drove her to his apartment.

"My friends are college students, and they're a little strange."

"Strange?"

"They're computer geeks."

"And?" she asked.

"They just kind of keep to themselves. They're not into partying and that kind of thing."

"Partying?"

"They don't drink or take drugs; they just like to hang out together. Bill and Lisa are Christians and spend time reading their Bibles and studying. Mark is some kind of a math genius, but he doesn't like math and doesn't want to study it."

"What does he like to study?"

"History …."

Lisa dropped her pan of stir-fried rice onto the stove when she saw Liana. Cindy left chicken frying and stared, as did Mark and Bill.

"This is Liana," Tim said quietly. Cindy came up, hugged her, and asked if she wanted to help them make dinner. Cindy saw Bill and Mark staring.

"You can go back to playing your game now!" They tried to go back to their game but found themselves stopping and staring at her.

"We didn't know what you liked, so we made a little of everything. You can make whatever you like," Cindy said. Liana found a head of lettuce, some Italian tomatoes, cucumbers and celery. She took a small pot and placed olive oil and a collection of herbs into it, adding one spice after another until the kitchen had fragrances no one could imagine. At the very end, she added red wine vinegar to the pot and placed a lid on it.

"When Tim said a Russian girl, I expected a two hundred pound wrestler, but my God she's really pretty!" Cindy whispered to Lisa.

"And tiny!" Lisa whispered back.

"Liana, what do people eat in Russia?" Mark asked.

"We eat the same foods as you do here, but most families just stick to basics. We have, and grow, cabbage, potatoes, vegetables, onions, garlic and tomatoes, but there is little of them. Chicken is hard to find, and the food is very expensive. In Russia, food is sold on the black market, so little makes it into the stores. If you want something you can't find, you hire a taxi driver and he takes you to get it for a fee."

It was now time to eat, and everyone gathered at the table. Bill noticed Liana's tiny cross.

"Can we all hold hands?" Lisa asked. Liana held Tim's hand on one side and Cindy's on the other. After the blessing it was time to eat dinner, which was more of passing pots or dishes around. No one really understood what Liana made on the stove, and now it became clear. She had made a hot dressing that, just before serving, she poured over the salad. Everyone loved her salad.

After dinner, everyone gathered and played Uno for over an hour. Liana had never played the game before but quickly caught on and began slamming cards down and joking around. She felt very comfortable with everyone and was able to relax. Later in the evening Liana was able to talk with Mark.

"I understand you're a genius at math?"

"That's what they tell me, I really couldn't care."

She began scribbling a long calculus equation on a notepad and asked if he could solve the equation. She knew it would take her several hours with a calculator to get the solution. He solved the equation the moment she stopped writing and did it in his head. She didn't need to check if he was right. She just knew it.

"Liana, please no more math. Can we talk about Russian history or computers instead?"

"You know about computers?" she asked.

"Yeah, why?"

"I am having some trouble with a laptop computer; do you think you could fix it?"

"Bill's the real computer genius. Bring your computer over, and we'll take a look."

"I have to leave soon for work but I'll bring it back," Liana said.

"Tim, could you drive me home?" she asked. As she went to leave, Lisa and Bill followed her and Tim outside.

"Liana, can we pray for you?" She did not know what to say or how to take this.

"Okay," she said. Lisa began praying aloud and asked God to protect her. The prayer stunned Liana.

After Liana left, the whole conversation in Tim's apartment turned to her.

"I never thought a Russian girl could be as pretty as she is," Cindy said.

"She definitely sent me for a loop," Lisa admitted, "She kind of reminds me of a junior high cheerleader." Mark and Bill knew that the less the two of them said the better off they would be.

Liana brought her laptop computer over on Friday.

"Liana, your laptop is terribly underpowered, you're trying to drive a Porsche with a motorcycle engine," Bill said.

"I don't have much money to spend, what can I do?" Bill went out to his car and brought in a large red box.

"Do you need special tools?" she asked.

"No, you need ram." She watched as he sorted through the red box and came up with ram chips that would power her computer.

"We want to copy your hard drive onto a faster model," Bill said.

"Okay." Liana sat down and watched TV as the guys worked.

"Try your computer now," Mark said.

Her laptop computer started so quickly that it stunned her. Using Tim's wireless, she surfed the net faster than she could type. She tried, for just a moment, to bring up the Polish gaming site.

"Oh, wow, what a ridiculously cool site. Some Polish guy wrote that!" Mark said.

"The ram, the hard drives, the time … how much?" she asked. Bill looked at Mark as if he did not understand. He just shrugged his shoulders.

"She wants to know how much you want for upgrading her computer," Tim said.

"No, really, how much for all that, the parts and all?" Liana asked.

"The parts are all scavenged from junked computers, and we're staying at Tim's for free...."

"Thank you so much!" she said. "Where did you meet Tim?"

"We met at Temple University in Philadelphia," Mark said.

"Oh, that's nice. I've heard a lot of nice things about Philadelphia."

"Well, I lived in a bad area, so actually Philadelphia was terrible."

As Liana fell asleep that night she remembered Mark's words about Philadelphia.

*Philadelphia is the City of Brotherly love. Grozny was terrible. Momma and I ran for our lives...*

## GROZNY

Grozny is the capital city of the Chechen republic and, in Russian; the word means "Terrible." Sarena and Liana fled their cottage taking nothing with them. With great difficulty they found Aslan in a city under siege.

"Liana, we must find an underground shelter, perhaps a basement in an apartment building, something that will protect us if the Russians bomb the city," Sarena said.

"I'll look around and find a place for us," Liana said. "See if you can gather any food and supplies."

Liana found a perfect spot, a supply room three stories underground at a large building. They stocked the room with food, water and supplies and waited for the Russian assault to begin.

"I found work at the hospital," Sarena said. "No one has cash, but they can pay me with food and medicine. Most of the nurses have fled the city, so it will just be myself and some Red Crescent nurses."

"Momma, we should be all right," Liana said.

"No, we will not be all right. We should have never come. Your grandfather was right. I didn't expect the amount of death and hurt that I've seen, but we have no choice now. If the Russians capture us, they will use us as pawns against your grandfather. If we face capture, we must promise to shoot each other. Death will be much kinder to us than the Russians." Liana acted shocked at her mother's words but knew it was true.

"Momma, all we can do is to keep fighting the Russians and pray for a miracle."

"Yes, but I don't see how you slipping out with your sniper rifle, or me laying land mines really changes anything."

"Grandpa says that if we can hold Grozny then the Russians will have to return to negotiations," Liana said.

"Yes, but what if they overrun the city?"

"Then we will have to fight somewhere else," Liana said.

"Liana, if Grozny falls then we lose the war and we're all dead."

Liana joined a three-person hunter/killer team. The teams consisted of militiamen who carried rocket-propelled grenades (RPG'S), AK-47s, and snipers. Three to five teams worked together and could take on sizable Russian forces.

"In Stalingrad we found that you could train a soldier for three months and hand him a bolt-action rifle or you could hand him a machine gun and he could fight today," Aslan explained to the men. "You can fight against the Russians only if you attack them at point-blank range. If you do not their artillery and aircraft will kill you all. You must keep moving, or they will pinpoint your positions."

The Russians that Liana encountered were recognizance units that probed the Chechen defenses and radioed information back to the command. Her hunter/killer teams attacked the Russians daily, and each side suffered terrible losses.

"Momma," Liana explained to Sarena one evening, "we encountered something new today, Chechen militia forces allied with the Russians. Won't these men know the city like we do? It's one thing to shoot at Russians, but now I'm killing Chechens? So many men have died fighting alongside me that most are frightened to be around me. I think it might be safest if I fight alone."

In early autumn Aslan warned everyone that the Russians would flatten the city with bombs and artillery. The other militia leaders insisted he was wrong.

"The Russians will come right in like they did before, so we must keep our men out in front of the Russian army," the other commanders told Aslan.

"If you try and fight the Russians head-on they will call artillery and air strikes in on you. You need to hit and then flee, divert the Russian attack. Your men will be wiped out if you use conventional tactics," Aslan said.

Using the sewers that the Russians had attempted to seal, Liana slipped close to Minutka Square. She found a spot amid some rubble with a good escape route. She saw militiamen moving in groups of twelve to fifteen men, but had not seen anyone near the square. She slipped into a tiny hole and waited for an oncoming Russian column.

*The Russian column must be stopped; I will shoot seven times and disappear into the sewers.*

As she waited, a Russian recon unit came toward the square. She fired her seven-shot sequence. When she got up to slip away, someone struck her on the back of the head, pulled a hood on her, and dragged her away.

Liana awoke to the sounds of screaming and moaning.

*A hood covers my head, and shackles are on my hands and feet. I'm chained to a wall in an awkward position. Where am I? Who captured me? Please let my captors be Russian and not one of their militias.*

After a very long wait, Liana heard footsteps coming toward her, and a man shouted at her.

*The man does not sound Russian!* The man seemed enraged and began slapping her through the hood.

"Get her to the hoist!" he screamed.

She felt a rope on her feet, and a winch pulled her into the air. The questioning and slapping went on, but she remembered little as she kept passing out from the blood rushing to her brain. She awoke later but had no idea where she was.

*I still have the hood fastened on my head, but I must be lying on a concrete floor. My head still throbs from that blackjack. Why is everyone still screaming and moaning. Perhaps if I hold my breath long enough I will die!*

Liana heard footsteps approaching her.

“Stand her up. Let’s see what we have.”

She felt hands grasp at each arm and felt a bench under her. She felt someone’s fingers at her neck and heard a metallic click of a lock. Someone pulled the hood from her, and the bright light jolted her. A man sat in front of her dressed in camouflage fatigues.

The man opened a manila folder and stared at it.

“Your name’s Liana; your mother is Sarena. Aslan Yastrz is your grandfather! You were born in southern Russia, and you know several languages including perfect Russian! You know Russian customs, and grew up with Russian girls. Your mother is a nurse working in Grozny; we’ve been watching her! You kill Russian soldiers with sniper rifles!”

“How do you know all this? Who are you?” Liana asked quietly.

“I am of no concern to you. What you need to concern yourself with is keeping your mother alive.”

“My mother?”

“Yes, your mother Sarena, the nurse! You decide whether to let her live or die.”

“How do I do that?”

“By doing as instructed. Get cleaned up!” The man pointed to a bowl of water and a small towel.

“Now?” Liana asked.

A small set of fatigues sat on the bench. Liana washed and put the fatigues on as men watched. They marched her out of a basement full of cells. Each cell seemed to have one moaning or screaming prisoner in it. She saw daylight ahead, and found she was still in Grozny. Tape players blared sounds of wounded and tortured men and women across the city. The vehicle stopped at a mound on a corner, and the man pointed at it.

“Do you recognize them?” the man said to her. Liana started to look down but was repelled back in horror. The mound was a series of heads pointed north, a cruel display someone had set up.

“You should recognize the faces. You shot those Russians.”

“You’re not Russian allied militia?” Liana asked.

“No, we’re the CDF.”

*Can it possibly get any worse?*

The CDF or Communist Defense Force traded heroin to finance their war and sold any girls or women who would not join them into prostitution. The group would shoot Chechen men simply for praying.

The CDF excelled in the use of psychological warfare and regularly tortured to death captured Russian soldiers and videotaped the act. The group placed the decapitated heads of Russian soldiers on street corners facing out so advancing Russians had to look at them as they advanced.

"You're a sniper; this is how we shoot Russians!"

She could see a sniper sitting behind a tarp with a rifle in front of him. The tarp began to move, and Liana, to her horror, realized the "tarp" was a wounded Russian soldier hanging by his feet.

"We shoot at the Russians. If they shoot back at us, they shoot their own wounded comrades."

She did not want to see any more. She knew the CDF would not stop until they completed their goal of a Communist Chechnya. The fighting would not stop if the Russians left, but would turn to Chechens as well.

*There are Russians hanging in the square now. If these men have their way, we will all be hanging in the square.*

"What do you want of me?"

"You'll soon find out ...."

They took her back to the basement and placed her in a cell. They gave her some moldy bread and weak tea. The next day they took her to a four-wheel drive vehicle and handcuffed her to the door. Three men sat in the truck, and they sped through the town to a minefield.

"Drive on!" the commander bellowed. They headed right across the minefield.

*The Russians would not expect anyone to drive across a minefield ....*

They drove back roads and side trails, avoiding Russian patrols as they went. Liana noticed a package sitting on the seat of the truck and wondered what was in it. The men finally stopped the vehicle and pulled her out.

"There's a Russian compound in that village, and in that compound a Russian Colonel has set up his command post. Kill the colonel, bring me his head, and your mother will live. If you're not back in one week, Sarena will die ... and it will be long and bloody."

"How can I get to a Russian Colonel? They will kill me on sight!" Liana protested.

"Open the package!" he screamed. She opened the package and found it held a Russian schoolgirl's dress.

"Put it and the necklace on!" The necklace was a small silver cross that signified she wasn't Muslim. The man took her fatigues from her.

"Your name's Sashi Kamikov, a Russian girl who was taken captive by the CDF but escaped after being beaten. You lived at Minutka square. Your parents are dead."

She looked at her swollen wrists and ankles and felt her swollen face.

"The girl … the Russians will check out my story?"

"It will be correct. There was a Russian girl Sashi Kamikov, she did live near Minutka Square, her parents were Boris and Maria Kamikov, and all three are dead."

*I'm wearing a dead girl's clothes, and this man killed her and her family.*

"How do I get to a Russian Colonel?"

"The Russians will take pity on you and take you in; they will believe your story."

"And the Russian Colonel?"

"Seduce him and kill him!"

"Seduce him? I don't know how to do that!"

"You've had boyfriends!"

"No," Liana said without thinking.

The man thought a moment and motioned to the men behind him.

"Take her and teach her about sex. Being raped will just make her story more believable to the Russians."

## THE HUNT

The CIA placed a bounty of ten million dollars on Walid Hatab. "The CIA, MOSSAD, the KGB -- they all want me dead," Walid described to Ali, his security officer. "I'm in hiding all the time, my operations in Tampa, Chicago, Mexico City, and South America are shutdown, and I have no idea who's killing our men."

"They are a rogue group of Israelis, American citizens that fought for the Zionists and later returned to America. For a price we can get their photographs from Hamas," Ali explained. "Do you want me to track them down?"

"Have Hamas send me their photos, but concentrate on the Toronto operation. I have men who will deal with the Zionists."

Walid received the names and photographs of four men and two women. He sent three of his men, Saleh, Yasin and Hamid, to hunt them down.

"We have verified that one of the women in their group is living in Duluth, Minnesota. Her name is Mara, and she was once captured by Hamas and traded for believers held by the Israelis. Some of the Israelis are believed to be living in New Mexico," Walid explained to Saleh. "I have rented a camper and a van to pull it for you. You will live as tourists. I have an agent named Tari. She will help you in New Mexico. She is Indonesian and very dedicated. You will fly into Mexico, travel by foot across the border, and call her to pick you up. She will have the van and the trailer."

One week later the three men easily crossed the border into New Mexico and contacted Tari.

"I have your identification and papers," she explained. "Your van and camper are waiting. I have the weapons you requested. The Zionists do kitchen remodeling as a cover and to pay expenses; they travel a lot."

"You could call them and ask to have your kitchen remodeled; I could give you the cash for a down payment?" She agreed and made the phone call to the contractors. Saleh and his group went back to the campground.

"Saleh, the men are coming Tuesday to give me an estimate. Can you tail them?" Sari later explained. He followed the men until they came to a Super 8 motel, where they went into room 133.

"Yasin, the Israelis are in a Super 8 motel, room 133. Go in and quietly kill them both and make it look like a robbery." Yasin attached a silencer to his pistol.

At three in the morning he drove to the Super 8 motel and used an electronic device to open the door. He saw the two men in bed and shot both in the head twice. He ransacked the room to make it look like a robbery. Yasin turned one of the bodies over and found that he had shot a Chinese couple. He took the man's wallet and dumped the woman's purse.

"Saleh, the two I killed at the motel, they were Chinese." Yasin showed him the wallets. He studied the ID'S that Yasin had brought back and realized that the Israelis had given them the slip.

"We must have spooked the Israelis. They must have checked out early! We must leave now. The Israelis will hear about the Chinese couple found dead in the motel and know we are after them," Saleh said.

Saleh drove north as they sped out of town. In the morning they heard the news of the Chinese couple found shot to death. The news reported another murder also. Tari was dead.

"The Israelis must have known she was helping us. Do you think she talked to them before she died?" Yasin asked.

"I don't know, but getting out of town was the wise thing to do," Saleh said. They drove north toward Minnesota in hopes of catching Mara, before she too slipped away.

Three days later they arrived in Duluth, Minnesota. They tracked Mara down and found she worked as a beautician. Saleh learned she was leaving for Chicago that night. The time to kill her was now. He decided to do the job himself….

***

John Kline flew into Washington, D.C., and got a room downtown. He went out to dinner and afterwards decided to go for a walk. As he walked, a black Lincoln pulled alongside.

"John get in," a man called. He found two Israeli intelligence officers in the car.

"Are you a complete idiot, or just incompetent?" the officer asked. "First we hear of the shoot-out in Florida, then of the dead men in Toronto. How could you have bungled things so badly? Do you know the CIA is trying to track down your group, the Danite's? I don't know why, but we have decided to let you continue your work. We have a new list of enemies for you -- they live in Los Angeles."

"What is going on in Toronto? What are the Pakistani's doing there?" John asked. The two officers looked at each other but did not say anything.

"We sent your remaining men back to Israel. When your mission is complete you will be brought back also. John, you must go underground for a while and not be seen. The CIA intercepted a communiqué from one of Walid Hattab's men; it contained pictures of all of you, and now Mara's dead. We have a safe house arranged for you two in Kansas City. Stay there and for God's sake keep quiet!"

"Mara's dead? What happened? Who?"

"Walid received her picture; he must have ordered the hit."

"I need to know about Toronto. What is going on in Toronto?" John asked.

"I don't want to guess, but it could be the end of us all," the officer explained.

## THE PHOTOGRAPH

Cathleen Hale intercepted a communiqué containing a short message and pictures of four men and two women wanted by Walid Hattab. She had a facial recognition go out among all known databases, but nothing came back. It seemed that the trail had gone cold when she received a call from Tom Eberly.

"Cathleen, I think we have a positive hit on one of your pictures."

"Really? Do you have someone in custody?" she asked.

"No, but we have a woman in the morgue who bears an incredible likeness to one of your photographs."

"Where is she?"

"In Chicago."

Cathleen decided to fly to Chicago and meet with Tom. He took her to the city morgue and asked for the woman known as Jane Doe #176.

"Look at her arm," Tom said. Cathleen looked at the woman's arm and saw that the woman had a series of numbers tattooed on it.

"Does this make any sense to you?" he asked.

"Yes."

"Please don't tell me she survived the concentration camps or something," he said.

"No, but close. In some of the more radical kibbutzes in Israel the youth tattooed themselves to show support for older members that survived the concentration camps."

"Do you think she is an Israeli?" he asked.

"No, she looks American to me, but I think she was an Israeli soldier," she stated. "Tom, the shoot-out in Florida?"

"How could I forget?" he said.

"Didn't you say that a woman was involved with the bank robberies? Check this woman's DNA against the body armor and see if you have a match," she asked.

"The woman, do you believe she was one of the Danite's?" he asked.

"Yes, I do. I believe the photographs I intercepted were all members of the Danite group."

A week went by and, acting on a hunch, Cathleen requested records of American citizens who had left the U.S., became Israeli citizens, and then returned to the U.S.

"Cathleen," a worker asked her.

"Yes?"

"These four seem strange. They not only did everything that you asked but also returned to Israel and became Israeli citizens again," the woman explained. Stunned, she looked through the group and saw that indeed the four had left the U.S., became Israeli citizens, gave up Israeli citizenship, took U.S. citizenship again, and then returned to Israel.

"When did these four return to the U.S.?" she asked. Records showed they had all come to the U.S. within a week of each other.

The next week Cathleen received a phone call from Tom Eberly.

"Cathleen, you were right. The DNA in the smallest suit of body armor matches the woman in the morgue."

"Tom, I think I have the woman's name, Mara Levin, and I think I know the name of the ring leader of the Danite's, John Kline and his wife Sarah. They were living in Chicago, last anyone knew," she stated.

"Cathleen, the four that returned to Israel, how would we go about questioning them?"

"Little chance of that! Unless they leave Israel and return to the U.S., you'll never get them."

"I guess we need to concentrate on the two remaining in the U.S."

He requested search warrants of John Kline's apartment and phone records. Tom, Shawn and two other agents' raided the apartment but found nothing. A search of John's phone records showed nothing also.

"Shawn, Cathleen had pictures of John Kline in Toronto, but his credit cards show nothing. He must be traveling using fake ID's and fake credit cards."

"It's a long shot, but if we show John's picture to the workers at the motels and restaurants around where these guys were killed, maybe someone will recognize him and give us his alias," Shawn said. He flew to Florida to see if anyone remembered the two. Tom flew to Toronto and did the same. He was sound asleep when Shawn called.

"Tom, I think I have something."

"What?" Tom asked in a stupor.

"The shoot-out in Kissimmee, I think I placed John and Sarah Kline at the scene."

"How ….?" he said getting out of bed.

"Well," Shawn said, "I took the photographs of John and Sarah Kline to the local cops that were at the shoot-out, but none of them remembered them. I started thinking about the news crews that had come upon the scene, and I went and interviewed them. One of the women that covered the shooting distinctly remembered seeing the two sitting in a car near the scene."

"Go on."

"She saw them open their car door to help a woman who was looking for a safe place to hide during the shoot-out."

"I see…."

"I spread our pictures out, and she identified Mara as the woman that got into John's car, and her camera gave a short glimpse of the car John was driving."

"Were you able to identify the car?" Tom asked.

"I believe so, sir. It looks like it was a rental charged to a Robert Shank."

"Shawn, I'm flying to Orlando tonight. Try and find any records you can on a Robert Shank, licenses, credit cards, phone records, anything. I'll be there soon." Tom sat up in bed, stunned. Shawn had finally come through.

## UNDERGROUND

Secure in a safe house in Kansas City, John and Sarah waited. On a Monday morning a message arrived that struck fear in their hearts.

"Three of Walid Hattab's men are trying to hunt you down. They killed Mara and tried to kill several others. They're living in a campground outside Chicago, waiting for you to reappear," the message explained.

Two names on his original list remained. From what he could gather, the two smuggled drugs for Walid Hattab.

"Sarah, I need to go to California and finish off the two Arabs. If we can stop Walid's flow of drug money, Israel will be safer."

"John, the men in Chicago are looking for you, not a pretty blond woman."

"And…?" he asked.

"I can dye my hair blond." John slowly came around to what she was asking.

"Sarah, what you're asking is too dangerous."

"Is it anything different from what I've been doing?"

"I'll get fake ID for you," he said, reluctantly. Sarah dyed her hair blond. He would be traveling to San Diego to find the two smugglers, and at the same time Sarah would be traveling to Chicago to find Saleh's crew. She would be traveling as Carol Baxter. Sarah, now seeing herself blond, could hardly even recognize herself.

She flew to Chicago and rented an SUV under her fake ID. She paid a thousand dollars in cash and bought a used pop-up camper. She stopped at a Wal-Mart and bought some camping equipment, a sleeping bag and a cook set. The terrorists were reportedly staying in a campground named Sugarhill. She hitched the camper to the SUV and headed east toward the campground. Arriving she attempted to set up the camper.

"Hun, do you know how to set-up a camper?" a man asked Sarah.

"No."

"I'll help you. What's your name?" he asked.

"Carol…," she replied.

"Carol, do you want to get together for drinks later?" She started to say that she wanted to be alone but realized that the man, or his cover, could be useful.

"I could go out for a glass of wine…."

The man's name was Frank and the two went to an Italian restaurant for dinner. Sarah insisted upon paying for her own meal, and he agreed. The man seemed to be decent enough, and she had a good time.

"Can we take a walk through the campground?" she asked, after they returned.

"I'd like that."

"Frank, I just got divorced and I'm having trouble adjusting."

"I understand. I went through that also."

"Are there any other singles staying at the campground?" she asked.

"Only families, no other singles … well we have three guys in the red camper, keep to themselves," he explained. She studied the red camper at length.

"Tomorrow I'm heading west to Minnesota; you're welcome to come along," Frank offered. She seemed to ponder the invitation.

"I'm sorry, I can't … I really just need some time to be alone."

"I understand. Here's my cell phone number. If you change your mind, I'd love to see you again."

The next morning Sarah went to the women's bathroom nearest the red camper. She left the bathroom and walked past the men. One of the men brazenly whistled at her. She smiled back, took a good look at the three men, and confirmed that they were all Arab.

She looked around the campground and tried to decide if she could blow up the camper without killing any of the other people in the campground. It seemed like a good plan, but she needed to contact her husband since he could get the explosives she needed.

"Sarah, the explosion must look like an accident. You need to make it look like they were making a bomb to kill someone else, and it detonated accidentally." He had one of his contacts design a bomb which could be detonated by cell phone.

***

"You arm the bomb by throwing this switch," the man described to her, "and then dial the number when you want the bomb to detonate."

Saleh's crew left around ten in the morning. Sarah entered their camper and placed the bomb in a cupboard near the kitchen table. Around five that evening Saleh, Yasin and Hamid returned. Sarah waited and saw the three sitting at the table. She pulled her cell phone out and dialed the number as instructed. Nothing happened. She dialed the number again and again nothing happened. She called her husband.

"I set everything correctly and dialed the phone number, but nothing happened," Sarah said in a panicked voice Saleh, Yasin and Hamid got out of their trailer and laid mats on the ground to begin their evening prayers.

"Get out of there now!" John screamed back over the phone.

Sarah saw Saleh, Yasin and Hamid staring at her. Saleh, now done with prayers, had arisen and had begun to walk toward her. About twenty feet shy of her SUV, Saleh's trailer blew apart. She sped out of the campground with Saleh screaming at Yasin and Hamid to get into the van.

She sped out onto the road and for almost an hour just kept taking one side road or another as she drove on. Many hours later she abandoned her car in Minnesota. The best thing for her to do now was disappear. She called her husband.

"Things went bad. I'm going underground for a while," she said over her cell phone. She threw her cell phone into a lake and walked to a pay phone.

"Frank, hi, it's Carol. Are you still in the area?" Frank came and picked her up.

"Do you believe my slimy husband took my SUV and camper?" she told him.

"It sounds right to me. My wife cleaned me out five years ago; you just have to start fresh and go on." She did not like the situation of being with him, but she felt she had no choice now. The wilds of Minnesota would hide her from those searching for her.

## THE TRAIL

Tom Eberly received word of a trailer blowing up near Chicago. The local police felt that a propane leak caused the explosion and that it was an accident. The men staying in the camper had not returned and that mystified them. Tom thought it was unusual and asked Shawn to check it out. He flew out that afternoon.

"Tom," Shawn explained the next morning, "the police towed the camper from the scene to a deserted section of the Sugarhill campground, and other campers pilfered it. I'm not a bomb expert, but this is no propane leak."

"Who was staying in the camper?" Tom asked.

"Some Arab guys," Shawn explained.

"Arabs?" Tom exclaimed. With the revelation that the men were Arabs, he knew he had to call in everyone.

Three hours later there were FBI agents interviewing everyone at the campground. Tom flew in to interrogate both the local firefighters who had responded to the explosion and the police who first entered the trailer. As he suspected so many campers, firefighters, and onlookers had entered the trailer before him that the crime scene was a disaster.

*I bet thirty guys left their fingerprints in the camper.*

"The Arabs paid cash at the campground," Shawn explained. "The addresses given, and the copies of their ID'S, were fakes. We have three badly copied photographs of Arab men. Maybe our guys can enhance them."

The FBI flew their explosives experts to the scene.

"Were the Arabs planning on blowing something up? Did the bomb go off early?" Shawn inquired.

"Arabs usually use large bombs to destroy buildings. This bomb was small and shaped to explode straight out and do little collateral damage."

"What do you think happened?"

"I think someone set a bomb to try and kill these guys as they were eating dinner," the agent told him.

"A planned hit?"

"That's my best guess."

"Shawn, get the campground manager and find out who left in the last day or so," Tom said.

"I had a single man staying here, Frank Silva. He said he was heading on to Minnesota. I also had a cute blond woman, Carol Baxter; she left the morning of the explosion," the manager explained.

"Shawn, I want everything possible on each of them. I'm sure this was that Israeli crew, the Danite's, again and I believe the Arabs they are after are the same ones that killed that woman Mara. We lost three days and now the Arabs, and the Danite's, had enough time to hide or leave the country."

That afternoon Tom found a thick file waiting for him on Frank Silva but really nothing on the ID given for Carol Baxter.

"Tom, the only thing we have on Carol Baxter is a copy of her ID and a few credit card receipts," Shawn said.

"Anything special on the credit card?"

"A rental car and some gas. The police found Carol's car and searched it for evidence, but found nothing. I had our agent check the fingerprints from the rental car against the slew they found in the bombed-out trailer, and they say they have a match," Shawn explained.

"Frank Silva, anything recent on him?"

"His credit card showed he got gas in Minnesota," Shawn said, "but nothing else."

"He's camping .... We need to travel and probably camp in Minnesota. Set it up," Tom said. *It's going to be a long week ....*

***

Sarah and Frank camped in Minnesota, and at her insistence, never stayed more than two days in any area. She also insisted they stay in the most remote sections. When Frank stopped at a small supermarket and bought some groceries, she stayed inside the camper. He decided to surprise the woman he knew as Carol and bought a dozen roses and a bottle of wine at the store.

"Carol, I bought you something for tonight, a surprise." He got into the camper and drove off heading west. He drove for ten miles and stopped at a gas station. She spied the roses and wine he had bought. She looked at a map and saw that southeast of the grocery store lay a wilderness prairie.

"Frank, we missed the prairie east of here!"

"Really? But it's back from the way we came?"

"Frank, they have deer and being out on the prairie would be really romantic." He stopped the camper and turned around. They were now heading some thirty miles east of the store.

Frank surprised Sarah with the roses and the wine.

"Frank, it would be really special if we could camp out on the prairie. That way we'd truly be alone. Could you drive this off the road?"

"I guess so," he said.

"I'd like to watch the sun set if we could."

***

It took Tom and Shawn a full day to drive into Minnesota. They stopped at a Wal-Mart and bought a tent, sleeping bags and camping equipment in case they had to camp out. Tom wanted to follow Frank Silva's trail, and the only thing they had to go on was his credit card receipt. They were ready to stop for the day when Shawn's cell phone rang.

"Frank was at a food store about thirty miles from here earlier today," Shawn explained.

"Get us there as fast as you can," Tom said. Forty-five minutes later they were at the grocery store. Shawn sorted through the store's credit card receipts and found Frank Silva's slip.

"Can you tell me anything about this guy?"

"The guy bought a lot of groceries," the clerk said.

"Anything else?" he asked. The woman's face turned red.

"He also bought some wine and red roses."

"Did you see a woman with him?" Shawn asked.

"The woman, uh, just a glimpse, a blond woman half his age. He called her Carol," the clerk said.

"Carol?" Tom asked.

"He said 'Carol, I have a surprise for you,'" the clerk said.

"Which way did they go?" he asked.

"West. He said they were heading to the badlands in South Dakota."

"Is this the woman?" Tom showed the clerk the copy of the driver's license.

"I guess it could be her."

They headed west down the highway toward South Dakota and almost immediately Shawn's cell phone went off again as Frank had purchased gas right up the road. They stopped at the gas station and quizzed the operator but found nothing.

"The guy used his credit card at the pump. I never saw him," the clerk said. They went to leave, and Shawn spotted something.

"Tom, turn around," Shawn said.

"Why?"

"They have a camera monitoring the pumps."

They watched the video of Frank's camper entering the station and got their first good view of it. They also got a very good close up of the woman riding with Frank.

"She is pretty, and much younger. Cheap hair dye, though," Shawn said.

"Hair dye?"

"Yes, and not a good one." They watched the tape over and over again.

"Tom, the two don't look right together."

"Right together?"

"She looks uncomfortable around Frank. She just doesn't seem relaxed like a camper should. You know like when you meet a girl for a one night stand and then have to say good-bye."

"I wouldn't know," Tom said. "Are you saying he really doesn't know her?"

"That's the feeling I get," Shawn said.

"Okay, this woman, Carol, travels to a campground and finds an admirer. The woman tries to blow up these Arabs, but everything goes wrong. The woman needs to hide, so she calls this older guy. She guides him here and there and keeps him moving, and all the while he's unaware of who she is," Tom said.

"And now they are heading for the Badlands …," Shawn said.

"Are they? She's not stupid and knows that by now she has the Arabs and us after her. She can't take any chances and figures by now that we know about Frank. Shawn, get a map." He laid a map on the gas station counter. Three remote camping areas lay within fifty miles of the gas station.

"They're at one of those three; we need to visit all of them tonight, quietly. Have someone forward pictures of the trailer and of "Carol" from that video so that we can pick them up."

Shawn drove through the Minnesota darkness toward the first likely camping area. He stopped at a copy center and picked up the photographs. An hour later he drove into the first camping area.

"Shawn, you drive through the campground and quietly look for Frank's camper, I'll see if the staff remembers these two." No sign of the camper or Frank and Carol was found.

At around one in the morning, Tom woke the park ranger who cared for the second wilderness area and inquired about them. The ranger could not recall seeing them. Shawn drove all over the area but found nothing.

In the early morning hours they drove into the last area, a long rolling prairie. Tom decided to go to this area last because, being prairie, it was the last place he expected to find the two. He woke up the park ranger at four in the morning.

"I haven't seen anyone like those two, but I've been at a meeting. You're welcome to look over the campground," the ranger explained. "With all the hills and swales they could be anywhere out there."

Though exhausted they headed out anyway. Shawn drove up and down trail after trail throughout the park without seeing any campers like Frank's. At five-thirty in the morning Tom found he was too tired to function.

"I'm getting too old for this; my hunch was wrong. Let's call it a night." Tom set up the tent, and they crawled in. Shawn didn't care at this point; he was so tired that he would have slept on the bare ground. Had they waited until dawn they would have seen Frank's camper glittering in the morning light out on the open prairie.

***

At dawn Sarah left Frank asleep in bed, took her binoculars, and walked out. She hoped to spot a deer and found a group of whitetails going from thicket to thicket. She looked north and saw a car shimmering in the morning sun.

*That car wasn't parked there last night.* She hiked to the car and looked inside. Sitting on the seat of the car was a picture of herself and one of Frank's camper. Literature lay on the back seat, and "FBI" was visible on the top page. She looked across the prairie to where Frank was sleeping in his camper. If he tried to drive past the FBI agents in the tent, it would awaken them. If she went to his camper, he would not understand her concern. She couldn't return to Frank's camper.

*All I can do is hike out of here and somehow get a ride from someone.*

She began walking straight north keeping the road in sight but herself hidden from prying eyes.

*I've got my wallet, my fake ID, and about five hundred dollars.*

She continued walking and saw a farm truck coming up the road. She flagged the driver down.

"Could you give me a ride to the truck stop? My car broke down at the campground." He let her in.

At the truck stop, Sarah ordered coffee and sat staring at the drivers. One of the truck drivers had a "Tommy's Chicken" logo on his shirt.

"Where is Tommy's Chicken located?"

"It's in Berlin, Maryland," the driver said.

"Where?"

"It's near Ocean City."

"Are you heading there?"

"Yeah, wanna come?"

"Yes, I would." The truck driver almost fell off his chair but managed to wave her over.

"When will we be in Maryland?"

"Two days." They climbed into the truck and took off.

***

Tom had a bad night and lay snoring in his sleeping bag. Shawn got up around eight in the morning and stumbled out to the car. He reached in and got his cell phone to see if anyone had called. He looked south across the open prairie and saw Frank's camper sitting a mile or more away.

"Oh my God, Tom, you're not going to believe this! Tom, wake up. Tom!"

*At this point nothing would surprise me. I better get up and see what he's got.*

"Shawn, this better be good."

"It's the camper!" Shawn stated. Tom crawled out of the tent but could hardly see in the bright sunlight.

"Where?" Tom asked. Shawn pointed out on the prairie. He could see nothing.

"Are you sure?" Shawn nodded yes. He slid into the car.

"Shawn, get in." Shawn got in and Tom drove toward the camper on a very rough dirt trail.

"Get my pistol out of the glove box," Tom said.

Shawn drew his own pistol and took the safety off.

"Keep the safety on. I don't want to get shot when we hit a bump." He drove as quietly as he could the last half mile and stopped about fifty yards from the camper. They snuck around the camper and came to the door. Tom opened the door and slid in. He heard snoring and walked up to Frank, who was still asleep.

"FBI! Don't move!" A moment later Frank found he was lying in bed handcuffed.

"Where's the girl!" Tom screamed.

"The girl … Carol, was asleep here this morning," Frank said. "What the hell's going on?" Tom and Shawn searched the trailer but did not find the woman. Tom interrogated Frank for almost an hour. Frank knew almost nothing about the girl.

"You mean Carol's gone? Where did she go?" Frank asked.

"Shawn we screwed up!" Tom said, furious. "We missed catching the girl last night, and now she slipped away. Call in a helicopter and tracking dogs, and search the area." The dogs tracked Sarah to the road.

"Shawn, I want everyone questioned who drives this road on a regular basis. Check with all the locals." Tom had not really slept at all last night and had a bad headache. The sound of the helicopters overhead caused his headache to be much worse.

"Tom, I found out what happened to the girl."

"What?"

"She got a ride to a truck stop with a farm hand," Shawn said.

"Then she's gone. We might get lucky if we know who she left with."

They drove to the truck stop. The waitress remembered seeing Sarah but could not remember whom she left with or when. No one else remembered seeing her at all. Tom was too tired to go on.

"Shawn, let's call it a day and get a motel. Tomorrow's another day." Shawn rented a motel and each headed to their rooms.

***

Frank hoped Carol would return and explain herself. The FBI, their helicopter, and their dogs had left. He sobbed himself to sleep that night after drinking a full glass of scotch.

*I'm going to miss her!*

The next morning he heard a noise in the kitchen.

"Carol is that you?" Excited, he stumbled out of bed and came face to face with an Arab man carrying a pistol.

"What the hell!"

"The girl, where is she?" the man asked.

"I don't know. She left yesterday morning. The FBI was here!"

"Where did she go?" the man screamed at him.

"They said she made it to the truck stop, but I don't believe it," Frank explained. A few moments later, a shot echoed across the prairie and a van drove away from the trailer. The gunshot awakened the park warden.

"That guy Frank was so upset over losing that girl; you don't think he shot himself?" the warden said to his wife. He decided to go and see for himself.

Shawn had slept about four hours when his cell phone went off. He answered the phone and found the warden on the line.

"That guy Frank that you talked to yesterday, he shot himself."

"What? We'll be right over." Shawn awoke Tom again and was glad he was outside of range of his fists, as he was angry.

"Frank Silva, the guy with the camper, he's dead," Shawn said.

"Wake that yokel up; tell him no one goes into the camper until we get there okay?" Tom demanded. Shawn called and explained to the warden that no one was to enter the camper until they got there.

It took over an hour to drive out to the prairie campground. Tom could see people milling around the camper when they arrived.

"Oh my God, you called them, right?" He looked ahead and saw people and officers walking in and out of Frank's camper.

"Why not just charge admittance and get it over with!" He found that local sheriffs, the park service, firefighters, the local press and even the coroner had already been in the camper before they arrived.

"I don't see what jurisdiction the FBI has here," a local sheriff said as Tom got out of the car. "The suicide of a depressed man …."

"Where's the gun?" Tom said.

"The gun?" the sheriff said.

"The gun he shot himself with?" he asked.

"Who has the gun?" the sheriff called to everyone at the scene. No one answered. Tom was fit to be tied.

"Another crime scene down the toilet!" Tom called for the helicopter crew again.

"Why kill Frank?" Shawn asked.

"The killer came for the girl, she wasn't here, but they wanted no witnesses."

"Oh my God, the truck stop!" Shawn said. The helicopter flew them over.

Tom found the waitress he had talked to yesterday morning.

"You're back. I talked to your other agent this morning," the waitress said.

"The other agent?"

"The dark-skinned, handsome one. He asked about the missing girl, and a driver sitting at the counter remembered seeing her leave with someone yesterday morning in a white truck."

"The driver he talked to, do you know him?" Tom asked.

"No, but he's been coming in these last mornings. I think he likes me." Tom had no choice now but to wait until morning.

"Tomorrow morning, I don't care what you do, but don't let him leave until I get here. Shawn, I've never seen a case as screwed up as this one. I need to retire before I'm demoted to desk clerk!"

The next morning they found out that Sarah had ridden out of town with a Tommy's Chicken driver. Tom called their office and found that the trucker had arrived in Berlin, Maryland, and had gone home.

Tom and Shawn flew into Maryland, and interrogated the truck driver. The truck driver said he was sure that the girl he knew as Carol headed to Ocean City. Tom and Shawn drove down to Ocean City and began canvassing hotels for any single women that just arrived.

***

"Saleh, Hamid, we just missed the Israeli. She is traveling in a chicken truck," Yasin explained. All three men piled into their Dodge Caravan to drive to Maryland.

"We must complete the task; Walid will not stand for this nonsense!" Saleh said. "We need to find the truck and the Israeli. Perhaps we could cause the truck to crash or at least run it off the road. We can't stop to rest until we find her." It took them two days to drive to Maryland.

Saleh and his crew had not eaten much the past few days, and they decided to stop at a Wal-Mart and get food. Saleh and Hamid had already gone inside and Yasin was going to follow them in. He looked and saw the Israeli woman right in front of him talking to an older guy in a camper. He went to get Saleh and Hamid but saw the camper leaving. He ran, jumped into the mini van, and followed the camper south to Assateague Island. He observed as the man paid the park service to enter the National Seashore. Yasin, from almost a mile distant, watched the Israeli woman help the man set up camp. He got into the mini van and headed back to the Wal-Mart.

"Saleh, the girl is setting up camp on the island right now!" Yasin said.

"Then early tomorrow morning we send her to hell where she belongs." Saleh drove into Ocean City to rent a room for the night, hoping that their cover had not been blown. The clerk seemed nervous when he entered the motel.

"Did something happen?" he asked.

"Yes, the FBI was just here and checked my list of names; they must be looking for someone." Saleh felt his knees almost give out on him.

"The FBI must be searching Ocean City for us," Yasin said. "Driving out of town is pointless. They will be watching for that. What can we do? Who will hide us?"

"I know of someone who is close by," Saleh said.

## WASHINGTON

Liana learned to trust Tim. He wanted to take her to the Smithsonian museums. She asked at work if she could go on her day off, and everyone encouraged her to.

"Liana, relax in Washington and have fun with Tim."

Tim picked her up at six in the morning, as they wanted to get an early start. She wore a knee length blue dress that seemed to shimmer in the sunlight.

Liana spotted the blue dress in the petite section of a boardwalk store. It was very light and made of a fabric similar to silk. She ran her hands over the fabric and loved the feel of it.

"Tim I barely slept last night! I can't wait to see the museum exhibits."

The trip from Ocean City to Washington took about three hours, and they talked the whole way. On the way she looked into his glove box and pulled out a handful of homemade compact disks.

"Will you play this for me?" she asked.

"Liana, please no, it's embarrassing."

"Are you keeping a secret from me?" She shoved it into the player and music filled the car.

"Tim, your big secret is that you listen to Mozart!"

"Most Americans don't like classical music," he explained.

"I do. It's universal and cuts across all languages."

Tim drove through Washington explaining each monument.

"That's where the President lives," he said pointing. She could not believe she was driving past the White House.

"That giant tower is the Washington monument."

"To honor George Washington?" she asked.

"Have you heard of him?"

"Let's see … Washington was your first president. Before that he was an officer in the British army who fought the French and Indians. He lived in Virginia, and his wife was named Martha … I love to study history," she said.

They went to the American History museum first. Liana was surprised at the amount of displays and the detail that went into them. They walked floor after floor, going to one exhibit after another.

"How did they save so many artifacts?"

"From the beginning of our country, the need was known by men like Thomas Jefferson that everything had to be preserved."

They stopped at the Natural History museum. Liana viewed actual bones and skeletons of dinosaurs.

*Things I only dreamt I would see!* She walked on and saw a giant Blue whale.

"When I was a girl, they told us Blue whales were extinct. Are they?"

"No," the museum guide explained, "there are some left, but we wish that more survived."

On the street Liana noticed that everyone turned to stare, and she did not like it.

*Being noticed no longer means being shot. Relax ... maybe everyone's just admiring the blue dress.*

The next stop was the National Gallery of Art. Seeing paintings made by great artists made her cry.

"Liana, why are you crying? Tim asked.

"It's just me, I get overcome sometimes."

Liana viewed art by Picasso, Goya, Raphael and Verne.

"Tim, so much of your art is based on the death of Jesus. I had always been told that America was a godless, immoral country." She realized that she was saying too much, as a Russian would not comment like this, but a Muslim would. Tim said nothing, and she realized he did not catch her mistake.

They stopped to eat lunch near the Capitol. They watched a street performer as they ordered hot dogs.

"Don't worry," Tim said to Liana as he handed her a huge hot dog, "it's all beef." She bit into the hot dog before she realized what Tim had said and it worried her. Did he suspect she was Muslim?

"Tim, why all beef?"

"Beef, oh the hot dog! So many hot dogs here are made with chicken or turkey that they don't taste like hot dogs should. I just wanted you to have one that tasted good."

"I like the hot dog; next you'll convince me to eat pizza and french fries on the boardwalk."

They went on to the Air and Space museum. She saw the space capsules and the Spirit of Saint Louis. Liana sadly looked up at a jet fighter, remembered her mother and her being strafed, and once again it brought her to tears.

They ended up back at the car and drove around Washington. Tim drove through sections he had never been to before. As he was driving, they could again see the White House. He drove past a black granite monument that she did not recognize from her history books. Tim saw a huge collection of parked motorcycles.

"What's that?" she asked.

"I really don't know." They walked down and saw "The Wall."

Liana did not understand what she was looking at and walked right up to it. Huge bikers stood around the wall, crying and laying flowers next to the black granite. Men partially dressed in military uniforms felt the names on the wall with their fingers. Women made rubbings of names using thin paper.

"What this is?" she asked.

"The names of fifty-six thousand Americans who lost their lives fighting for our country," a biker said to her. Liana ran her own fingers across the black granite and felt the names.

*Someday one of these will be in Chechnya and my grandfather's name will be on it.* She stared at her own fingers.

*In Russia my friends are sketching names of those who died, and I pulled the trigger that killed them.* Liana broke down sobbing, and Tim was unsure of what to do. The biker picked her up and hugged her, and they both began crying. Tim had no choice but to stand and take it all in.

"I am sorry, Tim. It's just that there's been so much death and fighting. I guess the thought just overwhelmed me."

"I understand. It's a lot to take in." The day had been one of marvels and wonders for her. For the first time since she could remember things seemed positive in her life. On the ride home Liana realized she'd accomplished something she had wanted to do since childhood, see Washington and the Smithsonian museum. She slid across the seat and wrapped her arms around Tim.

"Tim, I now have something I've never had before"

"What?" he asked.

"A boyfriend." Later he stopped at her hotel and they had a long kiss before she got out of the car.

"I will see you soon!" she said. Tim got out of the car and surprised her as she headed for the hotel door, giving her another kiss.

"Tim, the girls I work with will see!" He blushed and went to return to his car. This time Liana surprised him and caught him before he got to his car, giving him a kiss.

"Tim, please go now!" She composed herself and walked into the hotel. As she entered the doorway, she saw several girls she knew and they were giggling. Liana just held her hands up as if to say "Oh well!" and walked toward her room. She entered her room, went to hit the light switch and felt something pulled into her mouth from behind. She bit down onto a pair of socks that stopped her from screaming. Hands grabbed her from the darkness and seemed to come from everywhere at once. She tried to scream but couldn't. She didn't have one set of hands, but several grabbing at her. The hands felt cold and slimy, and she realized her thin dress had torn off in the struggle. She clawed and kicked at whatever was in front of her. She felt herself lifted into the air as she fought.

*The boys in the car that Tim fought with, they must have followed us home!*

The hands holding her were slippery against her bare skin, and she twisted this way and that in them. She was able to claw out again and felt her fingernails tearing at skin. In the next instant she felt a gun muzzle against her head and heard a pistol's hammer click.

"Liana, survive!" her mother seemed to call out to her again.

She had to survive and stopped struggling against her attackers.

*I remember surviving this with the CDF. I will survive this again. The Chechen militia left me near the Russian hospital almost dead ....*

## THE RUSSIAN HOSPITAL

When the CDF finished with Liana, she had found herself stumbling and almost at the point of collapse.

"Stop, Stop!"

Almost in a dream-like stare, Liana saw Russian soldiers with their rifles pointed at her walking forward. She started to say something and collapsed on the ground.

She woke up two days later in a Russian army hospital. She wore a white hospital gown and found her wrists and ankles bandaged. An IV, attached to her arm, dripped fluid. She went to get up but found she hardly had the strength to move. Liana felt sore from her ankles to her head and had trouble bending her legs or elbows. A nurse in green fatigues stood nearby.

"Our angel is awake!" the nurse called to a doctor. The doctor walked down.

"Don't try and get up. You've been through too much already. Try and rest."

"Where am I?"

"You're with friends now, Russians."

"Where?"

"You're in a military hospital in Chechnya; an officer is coming over to debrief you."

An officer came up and they exchanged small smiles. The officer addressed the nurse as Lt. Anya Belova.

"You're a lieutenant?" Liana asked.

"Regular Red Army," the nurse replied. "Do you have some questions for our angel?"

"Why do you keep calling me your angel?" she asked.

"When the men brought you in I changed you out of your bloody dress and into a hospital gown. We washed you up and you lay there looking so innocent, and everyone who saw you said you looked like an angel, and you really did. You are our little angel!"

While the nurse and officer prepared themselves, Liana looked at her medical chart.

"Russian girl approx fourteen years of age, condition-stable … fracture to cranium … ligature marks on wrists … chain marks on ankles … right elbow reset … torture victim … rape victim … treated for venereal disease as a precaution."

She laid the chart down not wanting to remember the last five days. The officer and nurse came forward.

"Who are you?"

"Sashi, Sashi Kamikov."

"Where are you from?"

"The Russian School at Grozny."

"What happened?" the officer asked. She did not say.

"It's okay, tell him," the nurse said.

"The CDF captured my mother and me."

"Your mother?"

"Maria Kamikov."

"What happened?" the officer asked. She did not say.

"What happened to your mother?" the nurse asked her.

"She's dead. The CDF killed her," Liana said.

"Your father?" the officer asked.

"The CDF broke into our home and shot my father and dragged me and my mother away."

"What did they do to you?" the officer asked her. Liana simply turned away and said nothing. The room went silent for a moment.

"Will you show us where they took you?"

"Yes."

The officer came back with a map of Grozny, and she studied it in detail. The officer used his finger and traced up street after street. The officer's finger went past a street corner and she shuddered.

"What is there?"

"Heads!" she said in real horror.

"Heads?" The officer asked incredulous.

"They chopped off the heads of our Russian soldiers and piled them on street corners!"

The officer recoiled at the answer and could not believe what she was saying. The officer began tracing the streets again, and again she shuddered.

"Is this where they killed your mother?"

"No, it's a sniper bunker."

"And?" the officer asked.

"They hung wounded Russian soldiers by their feet so the Russian soldiers will have to shoot their own men to shoot them."

"Mother of God!" the nurse called out.

"Show me the location!" the officer demanded.

She traced the street with her finger. Liana expected that that they knew this already, but everything was new to them. One thing was certain to her, though. She hoped the Russians blew the CDF to hell.

The officer left after some additional questioning. Liana sat up on the edge of her bed unassisted.

"Sashi, stay in bed. You're too weak," the nurse said. "If I have to spend extra time with you, how will I care for the others?"

After a short meal Liana looked up to find the Russian officer returning, bringing with him a very bedraggled looking militiaman. Liana recoiled at the sight of the militiaman, as obviously he was part of a Chechen militia unit loyal to the Russian army.

"It's okay, he won't hurt you; he's a Chechen helping this country return to a civilized state. He's our friend," the nurse explained. "He has confirmed your story of the decapitated soldiers and wounded men. He wants you to point out where the CDF strongholds were located."

The Chechen officer looked at Liana with an air of suspicion.

"What I don't understand is how you escaped them," the militiaman said to her. Lt. Anya, to Liana's embarrassment, uncovered Liana to show her condition to the militia officer.

"It is a miracle you survived," he said.

The Chechen militia officer, the Russian militia officer and the nurse stepped aside, and Liana could hear part of the conversation.

"Do you believe her story?"

"Yes, I have no doubts. It's just that the CDF kills whoever doesn't cooperate with them."

Liana liked Lt. Anya, and they got along well.

"I'm going to try and get up," Liana said. "The exercise will do me good." She stood, shakily, and found she could hobble around the hospital tent. She found the Russian soldiers traumatized by the fighting in Chechnya. If a tray dropped or a spoon hit a pan, the men would jump and stare blankly.

On the third day Liana saw the Colonel that she was being blackmailed to kill. Colonel Temikov and a brunette nurse came to view the wounded soldiers and to try to cheer them up. Colonel Temikov was about thirty-five years old and very handsome. The hospital nurses all began whispering and teasing each other when he arrived. Liana saw the brunette nurse clinging to the Colonel.

*Skinny, tiny and wounded, I am supposed to lure him away from her?*

When the Colonel came her way, Liana was ready to head the other way, but Lt. Anya stopped her.

"You've heard of our little angel, haven't you?"

"No, I haven't."

"This is Sashi; she escaped from the Chechen murderers."

The Colonel glanced at Liana's swollen wrists and ankles, and tears welled up in his eyes.

"She's helping us in the hospital, but a girl her age should not view the horrors that these tents contain."

"She can help in the mess hall during the daytime, and stay here at night where she will be safe."

Liana began helping in the kitchen from ten in the morning until dinner. Her duties involved scrubbing and washing an endless array of pots, pans and trays. She did her best to stay away from the Russian soldiers, who tried to start conversations with her all the time.

Liana learned that the Colonel and the brunette nurse lived in a small house sixty yards from the mess hall. From the kitchen window she could see when the Colonel arrived and whom he brought with him. Liana also noticed the compound had guards everywhere and sections were mined.

"The Chechens attack the compound all the time. If any firing takes place, you lie on the floor until the all clear is given," a woman in the mess hall said. Liana looked around, automatic weapons and pistols were everywhere. It might be possible to steal one and kill the Colonel with it.

*Then what? I cut off his head and sneak through a minefield while I am being shot at?*

At lunch an obnoxious Russian soldier gave her a hard time.

"Go back to the barracks with me!" he demanded.

"Why do you want with that skinny thing when we have the Chechen girls on the hill?" another soldier replied.

Liana heard the comment and remembered that they trucked away the young women of her village. She needed to know the truth. She decided that, if caught at the hill, she would say that the chemical smells from the dish soap sickened her. After dinner she took the stroll.

She stepped out, and without much thought, began walking across the compound. The "Hill" was about one hundred yards away and she headed toward it. After crossing a series of tents, she had a clear view of a long set of barracks and headed that way. She saw a fenced yard, full of girls and young women. Liana knew by their dress that the girls were Chechen.

"Please help us! Please get us out of here!" they called through the fence.

She tried to ignore them and headed toward the hospital. About halfway two drunken Russian soldiers jumped out of a tent and stumbled at her. Liana screamed and ran to the hospital with the two soldiers chasing her. Other soldiers egged them on. As she reached the hospital tent Lt. Anya appeared carrying a pistol.

"Dear God, can't you see the child's had enough!" she screamed at the soldiers. "What happened?" she asked Liana.

"I was trying to get some air and two soldiers chased me."

"Don't think badly of them. I think they were just teasing you!"

*I must be very careful.*

Liana lay in the hospital tent trying to sleep but was having a hard time doing so.

*The Russian nurses are kind and nice to me; it's the Chechens, the CDF, which hurt me so much! Chechen girls, like myself, faced horrible abuse just a hundred yards away, could I help them? What about the CDF and my mission? If I don't complete it Momma and I will be dead. Two more dead Chechen women on a pile that reaches into the sky! If I do kill the Colonel, Momma might live. But how can I do it?*

"I have something for you," Lt. Anya said to her the next morning.

It was the Russian schoolgirl's dress, now washed and pressed.

"Thank you!"

"Let me put this back on you," the nurse said putting the silver cross back on Liana's neck.

"Be careful today and go straight to the mess hall!"

Liana spied a small backpack in the hospital tent. "Can I use that to carry my school dress and things in?"

"Yes, Sashi, you may have it. The Russian girl who owned it died from the wounds those Chechen murderers inflicted on her."

*I'm carrying a dead girl's backpack and wearing a dead girl's cross and dress.*

She noticed latex gloves at the hospital.

"Can I have a pair? My hands are getting red from the dish detergent." Lt. Anya gave her several pair.

"Now run to the mess hall! I'll watch you go. You will be all right."

Liana ran briskly toward the mess hall and stopped to look back. Lt. Anya stood watching.

The day started like other days with Liana cleaning pots and scrubbing pans. She ate black bread and soup with the other workers at lunch. She carried the backpack with her, which now held a few items collected in addition to her schoolgirl's dress. After lunch she spied at huge meat cleaver sitting on the counter.

"What is that for?"

"To cut beef brisket with when we make soup." She was tempted to steal the huge cleaver but knew that she could not explain it if caught.

After dinner Liana heard muffled gunfire and thought little of it, as gunfire seemed normal. Then gunfire exploded across the camp, and the sound of incoming mortars tore through the night sky. The already edgy soldiers panicked and ran for shelter.

"The Chechens!" a woman screamed.

An AK-47 stood in the corner. Liana picked it up and stepped outside into the confusion. A truck drove through the compound wire and headed straight for the hospital.

"Stop!" Liana screamed and fired on the truck.

The truck drove into Lt. Anya's ward. A huge explosion ripped through the hospital sending debris high into the sky.

*I just fired on another Chechen fighter. I have to think quickly. Bullets, mortars and rocket-propelled grenades are flying everywhere. Trucks full of explosives are driving into the compound from all directions and blowing up. The camp is total confusion.* She drew the latex gloves tightly over her hands, ran back into the kitchen and grabbed the huge cleaver, stuffing it into her backpack. A pistol lay where a Russian officer had been eating; she placed it in her pocket. She quickly changed into her schoolgirl's uniform and, wearing her backpack, walked toward the Colonel's cottage. He appeared from the doorway, screaming over a handheld radio. Liana walked up to him, drew the pistol and shot him twice in the chest. The brunette nurse appeared and screamed. Liana shot her twice in the head. She drew the huge cleaver and did as asked. She wrapped the Colonel's head in a black plastic bag, which she placed in her backpack. Total confusion engulfed the camp, but she could see where the truck had crashed through the wire.

*I can slip out of the camp by following the truck treads through the minefield. If I face capture, I'll kill myself. Grozny is twenty kilometers away, and I'll have to walk, sneak and crawl the entire way.*

Liana made it to Grozny before daybreak the next day. Russian artillery units now encircled the entire city. Blockades existed on all roads in and out of the city. She snuck around the blockades through the same minefield that the CDF had driven over. She descended into the sewers to enter the city.

Liana, still dressed in her schoolgirl's uniform, entered the CDF compound and found the man who had caused her so much pain. She threw the backpack on the table.

"It's done!" she exclaimed. The man viewed the gruesome discovery and compared it to a photograph he had.

"It is the Colonel! We have other missions for you, Liana!" He looked up but she was gone.

She made it back to Sarena's basement.

"Liana is it you or is this an angel I am seeing?"

"It's me, Momma, and I am no longer an angel."

"What happened?"

"Not now. We must leave here immediately. We are being watched."

"Where will we go?"

"Anywhere but here …."

## THE ENCOUNTER

Someone grabbed and gagged Liana when she entered her hotel room. She struggled and fought in pitch-blackness against the men who grabbed her. She felt a gun muzzle against her head and allowed her body to go limp.

The light came on. Someone tightly held a stocking over her mouth from behind. Another held her right wrist and arm. A third grasped her left wrist and held a pistol with a silencer to her head. She looked at the men and realized they were not the boys from the car, but middle-aged Arabs.

"We are from Walid," the man with the gun told Liana. The man holding her from behind ran his hand through her hair and it made her cringe. Her thin dress lay on the floor. The man holding her left wrist stood admiring her.

*I must remain calm and control the situation but I'm ready to kill someone!* She mumbled something, and the man with the pistol motioned to the man holding her. He pulled the stocking away.

"Get your hands off me," she demanded.

"You will do as we say?" the man with the pistol whispered to her. The men let her go. The man with the pistol still pointed it at her.

"Liana! Liana! Are you all right?" Margrite called.

"Let her in," the man with the pistol whispered.

*He intends to kill or rape Margrite!* She shook her head no. She grabbed her robe, put it on and slid outside. Margrite saw the red mark on Liana's face.

"Liana!" Liana put her finger to her lips.

"Shhhh! I snuck Tim in through my window. He almost fell and pulled me out too." Margrite's face changed from worry to amusement. Her doorway was open a little, and she saw her torn dress lying on the floor.

"Liana, your beautiful new dress!"

"Margrite, Tim and I are new to this and ... awkward? Please do not tell?" Margrite nodded yes, but Liana knew that every girl in the hotel would know Tim was here in the morning. Margrite left, and Liana waited in the hallway for just a moment. By being bold she had just saved her friend's life, maybe she could control her own future by being bold also.

Liana slid into her room, locking the door at the same time. She glared at the man who had gagged her.

"I am not afraid of you!" He turned to the man with the pistol.

"Now what?" he said. She turned a radio on to drown out their voices from prying ears. She pulled her covers away and slid into bed, turning away from the men. Liana kept a thin knife at her bed and now held it in her hand.

"Liana, I am Saleh. This is Yasin and Walid. We are following an Israeli agent, and she is camped near here. We are being followed, and this was the only place we could go. I remembered that Walid had a harlot ...."

"A what!" she exclaimed.

"We need to stay the night, and we will leave in the morning to get the Israeli."

"Do you know who I am?"

"Yes, through, how you say, gossip," Saleh said.

"You may have ruined everything. If you must stay then turn the light out and go to sleep."

*I'm so mad now I think my head will explode. Every time my life begins to make sense, something turns it upside down. Now I have killers sleeping in my room!*

"I sleep on the floor while the harlot sleeps in a bed, alone?" Hamid said.

*I can't believe this! I've spent years sleeping on rocks, in snowy, icy mountains, in rusty truck beds, in mud and always in danger. These three are sleeping on my clean, soft carpet, in a warm place, and complaining about it*?

"Hamid, this afternoon at The Wall I promised Allah I would never kill another man, but if you say one more word I will break my promise."

"This girl, this ... she threatens me!" Hamid said.

In an instant she held the knife against his throat. Saleh pulled her hand away before she could slice his throat. She stood holding the knife. Hamid's throat showed a cut mark. She slid back into her bed.

"Hamid, you were lucky. Many, many men have died by my hands, and I have nightmares about it every night. I want no more to die."

The night dragged on, and Liana wondered if she'd slept at all. The news came on her radio and said a nationwide manhunt was on for a woman thought to be a terrorist. Everyone thought she had fled to Ocean City, Maryland ....

***

Tom and Shawn searched the motels and hotels of Ocean City looking for the Israeli woman. They made every effort to keep things quiet, as everything about this case had gone badly so far. While searching, Shawn's phone rang. The Arabs had shopped at a nearby Wal-Mart.

"Great, all we need now is a shoot-out between the two, and a nationwide alert will probably go out." Tom received a telephone call from

Cathleen Hale.

"Tom, what's going on down there?"

"Down where?"

"In Ocean City, Maryland."

"Cathleen, how did you know where I was?"

"Tom, the Associated Press is releasing a story that the Israelis and Arabs have been chasing each other across the country, killing each other and blowing up campers as they go."

"They put that out on the wire!" Tom said.

"A news crew from CNN is in Minnesota interviewing the local police; they are saying that the two groups are killing each other off as they travel the country. Tom, they're showing pictures of three Arabs in a van at a Wal-Mart in Ocean City, Maryland, and saying that the FBI is searching the hotels for a blond Israeli woman."

Tom knew the case had blown wide open. As he talked, police cars began driving up and down the strip with their sirens on. He wondered how everything got out of whack so fast.

"Shawn, I think we're screwed," Tom said. "We'll probably get a call from Washington next."

***

Ali, Walid's security officer, wondered what the hell was going on. He kept his eye on Liana, and now it seemed that the Wrath of Allah had fallen upon Ocean City. She took the job at the hotel as directed. She tried to fit into her new lifestyle and did well. She dated an American boy, who Ali saw as being helpful as a cover. All seemed perfect this morning, and he did not have any inkling that anything was wrong. Now the news showed the FBI combing the city for Arabs and looking for a blond woman they were supposed to kill. It showed the van the Arabs drove and an all points bulletin put out by the police. Ali turned his computer on and brought up a web cam.

"I think we're finished," Ali said aloud, grabbing his car keys.

***

In the dark of her room, Liana saw a shadow against her wall. She turned abruptly and saw Saleh standing next to her with his gun drawn. She almost screamed, but Saleh put his finger to his mouth.

"Someone is at the door …." She slid out of bed, crept to the door and opened it slowly.

*Another Arab?* The man slid in. Saleh held his pistol on the man.

"Put that pistol down, you idiot," the man said to Saleh.

"Who are you?" Saleh asked.

"Ali, Walid's security officer."

"Are you Saleh?"

"Yes, and Yasin and Hamid," he responded. Ali shook his head in disgust. The three had brought this upon them all. An all-points bulletin was out on Saleh's van, and it sat in the parking lot.

"You idiot, you've blown everything, everything! How did you end up here?"

"We were spotted in town, so we came here to hide. We heard Walid had a harlot here," he said.

"A what?" Ali asked. He looked around the room. He saw fingernail scratches on Yasin's face and chest. Liana's new dress lay torn on the floor. Hamid's throat showed a razor cut. Grasp marks outlined Liana's mouth, arms and shoulders.

"Did they harm you?" Ali asked her.

"I am fine, but I almost killed Hamid," she said.

"Liana, can you swim?"

"Yes, I swim very well."

"We need to get rid of the van, and I am sure the police have road blocks at each end of the island. They would spot those three before they got to the van. We need to clean this up, fast! At any time the police will spot that van, search the hotel, and then we're finished," Ali said.

"The FBI is looking for you?" Ali said to her.

"No, they are looking for an Israeli woman, and those three know where she is."

"If those three are caught alive, the police will track them back to you. I don't know how they heard about you, but they will never see you again. Liana," Ali said putting his hand on his heart, "I am sorry."

For a moment the street was empty, and Liana, wearing gloves, drove the van across side streets to a deserted section of the bay. She floored the van, ran it off the road, over a dock, and into the bay. She swam back as the van floated fifty yards north, and then sank out of sight. She walked home in soaking wet clothes.

"Saleh, we'll deal with the Israeli now." Ali and Saleh's crew slipped out of Liana's room. It was 2:30 in the morning. Liana tried to sleep but had another nightmare. In her nightmare, she was escaping from Grozny through a minefield.

## THE BARRAGE

In an attempt to escape the clutches of the CDF, Liana and Sarena secretly moved their belongings into another abandoned basement in Grozny. Liana told about being captured by the CDF but did not go into details.

"The less you know about the CDF the better." Sarena, seeing the chaffed wrists and ankles, knew all too well what Liana had endured.

"All you need to know is that I had to kill a Russian Colonel and prove to the CDF that I did so."

"They forced you to go to the Russians?"

"They treated me much kinder than the Chechens."

Sarena did not want to know more. Liana wanted to burn the Russian schoolgirl's dress, but Sarena washed it and put it away.

"Liana, rest and eat!"

Liana rested and read books, trying to put the last weeks behind her.

At breakfast the next morning the Russians began a campaign to reduce the city to dust with bombs and artillery. Barrage after barrage of shells fell into the city. Liana climbed to the roof to see that the Russians were leveling the city yard by yard.

"Get them!" she screamed aloud as she watched a jet swoop in and fire missiles on the CDF compound.

"Liana, come down!" Sarena screamed. "Your grandfather has ordered everyone to stay hidden and wait out the barrage. They're safe underground. Most of the militia units believe the Russians will mount a frontal assault on Grozny. I think the other militias tried to meet the Russians head on!"

Three days later the Chechen commanders gathered to discuss the situation, as it was very bad. To her horror Liana saw the CDF commander walk into the building to talk to Aslan. She hadn't told her grandfather anything about her capture and had pleaded with her mother to do the same.

*He has enough on his mind now. Why trouble him with things he cannot change?*

"We lost over half our men in the initial attack," one described. "Some units were completely wiped out, but we must drive the Russians out of Chechnya! We will attack them and drive them back!"

Aslan's militia survived the initial attack by remaining hidden and away from the front lines.

"We cannot win this fight, and we should not fight as if we can," Aslan explained. "Our only hope is to hurt the Russians and cause them to negotiate a truce. Without a truce the city will fall and we will all die. The Russians have not even hit us hard yet, and we are wounded. What will we have when they attack with might?"

"They've pounded our positions, and you're saying that they are going to hit us harder?" a commander asked.

"The Russians will hit us very hard!"

"We must somehow attack the Russians!" they said to Aslan.

"Our only chance is to fire in a diversion, draw their artillery to where we want it to fall, and hit them very hard when they send reconnaissance. The Russians will be thrown off their plan constantly and will not be able to comprehend what is going on," Aslan explained.

"This is your plan for the war, sit and take it?" a commander asked.

"No, this is my plan for the city."

"Do you believe we can defeat the Russian forces by doing this?" a commander asked Aslan.

"We cannot win, but we can cause the Russians to think about the invasion, and again ask for a peace conference," Aslan said. "If Grozny falls and we have no agreement with the Russians, we have lost the war." Liana heard her grandfather's words and sat contemplating them.

*The Russian commander bragged that his men would be comfortably encamped in Grozny by Christmas. January is here and the Russians do not hold a single block.*

*I am so tired. Some of the Chechen forces believed they could win by an all-out assault on the Russian army. Grandpa warned them, but one of these took place. The Russians, seeing a large Chechen force in front of them, retreated and shelled the area into oblivion. Many of the fighters he desperately needed to hold the city were lost in the foolish attack.*

The Russians hit the city hard. Liana was lying asleep when a blast threw her into the air.

"What was that?" Sarena asked. Liana held a rag to stop a nosebleed. She climbed up the rubble of the apartment building to see what was happening. She saw a plane fly over and drop a bomb on the southern end of the city. The bomb was a fuel-air device that dispersed fuel in a block-wide area. The fuel mixed with oxygen in the air and ignited just before hitting the ground. The explosion was unlike anything anyone in Chechnya had ever seen, and it killed any man, woman, dog or rat on the ground, in a basement, or in a bunker under it. When the bomb exploded the blast tossed her onto a brick wall like a rag doll. She ran downstairs to find Sarena bleeding from one ear.

"We must get far underground!"

They crawled into their basement and covered themselves with mattresses and piles of carpet to cushion the bomb blasts. She later found out the Russians called these "Vacuum bombs."

By February Aslan did not have enough men left to resist the Russians. All the other militias had fled Grozny. The CDF had left but had given Aslan an ultimatum of sorts, a death wish.

"Fight to your last bullet, but do not leave Grozny!" Liana tried to understand what they expected of them.

*It's strange that a group that fled the city would order another to stay, but nothing about this makes sense. The Russians now hold almost the entire city and will reduce the rest to dust tomorrow.*

"Sarena, find a way out of the city through the minefields. We must leave the city," Aslan said.

"There is no way out through the minefields. We will all die trying."

"You laid the mines. You can find a way out!"

She spent the evening marking a very dangerous zigzagging path through the minefields.

Aslan called together all the men he could contact, about two hundred all total.

"The city is lost. We must flee for our lives, but we must not allow the Russians to capture anyone alive. Everyone must swear to shoot his comrades before he will let them be captured." Aslan thought of Sarena and Liana, but he did not change his mind. "We will leave at midnight. Be ready." The Russians did not wait until midnight.

At ten that evening the final shelling began. Aslan's men slipped through the sewers until they reached the minefield. Sarena crawled in first, followed by fifty men. The group wormed their way, zigzagging this way and that, the half-mile or so through the minefield to safety. Once they had crossed and disappeared, the next group of fifty started. Then Liana's group began to crawl also.

*I was in the third group, and things should have gone smoothly since so many others had already crossed. I was about halfway across the minefield when a Russian attack helicopter flew directly overhead. The helicopter swerved, entered the city and returned over top of where I was lying. The helicopter would have simply flown by, but one of the men in the last group, fearing capture, fired an RPG directly into the Russian chopper. The helicopter fell, and Russian Special forces jumped out firing at everyone. The other helicopter began killing anyone on the ground. The fighters with me began stepping on land mines and were blown apart.*

Through the chaos and insanity of the minefield, Liana began crawling again and somehow found her way through.

"Liana, you made it through that!" Sarena said.

"Yes, Momma. Let's go quickly!"

Sarena and Liana fled the flaming city of Grozny and at Sarena's urging headed into the southern mountains. A few miles east of Grozny they came upon a mass grave and a destroyed village. Sarena found a woman hiding in the woods who explained what happened.

"Our men surrendered the village to the Russians. They killed everyone and burned the village."

"Momma, I don't understand?" Liana asked.

"It means that once you have fought, there is no surrender. We have no option now but to fight or die a horrible death."

Liana awoke from her nightmare and realized she was in her hotel room in Maryland. She picked up the phone and called Tim.

"Tim, can you come and sit with me a few hours? I'm having a really bad night."

"Nightmares again … what time is it …?"

## ASSATEAGUE

Sarah and the old man camped at Assateague, as he wanted to fish a few days. The old guy enjoyed her company, and they had a nice dinner together. Around nine he headed to bed.

"Are you staying up?"

"A little, I'll see you in the morning."

Sarah turned on the satellite TV and sat down. She watched for a while and then turned the channel to CNN. The headline described a search in Ocean City, Maryland for her and the Arabs. The news showed the blown-up trailer near Chicago, a dead man in Minnesota and the truck driver from Tommy's Chicken. The news showed a picture of the Arab's van and a picture of her, blond hair and all.

*Frank is dead and I'm to blame. At any moment police cars will cross the bridge and I will be trapped here.* She gathered her things and found a large screwdriver. Cars sat in the parking lot, and she hoped to steal one.

*Where will I go?* She didn't want to dwell on it, as she had to get out of here. She began to tiptoe out of the trailer.

"You won't make it," a voice boomed out of the bedroom. She stopped for a moment and then went forward.

"Carol, you won't make it." Dejected, she walked toward the bedroom.

"The girl on the TV," the old man asked, "that's you?"

"Yes!" He reached down and took the screwdriver from her.

"You gonna steal a car?" She shrugged her shoulders.

"Carol, or whatever your name is, you'll find black hair dye in the bathroom. Change your hair color, and I'll break camp…." She walked into the bathroom and found the hair dye.

Sarah dyed her hair, and the old man escorted her to his bed.

"What do you have in mind?" she asked. The old man lifted his bed and Sarah could see a space underneath.

"You want me to hide in there?"

"Yes, lift the bottom board." She found that the board hid another chamber.

"The cops are sure to have a roadblock ahead," he said to her.

"Why did you build this?"

"Used to haul pot down from old Mexico. As soon as we're clear of town, I'll let you up." Sarah climbed in, and he covered her with a quilt before closing the chamber.

The road was rough, and Sarah, hidden under the bed, felt every bump in it. She felt the camper incline and knew they had crossed the bridge. The road turned smooth, and she knew they were on the highway. A half hour went by.

"This is it …. Hello, officer, what's the trouble?" Sarah heard someone in the camper opening drawers and closets. She lay, afraid to even breathe, and then felt the camper moving again.

*Suppose this old man's some kind of freak? I climbed into this coffin, and I could wake up in his own little torture chamber ….*

After another hour of driving Sarah felt the camper pull over. A moment later she saw the old man's face peering into the chamber.

"You can get out now. It's okay." She got out and joined him up front.

"If you could let me out at the next town, I would be grateful."

"You'll get caught."

"Where do you want to take me?"

"Home."

"Home?" she asked.

*Maybe this guy is some kind of freak. Why does he want me to go home with him …?*

Sarah sat back as the camper sped along the highway.

"You're Israeli, right?" the guy asked.

"Israeli? Let's not get into it."

"I mean you're Jewish, right? Why not just click your heels then and go home like Dorothy did?"

*Wizard of Oz? This guy is some kind of freak! Why does he need to know if I'm Jewish or not?* The camper sped on, but Sarah had no idea where they were.

"Any guns on you?" he asked.

"No!" To her amazement, he turned into the airport and parked.

"What are we doing here?"

"Click your heels!" he said. She looked at him bewildered.

"Look, El Al, the Israeli airline has MOSSAD security officers at every booth. Go up to them, tell them who you are, and go home."

"And why will they take me?"

"To save the embarrassment of having you caught here …." The idea worked for her. All she had to do now was cross a few hundred yards and get to the EL AL ticket counter.

"I don't even know your name," she said.

"Stan."

"Stan, I don't know why you're doing this; I mean you'll get caught."

"I'll get caught for chasing a young girl around and dropping her off at the airport. They can call me an old fool but not much else," he explained.

"But why help me? Are you Jewish?"

"Me, hell no. Look, I was with the 7th army, April 27, 1945."

"And?" Sarah asked. Tears swelled up in Stan's eyes.

"We liberated Dachau on April 27, 1945."

"The concentration camp?"

"I just don't want to ever see it happen again ...." Stan stopped short. The EL AL counter stood just ahead. Sarah went forward and talked to the staff. The woman at the counter seemed bewildered but went in back and then returned. A man escorted Sarah behind the counter, and she never reappeared. Two days later Sarah was home in Israel with her daughter. John had not shown up yet.

***

Ali drove Saleh, Yasin and Hamid to Assateague. The road west of them remained blocked, but he knew the road to Assateague was safe. He drove on guided by Yasin who had followed the old man to the campground. The campground was pitch black now, and Yasin had trouble figuring out which camper was which.

"It's that one!"

"Are you sure?" Saleh asked.

"Yes, the old man and the Israeli are in that camper!" Saleh got out of the car and walked up to the camper. He placed a silencer on his pistol. He found the camper unlocked and went in. Ali heard four thuds and knew that Saleh had shot both the old man and the Israeli twice in the head. Saleh got out of the camper and ran to Ali's car.

"Yasin, it's the wrong trailer, an African couple!"

"African? Then where is the Israeli?"

Saleh's crew had been an incompetent bunch of idiots since they had arrived, and Ali had enough of them. He headed south on the beach road.

"Can we get out this way?" Saleh asked.

"Yes, a sand trail leads all the way into Virginia on a deserted beach."

***

Tim awoke to the sound of a girl pounding on the door.

"Liana, you missed breakfast, but don't be late for work!" She looked at the clock; she had five minutes until she started work. She smeared face cream on and rubbed it in. The cream gave her face a tanned look and hid the red marks. Tim looked awful.

"Please go now!" Liana said.

"I didn't even comb my hair!" He slid out the door to find a group of giggling girls.

"Rough night!" one said to him, and they all laughed. Liana appeared next, and the face cream seemed to make her glow.

"It seems you had a good night!" one of the girls said to her.

"Please, let's get to work."

***

Two days later things calmed down in Ocean City. Liana's face healed, and the redness left. She tried to get her life back on course. On Thursday the news ran a follow-up story on the African couple found shot to death in their camper. A bird watcher photographed a Turkey Vulture, almost at the Virginia line. He returned to his camper to look at the photographs and saw an arm sticking out of the sand. The man called the police.

*Ali killed Saleh, Yasin, and Hamid because they stumbled across me and might have led the FBI here. He found a spot thirty miles from town on the bay side of a deserted island and buried their bodies. Foxes had partially dug up the bodies, and then the vultures joined in. I didn't want the Arabs around, but I didn't want them dead either. Why does it seem that it's always Muslims killing Muslims?*

Cathleen Hale met Tom at the scene of the murders.

"They're all dead now," she said.

"Did the Danite's finish them off?" Tom asked.

"I guess."

"And the Israeli woman?"

"I heard she's back in Israel."

"Then it's over?"

"No, at least one is still here and active. I think it's the missing woman's husband."

Two days later Tom received a phone call from Cathleen.

"Tom, the Arab men found dead in Maryland …."

"Yes."

"They fought with a woman just before they died," she said.

"Are you sure?"

"Yes."

"The Israeli woman?"

"No, the Israeli woman had her hair dyed blond. Whoever fought the dead Arab men scratched up one man's face and left a razor cut on his throat. A few long blond hairs were found on them, a natural blond, not a dye."

"Then someone else we don't know about is out there?" he asked.

"Yes," Cathleen said. "And, Tom, we found a rental car abandoned on Assateague Island, all the way down in Virginia."

"Great, just when the case couldn't become more bizarre."

A few days later a cabin cruiser hit something in the bay at Ocean City. It ripped a hole in its hull. A van came to the surface behind the boat and then sank. The FBI pulled the van from the bay and towed it to a garage for evaluation along with the abandoned car.

***

Liana sat on the boardwalk watching the waves on the beach.

"Liana," a voice called from behind her. She turned and saw it was Ali.

"I wanted to talk with you about your mission. I think you know it involves Washington."

"Washington?"

"Yes, that's why you went there, to the Capitol, to check it out?"

"Yes," she said, going along with him.

"In one week Senator Wright will be staying at your hotel."

"And?"

"He loves pretty blond girls," he said.

"And?" she asked.

"Show him a good time," Ali said.

"What?" She stared at the boardwalk. "I wish everyone would learn that I don't know how to do this." He stared at her for a moment.

"Ali, I've been fighting since I was a child, and I never learned the things others did growing up, but I'm trying," she explained.

"That explains the boy then."

"The boy?"

"Tim -- he is teaching you American customs, and you are rewarding him for helping you?" Liana was unsure of what Ali was saying, but nodded yes. She felt uneasy, as he had known about both the trip to Washington and Tim. He even seemed to know that Tim had visited her a few nights ago.

"I will provide you with cash to buy clothes. There are girls here that could explain how American women dress?"

"Yes, but what's my real mission?"

"I can't tell you that yet."

"What do you want me to do with this Senator?"

"Get to know him well. Make him want to contact you."

"Ali, if I do seduce him, won't he use me and throw me aside? A Russian politician would."

"Perhaps …."

"Then what you want is for me to start some type of relationship with him. To keep him coming back?"

"Exactly."

"I suppose I could find a way to do that."

"You must start monitoring the web site again. It may become too dangerous for me to meet with you, and you must stay in contact."

"I have been monitoring the web site but finding nothing."

"Search the clown's eye with your mouse, left clicking as you go."

"Liana, your mother …."

*Why remind me of that horrible day when I lost Momma ... and when I learned Grandpa was dead ... executed ...?*

## THE NEWSPAPER ARTICLE

After a long journey Sarena and Liana arrived at the deserted hut where Aslan had grown up.

"Liana, we have no food or money. How will we survive?"

"Momma, I'll gather wood for the fireplace, and we can get warm. When we are warm, we can go down into the village and buy some food."

"Liana, we have no money."

"Momma, I do. I saved some."

"Tell me how you got this."

"I didn't do anything wrong, if that's what you mean." She never told Sarena where the money came from, but she found it on the dead Russian Colonel.

Liana and Sarena walked into the village together. Surprisingly, with the country engulfed in war, the village was quiet and undisturbed. Sarena wisely bought as much cheap food as she could and was surprised that everyone was nice to her.

"Sarena, is that you?" She turned and saw a young woman.

"I'm Sarena."

"I'm Amanta, Amanta Katsa. I was at your wedding. This is my baby sister, Elisha." Sarena did not recall the woman.

"Aunt Sarena, I'm Aslan's granddaughter. My mother will be thrilled to see you. How is Aslan?" They walked down the street to a house, and Amanta escorted them in.

"Momma, look who I found at the market. It's Aunt Sarena!" A woman came around the corner, and Sarena instantly recognized her husband's youngest sister.

"Zara!"

"Oh, it is you, Sarena. How are you? Is Aslan with you?" Zara asked.

Sarena and Liana sat drinking Chia tea with Zara and Elisha. Sarena told in detail of leaving Russia and coming to fight in Chechnya.

"When I last saw Aslan, we had just crossed a minefield that I had laid with my own hands and we were under fire from the Russians. Aslan said he would join me here, so Liana and I fled," Sarena stated.

"I had heard that Aslan had a brigade in Grozny and that he fought until the end," Zara said. Sarena and Liana told of fighting in Grozny and the horrors of the battle. Zara was distraught by what Sarena told her and very troubled.

"Sarena, little Liana being forced to fight ... it troubles me so … will Elisha and I survive this war? Amanta is the lucky one here. Her husband holds a U.S. passport and they are traveling to Dagestan to get out. Sarena, what can we as mothers do? We have always been the peacemakers; what will this war turn us into?" Both women broke into tears and Liana felt very uncomfortable.

"We Muslims we have always been a loving and caring people. We have helped so many ... now I have found myself and my daughter fighting people we had called friends, Chechen and Russian," Sarena explained.

"That's enough for now. Let's get Liana and you some clothes. We have many extra!" Zara stated. Sarena protested, but they insisted. By the time they left Zara's home, they each had bags full of clothes with them, tea, cookies, fresh tomatoes and cucumbers, as well as the groceries they had bought.

Three nights later Liana woke up in the middle of the night and shook Sarena awake.

"Momma, I heard footsteps coming up the trail." Sarena got up and looked around, finding only a piece of firewood for protection.

"Whoever's out there, show yourselves. I have a gun!" Sarena called, bluffing.

"It's me, Aunt Sarena, and I have two of Aslan's men with me, and one's wounded," Elisha called back.

Elisha stepped out of the shadows and walked forward. Two men walked forward, one badly limping. Sarena went out to look over the men.

"It's true. These are two of your grandfather's men and one is wounded."

"I'm sorry, Aunt Sarena, but we have no doctors and if the men were caught in the village …."

"You were right to bring them here. Come inside for the night, too; it's dangerous for you to be out alone."

Sarena lit a lamp and found both men dressed in shreds of fatigues. Both men were very gaunt and looked dazed. The battle and retreat from Grozny had left the men badly shaken.

"I have their rifles," Elisha said. She stepped outside and retrieved two Ak-47s, which Liana took and hid.

In addition to being starved and shell-shocked, one of the men had a bullet wound in his side. The bullet entered near his shirt line and exited out the other side, evidently hitting nothing vital. The other man suffered a badly infected shrapnel wound in his foot. Sarena checked the man with the wound in his side.

"Your wound has healed itself, and there's not much I can do for you." The man with the foot wound was a different story.

"It's a ragged wound and badly infected … do you want to live?"

"Yes, I want to live and fight on," he said.

"What is your name?"

"I am Omar," the man said.

"I must cut off some of your foot. I have no chloroform or antibiotics. The amputation may kill you."

"What are the odds?" Omar asked.

"Fifty-fifty."

"Then what are you waiting for?"

Liana followed Elisha home and brought back a flat shovel, some vodka, and most importantly, a hatchet. Sarena stated boiling water to do the operation.

"Drink the vodka!" she ordered Omar.

"No, I am Muslim; I will not drink the vodka!"

"You must drink the vodka and not move around when I operate on you!"

"Momma," Liana said, "I will hold down Omar, and he will not move around." Sarena lit a large fire and boiled water. She heated the flat shovel until it glowed red.

"Let's do it," she said quietly. Liana propped his foot up with a large piece of firewood. She placed a stick between Omar's teeth to protect them.

"Hold him down!" she said. Instead of holding him down, Liana laid across Omar hugging him.

"Liana!"

"Momma, please, quickly!" she said. Sarena used the hatchet on Omar's foot and then almost immediately burned the wound shut with the hot shovel.

"Is he okay?" Sarena asked.

"Momma just finish please!" Sarena poured vodka over the wound and bound it up with clean bandages.

"You can let go of him now!" Sarena said.

"I don't have to. He passed out before you even used the hatchet."

The next morning Sarena awoke to see Omar trying to hobble around.

"You need to rest!" she demanded.

"You need firewood cut and I can at least do that!" he said. "Guna's a carpenter he can seal up your home from the winter winds."

Omar recovered so quickly that it shocked Sarena.

"How did you know Omar would not go berserk when I went to work on his foot?" Sarena asked Liana.

"Because Omar is one of the bravest men I have ever met." The statement frightened Sarena, and she wondered what might grow from it.

Omar and Guna told Sarena of the fighting that took place after they left Grozny.

"Aslan fought a rear action and allowed us to escape. We did not know where they went, so we came home," Omar stated.

A month passed and they recovered from the fighting in Grozny. Liana's cheeks filled in again, and Sarena grew as strong as ever. The woodpile and food stocks grew during this time, as everyone wanted to help them.

"We want to go out and see what's become of our families," Omar explained.

"Could you bring back some fresh vegetables or a chicken?" Sarena asked.

*I really hope nothing is going on between Liana and Omar, but when they leave I will know.* At the last moment Omar turned and walked straight back toward Liana. Sarena held her breath. Omar passed Liana, pulled his hat from his head and grabbed Sarena by her wrists.

"Thank you for healing my foot." With that, Omar was gone.

Sarena and Liana went back inside. Liana decided to read and Sarena to sew. The day went quietly as did the next two. On the fourth day Elisha came running up to the cottage saying that Omar and Guna were under arrest and awaiting trial.

"They're coming for you, too!"

"Who is coming … when?" She saw armed men walking up to the cottage. They surrounded Sarena and Liana and arrested them.

Armed men escorted Sarena and Liana back toward the village. The men, Sarena noted, were Chechens wearing skullcaps and scarves embroidered with "Allah is great!"

"We're being arrested by Chechens!" Sarena said flatly to Liana. Liana feared this to be the CDF, but these men seemed to be strict Muslims, wearing Muslim garb.

"What are we being arrested for?" Sarena asked her captors.

"The charges will be explained by Captain Atta," one of the men said to Sarena. They entered the village with the men and found it in an uproar. A crowd of villagers gathered, evidently chased from their homes. Liana and Sarena found themselves in a hut, captive, with five other women.

"What's going on?" Liana asked the women.

"The Wahabbi militia came into the village. They arrested two men and hung them. They said that they should have joined a militia and fought. They searched all our homes and beat anyone if they found vodka or magazines. They are declaring Shari as the law and are trying everyone in the Captain's Islamic court. The Wahabbi Militia has many Chechen men in it, but it's run by Arabs."

"Liana and I?" Sarena asked.

"Whores and rape victims," the woman said.

"What?" Liana said jumping up.

"Sit and calm down. We are being tried under Shari, Islamic law. You studied Shari. Try and remember what it says," Sarena said to her.

"Omar and Guna?" Liana asked. Sarena nodded.

"Do you know what happened to Omar and Guna?' Sarena asked.

"Arrested!"

"That's the law," Sarena told Liana. "If a man enters another's home while he is not home, then the man is guilty of rape. If we, as women, allow a man to enter our home, then we are guilty of being whores."

"At trial Guna and Omar will be found guilty of rape, or you and I will be found guilty of being whores," Liana said.

"The Wahabbi militia has also demanded that polygamy be practiced," the woman explained.

"What? Polygamy has never been practiced here. Our own laws prohibit it," Sarena said.

"But Shari encourages it," Liana said.

"The Wahabbi feel that there are too many single girls and widows, so they are ordering polygamy."

"Liana, they could order you to marry someone. If I am tried, then do as they say."

"I'm not marrying someone I don't love!"

"Liana, you must survive. Even if I and your grandfather die, you must endure and go on."

Chechens did not follow the Wahabbi version of Islam. Chechens dressed brightly, and women kept their faces uncovered. Unique in the world of Islam, Chechens considered women and children as equals to men. Women acted as the head of some households. They allowed dancing, music, and theater. Now, after years of war, the Wahabbi's demanded that Chechens practice Shari.

The Arab Captain's Islamic court tried villagers. A cleric who traveled with the militia held the trial. For small offenses he'd order the villagers' feet whipped until bloody. In other cases he demanded death, like those he hung.

"Your trial is next," a man told Liana.

Sarena, not wanting the Wahabbi's to hear what she said, talked to Liana in Latin.

"When we are brought in front of the Islamic court, say nothing. Keep your head covered with a shawl and make sure your hair is tucked under it. The trial is no joke. We could be executed."

The Wahabbi's dragged Sarena and Liana into a building. The cleric ordered the badly beaten Omar and Guna to kneel on the ground. An Arab cleric walked into the room and sat across from them. The Arab Captain walked in and sat down.

"These men have admitted to living with you and were found bringing food and supplies to you," the cleric shouted at Sarena. Liana went to stand up, but Sarena held her hand on Liana's shoulder. She coldly stared back at the Captain.

"Eyes down! Don't look at the Captain!" She continued her gaze.

"Who are you men that come here to judge us while real men are fighting and dying?" Sarena asked in Arabic. The cleric was stunned that she addressed him in Arabic and taken aback by her actions and rhetoric.

"Do you deny these men lived in your home?" the cleric shouted at her. She didn't answer but turned to the Captain.

"Liana, my daughter sitting next to me, has become a sniper and a killer. I am a nurse and a teacher, and I have found myself killing people that I once taught and cared for. My father-in-law is very old and should be resting but instead leads a militia. Liana was caught by the CDF and hurt badly by fellow Chechens, and she has not been the same since. My father-in-law, my daughter and I left Grozny only after the Russians had captured the entire city and it was in flames. We crawled through exploding minefields that I laid with my own hands. I arrived here in rags and had to begin living again. After we arrived, two of my father in law's men arrived wounded and hurt, and, yes, I took them in. Would you have me cast them out? Guna arrived with a bullet wound in his side, and I cared for him. Omar arrived with his foot half blown off and badly infected. Liana held him down, and I cut off half of his foot with my own hands. My father-in-law is missing, my daughter has turned into a killer, and you have beaten the men that I nursed back to health."

The Captain seemed shaken. He ordered Guna to move his shirt to expose his wound. He asked Omar to remove his boot and saw the wound that Sarena had burned shut.

"The law is the law!" the cleric explained. The Captain waved his hand.

"We are all fighting for Islam and are bound to follow Shari!" the Captain stated.

"I fight only because surrender means a horrible death, and there is nowhere else for us to go," Sarena stated.

"You and Liana will stay at the home of the traitor we hung. We will use your cottage as we see fit. Guna and Omar will join us to fight the infidels. We must leave soon. That is all!" The Captain ended without even looking toward Sarena or Liana.

"Momma, we must live in a dead man's home?" Sarena nodded.

They spent the next day moving their supplies from the cottage to the village. The Wahabbi militia left a week after their trial, leaving the rest of the cases unheard. The villagers buried their dead and quickly began to recover from the inquest.

"This war is destroying the fabric that holds Chechnya together," Sarena lamented. "Everyone who is alive is clinging to extremes; we have strict communists, strict Islamic's, strict nationalists, and strict socialists. Us women fight and die like men. Who will be left to go on?" Liana understood even less than her mother.

"Momma, what will we do when the Russians come here?"

"What can we do but fight them and hope to survive?"

Two days later Guna returned with a message for Sarena.

"One of Aslan's men is hiding, and he wants to talk to you," he explained. They grabbed their coats and followed him to the outskirts of the village. Here Sarena found Zara and Ammon, one of Aslan's men.

"Sarena, I really don't believe it. Aslan thought you were dead, and little Liana is here also. I have very bad news, and I wanted you and Zara to hear it. Aslan is dead. He was publicly executed by the CDF. I'm so sorry!" he said.

"Executed, why?" Liana asked.

"The CDF said they had ordered Aslan to fight to his last bullets in Grozny and that he abandoned the city," he said.

"The CDF left Grozny a month before Aslan did; he fought the Russians until the bitter end!"

"I was there. I know. The truth made no difference to the CDF. I crawled out of Grozny with Liana … the helicopter crash, the explosions …." They were all silent in the room. "I have the article from the Russian papers," he said.

"The article?" Sarena asked.

"A Polish journalist witnessed the execution. He recorded it all. The Russian papers picked up the story and published it," Ammon stated. He gave her the folded-up newspaper article. She unfolded the article but was too upset to read it.

"Momma, it's okay. I'll read it."

"Aslan Yastrz was executed by the rebel Communist Defense Force in Chechnya on April 17th. Yastrz was a former sergeant in, and hero of, the Red Army. He and a small group of Russian soldiers and sailors held off 80,000 Nazi troops in the battle of Stalingrad. Yastrz, along with his men, fought all the way to Berlin and helped to defeat the Nazis. He was awarded both the order of 'Noble sniper' and 'Order of Lenin' during his service with the Red Army. Yastrz had attempted on several occasions to negotiate peace in Chechnya. When asked by the CDF if he had any last words, he said, 'I am old and my country is in flames. Shoot me and put me out of my misery."

Liana and Sarena left to return home and mourn Aslan's death. They hardly had enough time to grieve before the war arrived at their doorstep again.

Liana awoke when she heard the sound of AK-47s firing near the village. She jumped up and found that her mother was already getting dressed. The sound of the AK-47s got closer, and she also heard helicopters. Sarena heard the sound of missiles firing and explosions. By now Liana was dressed also and they ran outside. The village was in a state of total panic, and they saw Elisha running.

"Elisha, what's happening?"

"Russian troops have cut the roads leading in and out of the village, and a column of armored vehicles is heading up the road." As soon as Elisha had spoken, a helicopter gun ship appeared over the village and began strafing them. Liana grabbed Elisha and pulled her to the ground. Out of the corner of her eye, Liana saw a rocket-propelled grenade shoot out from the trees and strike the attack helicopter. The helicopter turned sideways in the air, fell onto a hut in the village, and burst into flames.

Elisha, Sarena, and Liana collected what they could from their homes and gathered at Zara's home.

"Elisha, it's best you surrender and stay. Liana and I must flee."

"Stay and be captured by the Russians? I'm not going to be used as a prostitute."

"We must go now!" Liana said to Sarena. Elisha and Zara decided to flee to the Sarena's cottage.

"We can live there and if necessary flee into the woods, at least until things calm down. My husband, your Uncle Akhan, is fighting in the eastern mountains. He will take you in if you can reach him. He is leading the Aku militia." The sound of gunfire interrupted her.

"Elisha, we must go!" Zara and Sarena hugged, and then all fled.

Sarena and Liana both had packs full of food and supplies. They shouldered their packs and fled the village. As soon as the women entered the forest they heard shooting and screaming, as Russian troops had entered the village.

They walked east all day avoiding Russian checkpoints and patrols. At one point Sarena was ready to cross a small path when Liana pulled her to the ground.

"What is it?"

"Momma, the forest moved." They lay on the ground for almost half an hour without moving. Finally Liana saw a group of men dressed in strange shredded camouflage clothing. The camouflage clothing made them look like dead grass growing on a hillside. The group of men quietly moved east, passing them.

"Have you ever heard of such men?"

"These are Russian Special Forces, and I am sure they were sent to kill anyone that fled the village." A few moments later the forest exploded with gunfire. She again crept up and saw the same camouflaged men standing over dead bodies.

"Zara and Elisha, they will die!"

"They will have to slip away just like us," Sarena answered. She and Liana continued east through the night.

After walking for four days, they were deep inside mountains controlled by the Wolf Militia of Chechnya. In these mountains they found the men to be particularly fierce and the women strangely beautiful. They again found a small hut to live in.

Several boys noticed Liana and some of the local girls became jealous. A woman stopped by to talk to them one afternoon.

"Please, Liana, be very careful here. The vendetta is practiced in these mountains, and killings among families can go back several generations. Do not upset the women here, or things will go very badly," the woman explained.

"What should she do?" Sarena asked.

"Let Liana fight with those that have lost their wives already, not the young men," the woman answered.

Criminal gangs traveled throughout the mountains and traded in many things, but heroin was the primary commodity. It was often difficult to decide if the militia you were traveling with was a fighting force or a group of thugs.

"Do not fire upon the Russians in the valley any longer. The unit is a conscript unit, and we have reached an agreement that they will not attack us and we will not attack them," the commander said. Liana did not understand this as they attacked Russian troops whenever they encountered them.

"Momma, someone dug a tunnel in our root cellar. I'm going to find where it leads." The tiny tunnel traveled about fifty yards and came out at a rocky hillside. A flat rock covered the entrance and hid it. Liana thought that the tunnel might collapse at any time.

"The tunnel is very small and dangerous, but it might come in handy sometime."

The next afternoon a truck full of fighters pulled up to their hut.

"Liana, we are going on a raid against a Russian column. We need your help. We have a set of fatigues and a sniper rifle for you." She climbed into the truck. The truck slowly drove down the road and came upon the Russian checkpoint. A very dazed looking Russian soldier was at the checkpoint. The soldier waved the truck, bristling with Chechen fighters, through the checkpoint. She looked at the man that had asked her to come, and he described the situation.

"The conscript Russians do not like to fight us because they always lose. We bribe them with heroin and vodka, and they leave us alone. The

Russians are sometimes so stoned or drunk that they accidentally shoot themselves or their comrades."

The truck drove about ten miles farther, finally stopping near a small mountain pass. A Chechen commander stepped off.

"The Russians will come through the pass, and we will let them through. When the last vehicle has passed through our RPG men will fire upon the lead vehicle and stop the column. Liana will fire upon any officers from up on the hillside. She will wait for the first vehicle to explode before she fires. When the first vehicle explodes, the remaining RPG men will fire upon the last vehicle and move forward on the remaining vehicles in line. All machine gunners will pick targets in the column and fire upon them."

Liana climbed the hillside and found a good spot where she could see the entire area. She used a small shovel to dig out a depression to lie in and set up an escape route.

*I hear the sound of approaching vehicles. It's armored vehicles leading a column of eleven trucks. Second in line, and last in line, are heavily armored vehicles bristling with mounted machine guns. I didn't expect this much armor and equipment*! The column crept forward, and the lead vehicle, sensing danger, stopped short of the small pass. Several men got out and scouted ahead.

The Russians returned to their vehicle and an all clear given. The column began inching forward again. She waited, and finally the last vehicle cleared the pass. Just as described, she heard the whoosh of an RPG and saw the first vehicle explode. Moments later Liana heard a second explosion and saw the last vehicle explode. For a moment she forgot her mission and seemed dumbstruck. The sound of the mounted machine guns firing brought her back around. The Russians fired all over the area, strafing the woods, rocks and grass.

*A sergeant is barking orders at his men, my first target. Another is screaming at the Russians, telling them to swerve around the first vehicle and move on, my second target. Eight Russian soldiers are rushing the Chechens on the hillside; I'll begin firing from left to right as they come forward.* One of the Russian drivers freed his truck from the group and swerved around the other trucks. Russian troops ran up and climbed aboard. They sped up the valley and disappeared into the woods. There was a huge explosion in the woods ahead.

The mountain pass was now quiet, and a Chechen fighter began walking through the burning Russian vehicles shooting any remaining wounded Russians. The man finally gave an "all clear" sign, and the remaining fighters walked down to the burning vehicles looking for anything they could take. The men robbed the dead Russians of any weapons or food they found. One of the Chechen leaders walked up to Liana and gave her a small cap.

"This is yours; the man you shot was a sergeant."

"A truckload of Russians got away; won't they try and track us down?" she asked.

"No, they didn't get away. A woman mined the road ahead. The truck blew up and the men are dead," the commander said. They stopped to pick up a woman. It was Sarena.

"Momma, what are you doing here? You could have been killed!"

"I had to come; we had to stop the Russian column. Liana, so many dead and hurt, and at my hands." Liana understood as little about this as she did. The truck crawled on and again passed through the conscript Russian checkpoint before arriving home.

Two weeks later they were again asked to help in a well planned, organized attack.

*We joined a large group to go and stop the advancing Russian troops. Everyone who could carry a gun came to help. I was very worried because over half of the remaining fighters in the area were young boys. I joined the raid, as a good plan had been set up to counter the Russian advance.*

"Our fighters are positioned in a half circle across an area almost a mile long. The Russian column will advance beyond the hidden Chechen fighters and will be attacked at the very front. When the attack begins, the Russians will retreat toward the hidden Chechen fighters and the main assault will take place," the commander explained.

*It was a good plan, but the Russians knew the attack was coming. I was on the ridge almost behind where the Russian column traveled. Most of the Chechen fighters were far to the front, hidden in a half circle to trap the oncoming Russians. I watched and, down in the valley, a very large, heavily armored Russian column approached. The column came abreast of where I was and stopped. The next was almost a blur.*

*Two Russian jets appeared flying very low over the trees. The jets dropped napalm over the woods we were hiding in. I heard my fellow fighters screaming, and almost immediately three Russian attack helicopters moved in and began strafing the woods with machine gun fire. In the next instant artillery shells began falling precisely on our positions. At the same time the Russian armored vehicles began spraying the area with machine gun fire and liquid fire from propane cannons. Any Chechen fighter that arose to flee encountered flying bullets.*

*I knew that few of us could still be alive. I left my rifle and slid over the hilltop to flee into the woods. I knew capture would be worse than death and that I had to avoid the Russians. I panicked and ran through the woods. Almost as soon as I entered the woods, I saw that Russian soldiers on the far ridge had noticed me. I ran down a small embankment and made it over the ridge top. I saw a shape running which tackled me. I was fighting and rolling on the ground with my captor.*

*"Please don't fight me. We'll get caught!" I realized that my own mother had tackled me.*

"Liana, Special Forces are in the woods," Sarena said. Liana lay next to her mother for a moment and tried to calm down. She saw the same camouflaged men her mother and she had avoided some months back moving through the woods.

After painstakingly crawling almost a mile on their stomachs, they felt they were clear of the carnage in the valley and ran on ahead. After running almost five miles they came upon the conscript checkpoint.

"Momma I think it's safe to cross," Liana said.

"No it's not," Sarena replied. A Russian army truck arrived at the checkpoint and began talking to the men stationed there. Sarena heard the men talking, and one described that over two hundred Chechen fighters lay dead in the valley. As it turned out one of the drug gangs sold the news of the militia raid to the Russians. The Russians watched the Chechens from the time they had left camp until the beginning of the battle. Sarena and Liana crept back to their hut in the middle of the night.

"Momma, we must leave this area. Everyone else is dead, and in a few days they will be here for us!"

"Tomorrow morning we will pack up and leave," Sarena said.

Just before dawn the next morning they still lay on the floor of their hut when bullets tore through it. Men began screaming for them come out and surrender. Sarena looked outside and saw Russian troops on both sides of the hut.

"Liana, we have land mines and guns in the hut. Surrendering will be worse than death!" Liana picked up an AK-47 and began firing out of the hut.

"We need to get out of here!" she screamed.

"We are surrounded; there is nowhere to go! " Sarena said. "The Russians will torture us to death if we are taken alive!" Sarena heard the Russians screaming for someone to bring a flamethrower.

"Liana, we have no time. Give me the rifle!" Sarena held out the Russian schoolgirl's dress and tiny cross. She slapped Liana hard.

"Liana, survive, put the dress on and get out through the tunnel! You must survive. You know Russian life. Pretend you're a Russian girl again. Put on the dress. You have no time!" Bullets tore through the wall just over Liana's head.

"Liana, go now, before I blow up the hut!" Sarena screamed. Liana put the dress on and placed the cross around her neck. Sarena kissed her.

"Whatever happens to me, you must survive. Now go! Liana, survive!" Liana descended into the root cellar and entered the partially collapsed tunnel.

*I am Sashi Kamikov; I attended the Russian school in Minutka square in Grozny ....*

Liana made it to the end of the tunnel, slid out, and placed the rock back in place. She crept about fifty yards and hid against a burned-out truck. She looked back at her hut and saw it explode in a huge fireball. She knew that her mother had blown herself up. She saw four Russian soldiers running toward her. The Russians grabbed Liana and dragged her away kicking and screaming.

*Russian soldiers with flamethrowers walked from hut to hut setting them on fire, sometimes with my friends still inside. Women screamed and soldiers used rifle butts and clubs to herd them off. Russian soldiers lay dead either from my shooting or from Momma's explosion.*

The Russians dragged her to a small building where several soldiers and officers stood. An officer drew his pistol and shot a Chechen girl in front of Liana.

"Liana, survive!" She kept hearing Sarena's last words to herself as she stood next to the dead body of the Chechen girl. Shots rang out all around her, and she jumped each time one went off.

A Russian officer appeared and slapped Liana.

"Who are you?"

"Sashi Kamikov!"

"Who are you?" the officer asked, slapping her a second time. She told her name again and waited for the third slap to come. When the officer tried to slap her a third time, she caught the officer's wrist.

"I'm Russian, and you have no right to treat me this way!" She knew that timing was everything and she had clearly caught the officer off guard. He stepped back a moment and saw her tiny silver cross.

"You're Russian?" the man said to her in English. This was a trap since Russian pupils learned English in school.

"Of course I'm Russian," she said in perfect English, "I attended the Russian school at Minutka Square before Grozny fell; the Chechens captured me and have held me." The officer was unsure of what she was telling him.

*Things took a turn for the worse; a group of Russian soldiers escorted four Chechen girls toward me. I knew at least two of them would give me up during interrogation. I could see that the Chechen girl in the front was the same girl that had been jealous of me. I knew I was done for.*

"Russian bitch!" the girl screamed as she broke away from the soldiers and ran forward.

"Grenade!" one of the soldiers screamed as one of the girls dropped a grenade on the ground. She heard a series of screams and gunshots, and the Chechen girl fell to the ground close to her. The grenade went off, and she heard more firing and cries. She saw the dying Chechen girl lying inches from her and saw her mouthing words.

"Liana, survive," the girl breathed out and then died. It struck Liana strangely because it seemed her own mother's voice had slipped out of the dying girl's mouth and she did not understand it.

"Are you okay? She really wanted to kill you didn't she?" She said nothing. All four Chechen girls now lay dead on the ground near her.

"Sit here!" the officer said to Liana.

*I can hear a woman screaming and soldiers shouting. The voice sounds familiar. I better concentrate on proving my story to the Russians. This all happened so fast, I've got to keep my head and not screw up! What was it that Grandpa said about the front line soldiers .*

*"The front line troops are not the ones that kill and terrorize the local people as much as you think. It's the second and third waves of soldiers, the mop-up crews, that cause most of the atrocities." I must befriend these troops and either travel with them or escape before the others come forward.*

"You're Russian?" an officer asked her.

"Yes, of course."

"If you can cook, make us tea," the officer asked. The building she was in included a small kitchen. She lit a fire and found a pot and some water. The cupboard held Chia, which she avoided. A box of black tea lay in the back of the cupboard. There were cups on the shelf that Liana avoided also. Chechens drank Chia in cups; Russians drank black tea in glasses. The officer studied her as she made the tea, which she made very strong.

"Sir, do you have any glasses?" The officers held out aluminum cups from their mess kits.

"These will have to do," one said staring at her. She poured the tea into the officers' cups, kissing them on the cheek as she did so. The officers still seemed suspicious.

"Sashi," a soldier called out as he passed by. "Sashi Kamikov?" the man said walking up to the building.

"Do you want some tea also?" she said to the soldier as he came forward.

"You don't remember me?" the soldier asked. She had no clue how he would have known her.

"Do you know this girl?" an officer asked the soldier.

"Yes, sir," the soldier replied. "She's Sashi Kamikov. She helped care for me when I was in the hospital. She was our little angel. Don't you remember me?" It suddenly came to her, but not like he was saying. This soldier was one of two who had tried to catch her, only Lt. Anya had saved her.

"Yes, of course, I remember you and Lt. Anya. How is she?" she asked.

"Lt. Anya was killed protecting the wounded in the hospital. One of the Chechen bastards drove a truck full of explosives into the hospital and blew himself up. Lt. Anya was killed as she fired upon him." Liana began crying real tears as she mourned the Russian nurse who had helped her so much those first few days. The officers seemed relaxed now and sat drinking her tea.

A Russian soldier came in to make soup for the troops. He took a cleaver and began coarsely chopping beets and dropping them into a huge pot.

"That's not how you make borscht!" Liana, to the humor of the officers, drove the man away from the stove. "I'll make the borscht."

*I can hear the woman screaming again, and I wish she would stop! It's the soldiers interrogating a woman. The voice, it's Momma's! How could she have ever survived that explosion? The meat cleaver, I'll use it on the Russians! What were Momma's last words to me ..., "Liana, survive!"*

She laid the cleaver down and began crying and sobbing again.

"Sashi, your ordeal is almost over. We won't let the Chechens get you again," the officer told her.

"Do you have beef for the soup?" The officer gave her a small canned ham. She knew this was another trap, as Chechens would avoid anything containing pork. She opened the can and broke it into chunks before placing it into the soup. As she made the soup she was praying that her mother would die quickly.

*Liana, survive!*

The words again rang in her ears each time she heard her mother scream.

She poured the soup into bowls for the soldiers. The screaming stopped for a moment, and there was an eerie silence broken by a pistol shot.

*Momma's on her way to heaven now ....*

Liana worked at the kitchen of the Russian camp for two weeks; then that unit went forward and another unit moved in. As she feared, this group was even more abusive to the local people than the first had been. She found herself zoning out for long periods and this worried her. Once during lunch a soldier shook her.

"I've been waiting for you to serve my food! You've been blankly staring off into space. Are you thinking about your boyfriend or something?"

Her life became hell when the second group moved in. Coarse and undisciplined, they passed vodka around and ran through the camp like wild animals. She locked herself in the kitchen after dinner and slept on the floor. She found a baseball bat and kept it at her side at all times.

*At dinner a drunken soldier jumped over the counter and, while the other soldiers laughed, chased me around the kitchen. I grabbed my baseball bat, clobbered him, and he fell to the floor moaning and bleeding.*

*The other soldiers seemed annoyed and asked me to begin slopping their food again. I began filling the trays as I tried to avoid the bleeding soldier crawling on the floor.*

Liana needed to escape and now knew what to do. One of the Russian soldiers came to the locked kitchen every night, pleading for her to come out. He would be her key to freedom. She always locked herself in the kitchen right after dinner. She had ten hours after dinner, and before breakfast, to get away.

"Sashi, will you come out tonight and see me?" he called.

"If you get some vodka and a truck, we could drive up to the pass," Liana explained.

*I waited in the kitchen for dark to fall. I retrieved a stolen pistol, a small set of fatigues, some hard biscuits and a bottle of tea. I finally heard a voice calling softly through the window. I slipped unnoticed out the door, locking it behind me. I slipped into the small truck with the soldier, and we slowly drove out of the camp. Almost as soon as the truck got out of camp, I began pouring vodka for him. We drove through four Russian roadblocks on our way to the mountain pass. By the time we got to the pass he was singing and swerving all over the road.*

The soldier parked the truck at the top of the mountain pass. They got out, and she spread a blanket on the ground. The soldier staggered toward her.

"Lie down and rest." He lay next to her and she heard him snoring. She took her pistol out, aimed at him, but did not pull the trigger. If the Russians found his dead body they would track her down. If he walked back drunk and told a story of bringing "Sashi" here for a romantic evening, then everyone would assume that she ran off to avoid him.

Liana ground the gears as she drove the truck away. She did not know what was ahead or how far it would be until the next checkpoint. With her mother dead, her only hope was to find her uncle's militia, which was fighting near the border of Dagestan. She had no idea how to find her uncle, a man she had never met.

She shook herself back into the reality of where she was now. She wasn't in Chechnya but on the boardwalk in Ocean City, Maryland. *I've got to get my act together and somehow put aside the horrors of that terrible war. My mission ... the Senator.*

## THE AMUSEMENT PARK

John Kline returned to the safe house in Kansas City and waited for Sarah to return.

*The last I heard from Sarah she said she had to go into hiding. What the hell happened to her? I've no idea where she is. Is she dead?*

That night he watched the news and saw a report of Frank Silva's death and the camper blown up near Chicago. The report said a group of Israelis and Arabs were killing each other. The report went on to say a nationwide manhunt was underway for the Arabs and an Israeli woman.

*Sarah's running for her life ....*

The report stated that the manhunt had intensified in Ocean City, Maryland.

"The FBI conducted a door-to-door search on the island," the reporter stated "This is a video showing the Arabs and their mini-van." John watched the news all night long without learning any additional details.

Two days later he still had no new information on the Arabs or Sarah. As he arose from his chair an update came across his TV screen.

"This is where the bodies of three Arab men were found," the man said. The reporter said nothing about Sarah.

*Where is she at and why doesn't she show up?* Two days later a MOSSAD security officer contacted him.

"John, you have two open items, and then you must return home also."

"Have you heard anything about Sarah?"

"You haven't heard then?" the officer said to him.

"Heard what?"

"Sarah is safe in Israel with your daughter," the officer explained.

"Oh, thank God. Can I talk to her?"

"Yes, but make it very short," the officer explained, dialing his cell phone.

"Sarah?" he said.

"John is that you? You're okay?" she asked.

"Oh, thank God you're safe. Was it bad?"

"Very bad," she said. "John they say I must hang up now." A moment later he heard a click.

"John, something big is brewing, but no one knows what," the officer said.

"If you don't know what, then why the concern?" he asked.

"Because elaborate plans are being laid," the officer explained. "We want you to return to Toronto and find out what you can." The officer laid two sketches on the table.

"This one is working for Walid Hattab, and we don't know who he is. This one frightens us more than the other, a young girl. She was last seen by one of our agents at one of his safe houses in Saudi Arabia. Our agent said she spoke perfect English and Arabic. She's blond, has shining blue eyes, and she's pretty enough that she'll be able to go anywhere without suspicion."

"A blond terrorist?"

"John," the officer explained, "find these two and then go home to Sarah." The man in the drawing was Orman, and he was still in his bunker in Toronto building a nuclear bomb. The girl was Liana.

John traveled to Toronto and found an apartment. He contacted a private detective who would work for cash and not ask too many questions. He paid him fifty thousand dollars to find the man and girl he was looking for. He settled in Toronto and found the city similar to Chicago. The only thing different in Toronto was its large Muslim population.

John tried to melt into the culture of Toronto but found that without Sarah at his side, everyone was suspicious of him. He spent each evening at the park feeding pigeons and wondering if he had solved anything by coming to America. He missed Sarah, and his daughter, and wanted to see them soon.

*Finish my mission and return to Israel.*

John tried to get information on the girl in the drawing. His best guess was that she was any one of a number of British citizens who had converted to Islam and traveled to Toronto. He searched immigration files to no avail; the girl's trail went nowhere.

After a three-week wait he got a call from the private detective who asked that they meet at Dunkin' Donuts.

"John, I think I have a match on your drawing of the man, and a possible on the girl. The man's name is Orman, and he is a local college professor. He teaches nuclear science, but he has not been seen in Toronto for months."

"And the girl?" he asked.

"A girl like the one you're looking for works in Niagara Falls at a marine aquarium." John nodded and sipped his coffee. A man approached them and drew a pistol.

"Look out!" John screamed. He heard a pistol shot and felt his head blown back.

***

John woke up in a Canadian hospital and had no idea what he was doing there.

"You're a lucky man, but your friend is dead. The police think your coffee cup deflected the bullet. The police will be in shortly to talk to you. They have some questions about the shooting." He waited, and the nurse left the room. He got up, found his things, and slipped out of the hospital.

He made it down to the street and found a car he could steal. Whoever had shot at him was still out there, and he needed to leave Toronto. He drove the stolen car to an amusement park in Niagara Falls.

*The detective said a young blond Muslim girl worked at the aquarium here!* The aquarium had a killer whale in it, and the girl he was looking for cared for the whale. John paid the fee and sat in the crowd.

A clown came out and revved up the crowd by petting the whale and playing with some sea lions. A blond girl came out, explained about the killer whale and began her act. John sat and watched the show, which included the girl riding the whale, and the whale kissing the girl.

"Any questions?" the girl asked the crowd after the show.

"Are you British?" John asked.

"Yes, I've only been over here a few months. I was studying in Jordan."

"What were you studying?" he asked.

"I studied Islam and found it fascinating," the girl said.

When John went to leave, he found police swarming over the stolen car. He took a bus to the lake and stared across to the New York side.

*A small boat's tied up to the dock, and it has an outboard motor on it. New York is right over there ....*

Safely across to the U.S. side, John rented a car in Buffalo. He drove to the safe house in Kansas City before collapsing into bed. That night he saw his picture on the nightly news and it linked him to the earlier killings. The news showed a picture of the dead detective. He needed to stay hidden.

The MOSSAD agent visited John he next morning. He explained about the girl at the aquarium and about Orman.

"Do you think the girl is the one on the drawing?" the officer asked.

"Could be, I don't know."

"And Orman has not been seen in Toronto for a while?"

"Not for several months."

"John, it's too dangerous here. Go home!" He flew home to Sarah and their daughter. The Danite operation was now over.

## FASHIONS

Liana finished cleaning her hotel rooms but remained deep in thought.

*Ali seems to know everything I do! He knew about Tim, my trip to Washington, and that I sat on the Capitol steps. I don't think he's tailing me, I would sense it.*

Liana returned to her room and found an envelope stuffed with twenty-dollar bills. She locked her door and counted out a thousand dollars. She remembered Ali's instructions to go clothes shopping. Senator Wright would arrive soon and she needed clothes to impress him.

*Who would know the right things to wear? Margrite wears short skirts and dresses. Boys whistle at her. I'll stop by her room.*

"Margrite, I know little about fashion. Can you help me buy some clothes?"

"Oh, I'd love that. We'll have a lot of fun shopping!" Margrite took her to several women's stores and encouraged her to get some very tiny skirts and skimpy outfits. Liana tried on a miniskirt but felt so uncomfortable in it she decided not to buy it.

"Margrite, I would feel so ashamed wearing it, and I cannot sit down in it."

"I will show you how to sit down in it. You must learn to let boys notice you. It's a good feeling."

"Liana, do you mind wearing shorts, even little ones?"

"I'd rather wear those than this."

"Liana, try and get used to wearing this, and then when you feel comfortable with it, switch to the mini skirt," she said. The skirt she showed her was tinier than the other.

"I can't put that skirt on!" she said.

"Liana, it's not a skirt, it's a skort, and it has little shorts sewn in it." She checked the garment and found that Margrite was right; it did have shorts sewn into it. She tried it on and found that she liked the garment and did not feel as exposed wearing it. Margrite showed her other items, and she bought several dresses, skirts, blouses and shoes.

"We will try out your new clothes tonight, okay?" Margrite asked. At eleven that night she stopped by. Margrite wore a mini skirt and a low-cut blouse.

"Liana put your skort on and this blouse." Liana did as she asked.

"You look beautiful!" Margrite said holding her hands. Margrite led her out the door and up the boardwalk. Liana felt very uncomfortable and stared at the ground as she walked.

"Liana, look up and smile. You look cute!" Liana looked up and saw stares and leers as she walked. She could not stand being the center of attention. She spent so many years either in hiding or on battlefields, and being seen meant death.

As they walked up the boardwalk, everyone noticed them, and it made her worst fears come forth.

"Margrite, I can't, I just can't!"

"Liana, just walk and smile." She braced herself and did what Margrite said. She walked up the boardwalk with a smile on her face, but she was so frightened that she could not feel her feet touch the ground.

"Liana, let's go and talk …." Margrite motioned toward a group of wild looking boys standing just off the boardwalk. They walked over, and Margrite said hello to the boys. The boys and she talked, joked, and even teased each other for a few minutes.

"Doesn't your little sister talk?" Liana joined the conversation but felt very uneasy. Slowly the give and take of the conversation, the joking, and the teasing began to come to her.

"What do Russian girls do on Friday nights?" a boy asked her.

"Well, we don't stand on street corners and talk." She pulled Margrite's hand and they left.

"I'm sorry," she said to Margrite.

"About what?"

"About ruining things."

"No, you were right. It was time for us to move on. That's how it's done." Liana began to understand all this, but it was still hard for her.

On Monday night Liana called Tim.

"I need to know the correct way to eat at dinner. What silverware to use and when?" Liana asked. Tim agreed to try, and they went out to dinner.

"Liana the easiest way to do this is to watch what others do."

It was midnight when Tim dropped her off at the hotel. Liana put her skort on and went out onto the boardwalk alone. She watched the girls and boys on the boardwalk and the glances they exchanged.

Liana left the group of girls and turned back toward her hotel. Since all the girls were in groups or at least pairs, it made her feel very vulnerable but she plodded on. Several groups of boys stopped her as she walked home, but she was comfortable with them. She joked, or said she was not interested, and went on. She returned to her hotel around two in the morning.

"Liana, I'd like to take you out to somewhere nice," Tim asked one afternoon. She dressed in a dark black mini skirt, a blue top and high heels. As she entered the restaurant all eyes fell on her.

"She's really pretty," a boy said to his mom. Liana thought that the dinner had gone perfectly. Tim had seemed happy, but reserved, all night.

"Tim are you okay? You seem … uncomfortable."

"Let's stop by my apartment after dinner."

"Please Tim, I can't."

"We must talk."

"Can't we do that in the car?"

"No …," he said.

Tim kissed her as she entered his apartment.

"Liana," he said, "you know how much I care about you …." She relaxed and looked into his eyes. He looked a little frightened.

"Are you upset about my clothes? Did it bother you that the other men were looking at me?"

"Am I jealous? Yes! But that's not what I wanted to talk about."

"What then? Don't you like the clothes? I thought this was what men liked."

"You look fantastic; I think you look like every boy's dream tonight, but what bothers me is that this is not your dream. It's not what you want to wear."

"No, you're right. I feel very uncomfortable wearing these. I don't like the way men stare at me when I dress like this," she said.

"Rather than dressing how others would like you to, dress how you would like to." She had to consider what he was saying. If she had to look at ease, then her dress had to allow it. She realized something else and she didn't know what to make of it. Tim was looking into her heart and that meant something to her.

Liana found herself kneeling on the couch, first hugging and then kissing Tim. He felt tears on his shirt and just held her for a moment.

"Liana, are you okay?" She hugged him all the harder and slid her head against his chest.

"Tim, can't we just hug and say nothing?" He got up and turned the lights down. Later that evening he drove her back to her hotel. Liana went inside and saw several guys she worked with in the lobby.

"Liana, you look so cute dressed like that!" She stepped toward the elevator as one of the guys whistled at her. A group of men dressed in golf shirts and slacks was holding the elevator for her. Liana, trying to avoid being a spectacle, rushed for the elevator and entered it. Instead of having hit the "Up" button, she found all four men staring at her. She felt the same stares, and felt as uncomfortable, as she did during the confrontation with the Arabs. She reached through the men and hit the button. Staring at the floor she saw luggage with the name "Senator Wright" engraved on it. She felt fear, and her knees started to give out on her. She glanced up and smiled at Senator Wright.

Liana went to her room and collapsed on her bed.

*I can't do this; I can't keep playing this deadly game! Momma, what should I do?*

"Liana, survive!" She heard Sarena call out again, and she dreamed about the last time she heard her mother's voice.

## THE PHONE CALL

On the seventh day after fleeing the Russian army, Liana was sleeping in a refugee camp.

"Liana," one of the girls called to her, "let's go wash up. This tent is filthy." She got up, followed her to a well and drew water, as she had not bathed in several days.

"Liana!" She turned around to see Elisha and Zara.

"Aunt Zara, I thought you and Elisha were dead!"

"Liana, where is Sarena?" Liana began crying and telling them about her mother, the dress, the cross and her mother's attempting to blow herself up.

"Your mother died in the explosion?"

"No, a Russian bullet."

"We had a terrible time with the Russians also," Zara said, but did not explain.

"Liana, please stay with us. We are traveling to join my husband. It's said he is east of here." Two evenings later Zara woke them up around midnight.

"We must leave now before we are noticed. There are spies all over the camp." They slipped out of the camp, heading east. They walked through the mountains avoiding both Russian and Chechen patrols as they went. After five days of walking their food ran out.

"Aunt Zara, how deep into the mountains do we have to go?" Liana asked. "We haven't seen any Russian patrols in two days."

"There's a village ahead in the valley," Zara explained. "The militia is supposed to be there."

"I hope so. I'm close to collapsing now," Elisha explained.

That afternoon they came upon a camp hidden in the woods.

"Papa!" Elisha screamed and ran forward to hug her father. Zara came running also, followed by Liana.

"This is your Uncle Akhan!" Zara told her.

The militia gave the women food to eat and a tent to sleep in. All quickly passed out from exhaustion. For the next four days, the women ate, rested and gathered their strength. By the fifth day Liana felt well enough to ask if she could join her uncle's militia. Her uncle was not in favor of it.

"Liana, I wish you would stay with Zara and Elisha and be safe."

"I haven't been safe since I left Russia," Liana replied, "and almost all your fighters are teenagers."

"Many do not even shave yet," her uncle admitted. "Few are left to fight. I heard about Aslan's death. The CDF was all but wiped out when they tried to flee into our mountains. The vendetta is practiced here, and Aslan was greatly loved."

*The CDF met their fate for what they did to Grandpa and me. Vendetta? Revenge? I really don't even care any longer. It's just more dead and hurt people.*

"Thank you," she told her uncle.

"We attack Russians every night, and if you wish to join us as a sniper, I will assign you to a hunter/killer team. We will find a rifle and some camouflage for you. The Russians are afraid to enter these mountains as only we know the hidden passes and trails here," her uncle explained.

She joined two boys, one who used an RPG, the other who held an AK-47. Liana went on many successful raids during the next months.

"Liana, why aren't you married yet? You are very pretty," a boy asked. She thought about the boy's question, and it did seem odd to her. She should have married long ago.

"I've never had the time, or the wish, to find anyone."

Liana found herself zoning out for long periods. During one raid instead of lying hidden and using her sniper rifle, she stood in the open, holding her rifle at her side. Bullets flew all around her and RPGs exploded nearby, but she just stood in a daze.

"I think you are the bravest person I have ever met. You stood and stared at the Russians and just let them fire upon you. I've never known anyone like you," a boy said to her.

"Liana, you frighten me. You do not need to stand so that a Russian will kill you. Allah will call upon you in his own time," Akhan said.

Zara, Elisha and Liana often ate dinner together. Zara tried to fill the gap in Liana's life now that Sarena was gone.

"Liana you are spending too much time daydreaming. Do you want to talk? Is it the war ...?"

"I, ah, I ...."

"Yes, go on my child."

"My grandfather is dead, killed by Chechens and honored by Russians ... my mother is dead, by Russians ... I heard her screaming but could do nothing. My mother's last words were for me to survive, but for what? I kill the Russian boys I grew up with ... I've been molested by fellow Chechens ... I am fighting for a country I knew nothing of. I am fighting against a country I grew up in and loved ... the Russians have been kind to me, and I kill them. The Chechens have been brutal to me, and I sleep next to them. Every day dead Russians and dead Chechens ... the whole country is burning and destroyed. Every day I go out and fight with nice young boys, and every day I know some will not come back. Zara, you know as I do that the Russian army will come here also and we will either die or move on, but to where? We are almost out of Chechnya now. I mean, we're on the Dagestan border!" Zara began weeping, and so did Liana. The two hugged and cried.

After a time of relative calm the Russians struck the mountainous region they were hiding in with force. Helicopter gun ships began attacking any building in the area that looked like it could hide Chechen fighters. Russian Special Forces landed in remote mountain passes and ambushed Chechens heading to raid Russian columns. The area that Akhan's men could hide in shrunk to the most rugged sections.

"The Russians would never dare to enter this section of mountains!" militiamen said to her. To her the mountains she now lived in were a cold and dismal place. The dead bodies of Chechen and Russian fighters lay in each pass, small valley, and canyon. Burned-out trucks, cars and military vehicles clogged each road.

*My days have turned to complete drudgery. Each day brings hunger and cold. On a good day I might find a few hours to spend just looking out over a cliff or up into the blue sky. I remember being in southern Russia with my mother. The sun would be shining and it would be warm. Momma would be making bread, and the smell of the bread baking would fill the house. I would play with my Russian friends from school. Grandpa would return home from the tire factory in time for dinner. Momma would pray just before cutting the loaf of bread at dinner. After dinner we would tend our garden plot, and it was a fun time, with lots of laughter. We would then sit in the evening watching a pink sunset as songbirds flew from branch to branch on our tree.*

*The war is hopeless. The fighting is useless slaughter ....*

The militia shrank from around five hundred men to less than a hundred. The rest lay dead, wounded, or worse yet, captured, across the southern mountains. Liana became confident that the Russians could not penetrate the mountain stronghold.

One morning Liana sat studying the movement of Russian troops in the valley. She studied a new group of men through her binoculars. The men, dressed in tight fatigues, had bright bandanas tied around their heads. They all wore long hunting knives and carried their rifles casually, as if they had grown up with them. Packs of large cur dogs stood near them and she heard their mournful howls.

*Gypsies ... the Russians sent Gypsies to fight against us? I've got to tell my uncle about this.* Akhan seemed very troubled and climbed up to the ridge with her. She looked down on the men again, and Akhan did the same.

"Look at the dogs. I've seen men like these before!"

"Uncle Akhan … Gypsies?"

"I wish those were Gypsies. I think they are the death of us all. Those men are Cossacks, and they know these mountains as well as I do. They will not rest until we are all dead!"

Her uncle was right about the Cossacks. The ferocity of their attacks was unlike anything she had yet encountered. Once flushed out by the endless packs of dogs the Chechens would be fired upon as if the Cossacks were hunting wolves. It was very frightening. The Cossacks camped in the mountains wherever their attack ended. Reinforced by Russian Special Forces, the Cossacks drove the Chechens back.

Akhan's militia found themselves in an endless retreat east to the border of Dagestan. Akhan knew that Russians were waiting for him in Dagestan, but he did not have any other option. With great reservation, Akhan's militia fled into Dagestan, leaving Chechnya behind them. Liana waited until the last of the militia had entered Dagestan and then followed them, leaving Chechnya forever.

***

"Liana, I have been told of a farm that we can hide at," Elisha explained. "We will work at the farm. An old man owns it. We will be safe there. Dad and Momma have found a safe place to hide also."

About half of Akhan's militia decided to travel into Georgia in hopes of getting aid. Liana found that Russian security forces were everywhere, setting up roadblocks and raids looking for Chechen fighters.

"Elisha, you know farm work, but I don't. I've never lived on a farm. The daily chores of milking, tending crops, feeding chickens, shoveling manure and searching for eggs seem normal to you, but to me the work is awful."

A local boy stopped by to visit Elisha one day.

"My name is Valid, and I live on the adjoining farm. I have some books if you would like to read them." Elisha did not care about the books, but to Liana the news was a breath of fresh air.

"Elisha, the farmer drags the eggs, milk and vegetables into town once a week and sells what we've raised. The trip leaves him exhausted. We could sell much more in town than he is able to."

Liana, using a mule cart, began making the six-mile journey to the village. She found other farmers in the area who did not like to make the journey to the village, so she began selling their produce also. She felt it was wrong to have Elisha on the farm doing all the hard work, so they began switching back and forth between working the farm and going into the village.

"Liana, I found some scrap wood, and we can make our own market stand. We can sell everything from chickens to ducks," Elisha explained one day.

Valid stopped one night to talk to Liana. The conversation went on long into the evening, and she seemed to enjoy it.

"Valid, is there something you wish to ask me?" He looked very embarrassed.

"I am unsure of who to ask, if it is you or who?"

"Why don't you just ask?" she said.

"Liana, do you think Elisha would marry me?" The question stunned her as she thought he liked her.

"Ah … I don't know," she said. She couldn't help herself and began giggling and finally laughing, much to the embarrassment of Valid.

"Please don't make fun of me. I really admire Elisha," he pleaded. Liana understood his problem; he did not know where Elisha's father was to ask him for her. She was Elisha's cousin, and he had been trying to impress her. She agreed to talk to Elisha.

"Please come back next week, and we will see what will happen." He walked off, and she began laughing aloud again. She found it strange because she could not remember laughing in a long time.

"Elisha, Valid came by and he wants to … I'm sorry, he wants to marry you!" Elisha, overjoyed, contacted her parents and everyone approved of the marriage. Valid and Elisha would buy the small farm from the farmer. He was very happy to sell his farm and move into the village, as he was too old for the work. The marriage would take place that autumn.

Liana took the mule into town to sell their produce. She had a good day and headed back to the farm. Almost at the farm, she found herself surrounded by men and at first thought they were bandits. As it turned out it was her uncle's militia.

"Liana, we need to leave now!"

"Now, why?"

"Akhan and Zara have been captured by the Russians, and it's only a matter of time until they come for us also!" She could see the terror in their eyes and realized that they had not had the few calm months that she had.

"Let me talk to Elisha, and I will return."

***

"Liana," Elisha said, "I understand that my father and mother were captured, but I feel it's best that I stay here. The Russians know I am here, and they do not mind. I can help my father and mother best if I stay and, perhaps in time, I can raise a family here."

"I cannot stay here. The Russians will come for me soon," Liana said.

"I will never forget all you've done for us, and you are welcome here whenever you wish to come," Elisha said. She got the rest of her things and put them into a backpack. She had some clothes, some money, a few small books and her little radio. They hugged and Liana walked off into the night.

Liana caught up with the remainder of her uncle's militia, about thirty men in total.

"Where are we going, into Chechnya or Georgia?"

"We have been hired to fight with people of our own faith. They have promised to smuggle us out."

"Where are we going?" she asked.

"Afghanistan ...."

*Afghanistan, could it get any worse?*

The trip from Dagestan to Afghanistan was the most miserable Liana had known. They rode forever crammed in trucks. They walked through an endless mountain range that had freezing, cold summits and hot, dry valleys. Finally they joined the Taliban who were fighting against the Eastern Alliance in Afghanistan.

*The nights are so cold and the days so hot!*

"Afghanistan holds the poorest people I have ever seen. People actually live in caves here," one of the Chechen fighters explained to Liana. The country, after endless years of war, was completely devastated.

*The kids here beg for food constantly, and we are always hungry ....*

"Liana, you must cut your hair short because of the lice. It is better that way because we must convince the Taliban that you are just another dirty faced Chechen boy," her commander explained. "You don't want them to know you are a woman."

*Now I must make the Taliban think I am a boy. The Taliban are basically cutthroats anyway. They whip, beat or kill women for the tiniest infraction of Islamic law. All flee when they enter a village. I have descended into hell ....*

Liana always camped with the Chechen fighters, but she tried to sleep away from the remainder of her uncle's men. Tonight as she rolled out her bed, a boy with her group rolled his out near her. She dragged hers away. The boy dragged his toward her.

"Liana, please don't avoid me. I want to talk." She looked at the boy and guessed him to be about twelve years old. She remembered his name, Usef.

"Yes, Usef, talk ...."

"Please don't be curt to me. I'm troubled." She felt a little sad and just made a hand motion.

"Please talk ...."

"Liana, do you think we are doing right?"

"Doing right?"

"Fighting with the Taliban against the Eastern Alliance? The children here are terrified all the time, and the people are so poor, they beg food from me every day. It seems all the fields here grow nothing but dust. Doesn't it ever rain here? The food is bad, and there's little of it. A few shreds of bread, some bad tea and, if we're lucky, a piece of goat meat is a meal. We go days with nothing."

"Yes, it's bad here …."

"Liana, are we doing right?"

"No."

"No?" Usef repeated.

"No, we're not doing right. Now go to sleep."

"The Eastern Alliance that we're fighting against hold lush valleys and mountains. The area the Taliban holds is dry, worthless desert. Some of the villages show empty water fountains and deserted village squares that once flowed with water and bustled with activity. To me the Eastern Alliance are the good guys and the Taliban the bad. We fight against old men carrying shotguns, boys carrying bolt-action rifles, and terrified women and children," he said.

"I told you we are not doing right. Now go to sleep!" Liana said.

They did not get very far into the mountains when something she could not understand took place. A commander for the Eastern Alliance walked down out of the mountains and talked to the Taliban commander. The two sat and drank tea. The Chechens with her had no idea what was going on. At long last a Taliban commander explained what had happened.

"The Eastern Alliance commander has agreed to follow our lead, so they are free to take their rifles and go home. We will march north." The compromise meant that bitter fights to the death did not occur.

*This is the kind of peace agreement my grandfather would have struck with the Russians.*

"Liana we are heading south to rest in Kabul," her commander explained. "In one week we head north to fight the Northern Alliance, which is much stronger than the Eastern Alliance. Kabul is a large city, but it's been bombed many times. Most of the buildings have no roofs." As the Chechen militia entered the city they saw a Taliban checkpoint ahead with shimmering ribbons adorning it, the shredded remains of confiscated videotapes.

If the Taliban obeyed strict Islamic law while in the field, then they were fanatics in the city. A man could lose his nose if he shaved his beard. Liana felt unsafe here and dared not go out by herself. Her ruse of dressing as a boy did not really offer her any safety.

*The boys here are in just as much danger as the girls are.*

Liana still held her small shortwave radio. Using an earphone, she'd turn on the BBC and hear the news of the world. Tonight she heard The World Trade Center in New York had been bombed, and thousands were dead.

*More dead and hurt people .... The Americans will leave no stone overturned searching for Bin Laden. They will be here soon, and then no one will help us.*

"Liana, I know you're a girl, be very careful," an Afghan guide explained to her. "Anyone here can claim you if they wish." She understood Shari better than most Afghans did, but this statement floored her. When the Taliban invaded an area, they considered it their right to claim any women they wished. She decided to be very careful and wondered how long she could survive.

On a Monday morning, the Chechens joined Afghan fighters who were heading to fight the Northern Alliance.

"The Americans may attack us any day now also, but we will defeat them like we did the Russians," a Taliban officer explained to Liana's group.

The country the Northern Alliance held was beautiful with green rolling hills, farmland and even cattle. To her it seemed that the Taliban was like a plague of locusts, laying ruin wherever they went.

"Liana, please stay near me when the Taliban enters the village ahead," Usef asked. "I will try to protect you."

"Protect me?" Liana asked the small boy.

"Yesterday when we entered a village they chased down all the girls who tried to flee and captured them. When I asked why they did this horrible thing they explained that I was too young to understand. Their clerics have given them blank marriage documents. All they have to do to claim you as their wife is to capture you and write your name on the document."

"And you will protect me?" Liana asked Usef.

"Yes," he answered, patting his rifle.

***

After months of fighting against the Northern Alliance, the Chechens found themselves in a steep mountain range. The Northern Alliance held the mountains, and resistance from them was very strong. The battle had become a sniping war moving from rock to rock. In the confusion Liana found that the Chechens had retreated, leaving her with the Taliban.

The Taliban attacked the Northern Alliance near Mazar-i Sharif. No one gained the upper hand during difficult fighting. The battle took a turn for the worse; U.S. Jets showed up and began pounding the Taliban positions. Until that time they had not seen the Americans. Now they were flying over their heads.

The air power made the difference in the fight, and now the Taliban found that they were the ones asking the Northern Alliance for terms. A Northern Alliance commander told the Taliban to take their rifles and go home.

*My only hope was to head south toward Kabul and find fellow Chechens.*

*After walking for three days the retreating Taliban passed me on the road. When I entered Kabul I found the Taliban had abandoned its artillery, and its foreign fighters, and was now in a rapid retreat south to Kandahar.*

"The Americans will be in Kabul tomorrow. Come with us. We're fleeing into Pakistan," an Arab commander asked her. She weighed her chances, as without a doubt one of the Arabs would claim her.

"Liana, survive!" Sarena again called out to her.

"I will go with you into the mountains because I have nowhere else to go," Liana explained. The fighting in the mountains was very bad. Helicopters, jets and artillery pounded every spot the group chose.

"Who are the Afghans on the cliffs?" Liana asked an Arab commander.

"The Afghans have now switched sides and fight alongside the Americans," he explained.

*The local Afghans know every mountain pass, every cave and every peak in the mountain range. The local tribesmen can call in strike after strike on the area, and we can do nothing to stop them.*

Liana and the Arabs endured a thirty-six-hour barrage of rock-splintering bombs that started one morning and went into the next evening. After the barrage began, some of the fighters panicked and tried to cross the valley. They didn't make it.

*The Arabs who went insane during the shelling are lying dead in the valley, but I must try and slip away also.*

Liana began a long journey over the mountains into Pakistan. In Pakistan she found a Chechen militia fighting alongside the displaced Taliban. Afghan tribes loyal to the United States now controlled Afghanistan.

*The tribal regions of Pakistan are no different from Afghanistan. The tribes treat women as badly as the Taliban. The area is very remote and dangerous, and even the Pakistani army does not enter it. The springtime, which the Taliban called "The killing season," proved to be deadly to the Taliban crossing the border into Afghanistan.*

During the years that followed, few Chechens survived the raids into Afghanistan. The Afghans hated the Chechen militia and took great pleasure in slowly killing any Chechens they found. The Chechens who died quickly in Afghanistan were the lucky ones.

"Liana, we believe that we would be more useful fighting in Iraq. We are leaving as soon as we can make the arrangements," her Chechen commander explained.

"I'm staying. I'll try and slip into Islamabad and hide."

Liana found herself in the city of Islamabad, the first modern city she had been in since leaving Grozny. Against all odds she found a Chechen family and asked to stay with them.

A rich businessman who sold arms in the area contacted Liana's adopted family. The man's name was Walid Hattab.

"Liana, I need you in my organization."

"For what?"

"For our faith," the man said.

"I do not share your convictions of death and murder."

"I have an important task that could change everything for us here, in Mecca and even in Chechnya." She was Chechen, but Chechnya meant little to her now.

"What?" she asked.

"We can make the Americans stay home. Our Mullahs can govern the world from Mecca."

*As if I would want that ....*

"I'll think about it, but I still think the answer is no."

Time went by, and she gathered her strength. She could not live forever with the Chechen family. She had no passport, no identification, and the Pakistani's could arrest her at any time.

It was midwinter when Walid Hattab contacted her again.

"Liana, have you made your decision on joining my organization?"

"I have decided not to join," she said.

"I could help you in ways you couldn't imagine."

"Why do you want me to join your organization so badly?" she asked.

"Liana, you're Muslim, but you are also blond, blue-eyed and pretty. You will raise no suspicions."

"You said you could help me? What could you possibly do for me?"

"I could get your mother out of prison," he said. The statement stunned her.

"My mother is dead; you could bring her back to life?"

"Your mother, Sarena, is in prison in Russia, convicted of blowing up Russian soldiers," Walid said. Shaken by the news that her mother lived, Liana just stared at the ground.

"I heard the Russians finally shoot my mother … you mean she survived?" Walid handed her a copy of a Russian prison file. She read the report and tears welled up in her eyes. She suddenly thought of her grandfather and stories he told of similar ruses both by the Russians and the Nazis.

"I do not believe my mother is alive. Prove to me that she lives, and that you can free her, and I will do anything you ask."

"For now, accompany me to a safe house in Saudi Arabia, and I will get the proof you need."

"Mr. Hattab, I will accompany you to Saudi Arabia, but understand I will be no one's consort while I am there."

"I understand," he said.

Walid provided a passport and identification for her, and she flew with him from Islamabad to Saudi Arabia. In Saudi Arabia she lived in a large home, owned by a wealthy Sheik. All the Muslim women in the home, herself included, wore black robes. Liana, who already knew Arabic, was to study the Koran with the other women and learn Saudi customs. She did not enjoy the black robes and felt that the Arab women were subservient.

*The home is as much a prison as a safe place to stay. The Arab women live at the beck and call of their masters and have little freedom. The men forbid women from going out of the home on their own, and they only go out with an escort. I found out that American models lived here and I asked to meet them.*

The Sheik hired the models to attend parties. The women described the parties to Liana.

"We serve food, entertain guests, but mostly withstand jeers."

"Jeers?" she asked.

"The Sheik has parties and he sits at his seat shielded from the others by a sheer curtain. The other Arabs seated smoke hashish and throw insults at us; they scream and make a huge deal if they feel we've done something wrong. We often wonder if we're prisoners here ourselves." Liana did not like staying here but would do anything within her power to free her mother.

A young Saudi girl named Nusrat lived in the home. Liana often studied with the girl, and she was very intelligent.

"Liana, I know you suffered terribly during the war, but you must put that behind you and go forward. You believe that we here in the Kingdom have no say, but you misunderstand the effects us women, quietly, calmly, have on our husbands and country. We abhor the death, the destruction, the misery, just as you do. Do not fall into the trap of believing that Arabs are a wicked and cruel people. We are loving and generous."

Liana smiled at her because her words were almost exactly those told to her by her mother.

"Nusrat, please don't feel badly of me. It's just that I have lived away from other women for so long that I do not know how to cope around them," Liana said.

About the time that Liana began to feel accepted in Saudi Arabia, Walid Hattab came back.

"Liana, I have something to show you." He laid out four eight-by-ten-inch photographs of Sarena sitting at a table with a Russian guard behind her. Liana looked the photographs over. Her mother had a long scar on her arm that had healed over the years. Her brown hair had streaks of gray. She looked older and thinner than Liana remembered, but the photograph was definitely her mother. Liana stopped for a moment as the hope of seeing her mother again shot through her veins like a drug.

"Photographs can be faked!" she said to Walid.

"In Russia you can buy anything, at three o'clock I will prove it to you." She looked at the clock it was ten in the morning.

*How can I wait until three o'clock ...?* The day went very slowly. Liana decided to occupy her time by reading. Late in the day Walid walked up to her. She did not want to get her hopes too high but thought that he might have more photographs to show her.

Liana stared at Walid and a moment later heard a beeping sound. He reached into his robe and produced a cell phone. He spoke for a moment, and then handed the phone to her.

"Please, who is this?" the voice on the other end cried out in Russian. She knew the voice, deeper, sharper, but still it was her mother.

"Momma?"

"Liana, it's true! You survived!"

"Momma!"

"Where are you?" Sarena asked.

"I am in a safe place where there is no fighting," she said. She looked at Walid, and he nodded. "Momma, I am in Saudi Arabia."

"Liana, I'm so glad you're safe and that at least one of us made it out."

"Momma, I'm going to get you out also. I know how."

"Liana, I am fine. Do not concern yourself with me. You need to go on with your life."

"Momma, we will both be together again soon. Momma …," she said, but the line had gone dead. She handed the phone back to Walid.

"What do you want me to do?"

"I want you to travel to Russia and go to school. A girl, also named Liana, died at the age of two. She had no relatives, and would now be nineteen. I'm having identification made for her and your picture will be on it. You will visit doctors and dentists using her name. You will become the girl, Liana Yeglov. You will do well in school because you are a smart girl, and in time you will apply to go and work in the United States."

"The United States?" Liana asked.

"Yes, you will travel there and in time we will apprise you of your mission," he explained. "Liana, my security officers are everywhere. Do nothing foolish, and you and your mother will be safe. If you do everything I ask soon you and your mother will be in Cyprus, but if you do not obey ...."

"I understand," she said.

The following week she received a package containing a passport, driver's license and documents with her picture on them saying she was Liana Yeglov. The package also contained something she had seen little of in years, cash. She would study political science.

*Political science? That will be different from anything else I have studied ....*

Liana looked at the courses, which included English, algebra and chemistry.

*I am going to college, a month ago I wouldn't have dreamed ....*

***

Liana found herself in a tiny apartment in Volgograd, Russia. Volgograd, formerly named Stalingrad, was the city her grandfather had helped defend against the Nazis. A museum of sorts existed in the city, and she went to it. In it there was a collection of rifles, uniforms, photographs and artifacts showing the defense of Stalingrad during the war. Plaques on the wall listed the names of the soldiers decorated for service defending the city.

*My grandfather's plaque ... Order of Lenin ... Noble Sniper ....* She ran her fingers across his name, and tears came to her eyes.

The culture here was Russian, and Liana immersed herself into it again. She loved the academic environment at the University and almost wished she could live her life out here. She again wore the tiny silver cross.

*I am wearing a dead girl's cross and living a dead girl's life, but at least I am not wearing her clothes this time ....*

Liana loved the days studying and learning in school. She dreaded the nights. The years of war had taken their toll on her, and she would not easily forget them. At night the war came back to her, and it came when she least expected it. She woke up in cold sweats, screaming, as she remembered things she wished she could forget. She applied to go to the United States to work on the beach, during the summer break.

"Liana, you really should go to counseling and talk to someone about your troubles," one of her schoolmates explained to her.

*What am I going to say to a counselor? Am I going to say that I spent years killing Russians ... talking to anyone might be the death of Momma and me.*

The only dream Liana could hold onto now was the thought of her and her mother in Cyprus. The island had a large Muslim community.

*In Cyprus Momma could teach and I could go back to school. The island is awash in Greek and Turkish history. It has warm beaches where we could live out our lives in peace. Perhaps in time I could even marry, but first my mission ....*

Her mission ... Liana was now in Ocean City, Maryland, and her target, Senator Wright, was staying in her hotel. Liana awoke and her body shook with fear as tears welled up in her eyes.

## SENATOR WRIGHT

*According to Ali, Senator Wright dates blond girls. I'm supposed to meet him and develop some type of relationship? How long do I keep in contact with him; a week, a month, a year? Do I kill him, or use him for some purpose?*

*I need to take my laptop computer to Delaware and contact Walid. I need to find a hotel with wireless Internet.*

Liana took the bus to a hotel in Delaware. She brought up the gaming site and worked her mouse back and forth on the eye of the clown. A message, written in Polish, appeared.

"Any success?" She edited the message.

"Have seen catch, what hook, how long needed?"

The next afternoon Liana asked Margrite if she would come to the boardwalk with her, and she was anxious to go. She put on a bikini that she had bought and wore a tiny miniskirt over it. Margrite was dressed similar to her, but Margrite had a much better figure.

"I need to check a room on the way out." They knocked at room 531. A man answered the door, and Liana, for the second time in two days, came face to face with Senator Wright.

"We're the maids on this floor, and we just wanted to make sure everything was all right." Senator Wright stared them up and down. She felt herself blushing, but Margrite giggled. A blond woman appeared, dressed in a towel.

"We need more towels," the woman said.

"I will get them," Liana said, leaving Margrite at the room. A moment later she appeared with a stack of towels.

"Your names?" he asked.

"Liana."

"Margrite."

"Well … thank you!" he said.

*Well I screwed that up! Margrite handled the situation correctly and I didn't. She's been handling the attention of men, and boys, since she was young.*

"Liana, why did you take me to Senator Wright's? I mean we really didn't have to stop."

"I guess I just wanted to meet him."

"Liana, American politicians, Russian politicians, they are all the same. Did you think he could help you?" Margrite asked.

"Help me?"

"Yes, help you to stay here with Tim, you know, become an American citizen?"

"I didn't think that way."

"Then you are one of the few that wouldn't want to stay. A rich husband, a beach house, a nice car …." It never occurred to Liana that some of the girls hoped to remain here when the summer ended.

After work that evening Liana boarded the bus for Delaware, logged onto the Polish gaming site, and clicked her mouse over the clown's eye. A new message came up in Polish.

"Good … Whatever's Necessary … One month," was the message.

*Walid's happy I met Senator Wright. I'm to hook him by whatever means necessary, and hold onto him for at least one month.* She edited the message and included "Ok" at the end.

Liana returned to her hotel, as she needed time to think. According to the other maids at the hotel, a parade of pretty girls had been coming and going from Senator Wright's room.

*That's what I thought; he uses them and casts them away ….*

Liana needed to get into Senator Wright's life and, for now, she had to stay in his life. If he made an advance toward her, would she be emotionally ready for it? She knew Margrite would. She pulled her nightgown on and climbed into bed. Her phone rang, it was Senator Wright.

"Liana, will you stop by my room?"

"Please, is there a problem?" she asked, almost speechless.

"No problem. I have people over, and I thought we could chat."

Tears ran down her face as she dressed to go to Senator Wright's room. She looked at herself in the mirror and hated how she looked. She stared at the floor trying to compose herself because she was shaking like a leaf.

"Liana, survive!" Sarena called out. She calmed down and washed her face.

When Liana entered Senator Wright's room there was a full-blown party going on and she felt she could handle it. She mingled with several people and tried to meld into the mood of the party.

"Can I get you a drink?" Senator Wright asked her. Liana, like most Muslims, didn't drink; Russian girls did, a lot.

"A little vodka, with some orange juice."

"A screwdriver!" he said. She had no idea what it was called but nodded anyway. He and his friends had several connected rooms, and each was open. She wasn't the only girl here, but she was the only one who was supposed to be Russian.

"Tell us about Russia!" a girl asked, and Liana sat down and began answering questions.

The drink didn't hold a little vodka, as she had asked, it held a lot. She took tiny sips of the drink and put it down often. Whenever she or anyone else put their drink down someone would bring them another. Some of the people were already loaded, and she hoped things wouldn't get out of hand.

"Liana you're so cute and tiny. I always thought Russian girls were big and muscular," the girl said.

"You should see her friend Margrite, just as cute but stacked," Senator Wright commented. She knew everyone had too much to drink already, but she felt things would get worse as the night went on.

"An important man wants to meet you," a woman said to Liana. "This is Congressman Stevens." The woman left him standing next to Liana.

"Hello," Liana said.

"Hello," he replied. "I've heard a lot about you and your friend Maggy."

"You mean Margrite," Liana corrected.

"Liana, is your family okay in Russia? I heard bad things can happen to people there," he said. Liana thought for a moment, unsure of what she was hearing.

"I understand," she said.

"It's important to have friends to look out for you, friends that can make sure bad things do not happen to those we love."

*He's trying to blackmail me using my family as a pawn. What he was saying is the truth; if I had a family in Russia, someone like Congressman Stevens could make life very difficult for them. Russian politicians did this to girls all the time ....* The man put his arm around her, and she felt her skin crawl.

"I have a problem ...," she explained.

"I can solve it for you," Congressman Stevens said.

"I don't think so because everyone in my family is dead," Liana said, staring straight into his eyes. He blinked, as he had not expected that. She felt the arm fall from her waist and saw the man go to get another drink. She stood staring at the ground.

"Don't let Harry worry you." She turned and found that Senator Wright had been there the whole time.

"What he's saying is true, though. Having friends to look out for you is important. I'll see you to your room."

As they approached her room, she tried to slide in, hoping it would be easy.

"How about a kiss goodnight?" he teased her. Liana stuck her head out and gave him a cheek kiss.

"Goodnight!" she said. She heard his footsteps going down the hall and hoped she hadn't blown everything.

"Senator Wright?" she called. "I will consider what you said about, you know ... about friends."

"Of course," he said. She went into her room, changed and took a shower. This was all way beyond her.

The next morning Liana went to breakfast, but Margrite was not there. She ate alone and then began work. She hoped that Margrite had not overslept again as she was on thin ice with the hotel already. She decided to say nothing and just go on about her work.

*The seventh room up the hall is Senator Wright's room. Who is this hung over-looking brunette girl that answered the door? The room is a pigsty of empty bottles, half-smoked cigarettes, trash and empty pizza boxes. I need to get my work done quickly; I don't want to confront Senator Wright this morning.*

"Everyone's out playing golf this morning," the brunette girl explained.

"I just need to clean up the mess and vacuum the rooms and I'll be on my way," Liana explained. As she went toward the last room, she heard a small voice call out. The brunette girl got up, ran, and shut the door.

"This one's okay," the girl said to Liana.

"Are you sure?" The woman nodded yes. This section had a strange perfume in it, and Liana wondered where she had come across it before. She finished the room and went to the three remaining rooms on the floor. It took her about two hours to finish her work, and by that time she was nearly exhausted.

*I have to clear my mind and think! Why did things go badly last night? Why can't I concentrate? That weird perfume, it was Margrite's! Somehow, Margrite wormed her way into Senator Wright's room and spoiled things. She talked about having a house at the beach, a rich husband and a nice car in America. Is that why she went to Senator Wright's room? She may have ruined everything for me!*

*The man who tried to blackmail me last night? I had no family and was taken back to my room. Margrite has a family at risk. The room that the brunette girl shut, Margrite must have still been inside!*

*I did this! I introduced them! What can I do? What's done is done. I have my mission to complete.*

Liana thought she knew a way to keep Senator Wright in her grasp and now needed to get her idea to Walid. She got on the bus, rode to Delaware, logged on, and found the clown's eye.

Her mouse found a message, but it was only three dots. Liana edited the message.

"$50now,+more later, ok" Her note explained to Walid that she needed fifty thousand dollars now and more later.

***

"Liana, there you are. I'm sorry I missed you yesterday. I felt sick," Margrite said at breakfast the next morning. Liana knew better but said nothing. They cleaned their rooms, and she even seemed comfortable in Senator Wright's room.

They ate dinner together on the boardwalk. Liana felt her heart breaking but did not know what to say to Margrite.

"Liana, is everything okay?"

"No, I know about yesterday." Margrite was not shocked, nor did she blush. She turned to Liana with a knowing smile.

"Liana, you're so childish sometimes! I told you, Russian politicians, American politicians, they're all the same. Powerful men use their power." Liana understood what Margrite was saying. She expected this, and to her it seemed ... normal. For once she was glad she had missed this portion of her life in Russia.

Liana took one of her laptops and rode the bus to the amusement park. She sat on a bench and found a hotel with wireless Internet access. She brought up the Polish gaming site and clicked on the clown's eye.

"Good idea, do it, all you need," the hidden message read. She edited the message and added "Ok," on the end. Walid could get her all the cash she needed and approved of her idea. She needed to tempt Senator Wright with the bait. She returned to her room to think. She jumped when her phone rang.

"Liana, I want to take you out to dinner," Tim said over the phone to Liana.

"Tim, I'm too busy right now."

"Can't we at least meet on the boardwalk?" She thought that would be okay. They walked down to the arcades.

"I hope you understand that work has been very stressful for me lately," Liana said.

"I understand. Is there anything I can do to help?"

"No, not right now. Tim, can you kiss me good-bye here, instead of at work?"

"Liana, what's going on?" He left but seemed upset.

*Oh great, Tim probably thinks I have a secret boyfriend now!*

The next day Liana entered her room and found a cardboard box sitting on her dresser. It was the fifty thousand dollars from Walid. Unsure of what to do, she hid the money under her bed. She sat on her bed trying to compose herself, as she had never seen wealth like this before.

*Should I just take the money and run away? If I do my mother and I will be dead within a week ....*

Someone knocked on Liana's door, and when she opened it, Margrite stood there in a nightgown.

"Liana, we need to talk." Margrite was a beautiful girl and in some ways reminded Liana of her mother, as she was bold and courageous. "Many things about you have not made sense to me and I wanted to talk. Liana, you're not the girl you're trying to be." Liana stared at Margrite, and fear gripped her. "You are hiding someone inside and making us believes it is you?" Margrite saw Liana clench up and hugged her. Liana hugged Margrite back, unsure of what to do. Margrite kissed her on her forehead and stared into her eyes. "You have a secret you want no one to know?" she asked. Liana said nothing. By now Liana had no idea what was going on. Had she discovered she was Chechen? Liana sat frozen and unsure of what to do.

"Liana, I've seen how you react when men notice you. You look ashamed. When Senator Wright shook your hand, your eyes had the look like worms were crawling on you. It's okay. You can tell me the truth." Liana did not know what to say or what to do. "There is no shame in this, this fear, this secret. It's your decision," she explained. "It's okay you're a ... a ... a ...." Liana stared at Margrite. "You're a virgin aren't you?" Liana had masked herself as being someone experienced in love, and Margrite had seen right through it.

"Margrite, this is something that I don't talk about, I keep to myself. I am not a virgin, but I have never given myself willingly to a man either."

"I understand," she said. "And Tim? You had him over one night?"

"Perhaps someday when things are perfect."

"Liana," Margrite explained as she was leaving, "things are never perfect."

***

*I have one day left to lure Senator Wright; I must bait the hook tonight.* She looked at the clothes hanging in her closet and decided upon the blue dress that she had replaced after the Arabs ruined the other. She put the dress on and made sure she looked nice. She put on silver earrings and even a bracelet. She picked up her phone and rang his room.

"I've been thinking about what you said about friends, and I agree. We all need friends. Can you come to my room and talk?" she said to the senator.

"I've got some things to do, but I'll try and make it down." She made sure her room was neat, took the box of cash, and put it on her dresser. She then prepared herself to meet him. She heard a knock at her door and opened the door to see ... Tim!

"Tim, what are you doing here!"

"I just wanted to talk. Things don't seem right, and I love you, okay? I just wanted you to know."

"You must leave now, immediately!" she said. He could see she was dressed to go out, and it did not seem right to him.

"Liana?"

"I can't explain, but if you do care for me then leave now." He was distraught, and that was the last thing she wanted. Liana gave him a very long kiss.

"Does that answer your question? Now please go!" Tim left as asked. Liana heard the same knock at the door. She threw her hands in the air.

"Tim …," she started to say. She opened the door and stared at … Senator Wright!

"Did I miss something?" he asked.

"Please come in." She set a chair for him, but instead of sitting on it, he sat on her bed. She sat on the chair.

"I don't know if I explained this to you or not, but I am studying political science in college," she stated.

"You are? Do you want to be a Senator some day?"

"I want to be the President of Russia," she said.

"Is that why you called me to see if I could help you become the President of Russia?"

"Well, actually yes, in a way it is. I would like to go to Washington and study the political process."

"I see, a foreign student here to learn our American political process …."

"Yes."

"I think I could arrange something like that, but why should I?"

"The other day, we talked about having powerful friends that could help us; I have such friends that could help you." He stared at her for a moment, contemplating her words.

"And your friends?"

"They want to contribute to your upcoming campaign, fifty thousand to start." Senator Wright stared at her.

"An illegal contribution? Please stand up and turn around." She did not understand why he would want her to turn around, but she did as he asked. In one swift swipe he unzipped her dress from her neck to her waist.

"No, stop!" she shouted. He looked at her a moment and she started to talk. He put his finger to her mouth.

"Okay, have it your way. I'm leaving." Liana saw everything slipping away from her and did not know what to do.

"There must be a way." Liana stared at the Senator.

"Okay, you wore a skimpy little bikini under your mini-skirt the other day …."

"Yes …?"

"Put it on and come to my room, or this conversation is over." She had not expected this and had no idea what to do. Almost in a panic, she went to Margrite's room.

"Margrite?" Liana called, but she did not appear.

"Liana," a girl called to her, "I haven't seen Margrite since yesterday and if she is not at work in the morning, she will be sent home." Margrite was missing and about to be fired. Liana didn't need to worry about that right now. She returned to her room, put her bikini on, and stared at herself in the mirror.

*Momma, it's this or we die!* She pulled a robe on and took the elevator to Senator Wright's room.

Liana knocked at his door, and he appeared dressed in a swimsuit.

"We're going swimming!" he stated. She did not understand but followed him to the pool.

"The indoor pool is closed," she said.

"I called the front desk, and they said we can have the whole pool to ourselves." They entered the room, and he locked the door.

"Get in the water." She climbed into the pool.

"Deeper!" he demanded. She walked into the deep section. He reached across and took her earrings from her ears. He ran his fingers through her hair.

"Get under the water," he said. She did as he asked and prayed that he would not hold her head under and drown her. She came back up, and he ran his fingers through her hair again. They were in deep enough water now that she had to stand on her tiptoes to get air. She was very, very frightened.

"One more thing … your top." Liana undid her top and handed it to him. He threw her top into the deep water and slid close.

"Okay, you can talk," he said. She calmed down a little. He hadn't made an advance on her when he unzipped her dress. He was trying to see if she was wearing a recording device. She couldn't wear a wire in the pool, and he felt it was safe to talk. She was back in business.

"I have friends that need powerful men, friends with money."

"And your friends, they want what?"

"Influence," she said.

"They have a problem?"

"Yes, every fall Russian businessmen attempt to buy millions of pounds of poultry from U.S. growers, contracts are signed, and every year shipments are held up by your government's red tape. They lose millions of dollars. They need friends here who can see that the shipments are not interrupted."

"And the money?"

"They have cash that they can supply for your re-election campaign; I have fifty thousand in my room, a down payment."

"And you want to study politics in Washington, work with my staff?"

"Yes, I would."

“Done!” he said as he climbed out of the pool. “A man will stop by for the cash.” He unlocked the door and left. Liana swam over to retrieve her top. She was relieved on both counts: She hadn’t been touched, and she was in.

She went to her room and changed. She waited for half an hour, and there was a knock on her door. She opened the door and found a very scruffy looking man standing there.

“The money?” the guy asked. She picked up the box and handed it to him. He took the box and disappeared.

Liana sat on her bed trying to decide what to do. She got up and found her laptop. She rode the bus to the south end of town and found wireless Internet access at a coffee shop. She brought up the gaming site and ran her mouse over the clown’s eye.

“Success?” the message read. She edited the message.

“Hooked!”

Liana didn’t see Margrite at breakfast, and knew the hotel would send her home. She wondered if something bad had happened between her and Senator Wright.

*If he killed Margrite, then he might kill me also.* She left a message at the gaming site.

“Need Ali.”

***

Senator Wright spotted Liana in the hallway and stopped to talk..

“I’m checking out. You’ve been accepted as an intern for sixty days. Your paperwork will arrive tomorrow. You will have to find your own lodging and transportation. I’ll see you eight o’clock Monday morning at my office. And, Liana, you don’t have to hide your lover any longer.”

“My lover?”

“Tim, your boyfriend, he can have you back now.”

Liana went back to her room to try to think things out, as everything was moving too fast. A moment later she heard a knock on her door and opened it expecting Tim to be there. It wasn’t Tim at her door, but Ali.

“Ali, I am on my way to Washington. When will my mother be freed?”

“When your mission is complete you will both be in Cyprus together.”

“I’m frightened. My friend Margrite was sleeping with Senator Wright, and I think he killed her. She’s missing.”

“Margrite interfered with you and the Senator. She had to go.” Ali’s words hit her like a ton of bricks; he had killed her best friend. *More blood on my hands…*

“Where is she? What did you do to her?” she asked.

“She is not important … nothing. Concern yourself with your mission or ...." Ali waved his hand.

"I want to at least say good-bye to Margrite."

"Go to the ocean and say good-bye then," Ali said as he left. She crumpled onto her bed crying with the thought that Margrite was dead and somehow she was the cause of it all. She knew she could not take much more.

***

A wedding ceremony took place in the hotel. Liana cleaned the reception hall and noticed a huge pile of flowers in the trash. She took scissors and cut the tops off. That night she took the flower tops down to the beach and threw them into the ocean. Margrite's body lay somewhere out in the ocean, and this was the best memorial she could give her.

*Allah, take Margrite into your love ....*

Liana lay in bed thinking of the past month. Margrite and the Arabs both visited her room, and they were now dead. Ali seemed to know everything she did and whom she saw. Senator Wright visited her room and unzipped her dress in an effort to prove she was not wearing a recording device.

*Maybe Senator Wright's instincts are correct. Maybe my room is bugged. Straight above my bed I can see a smoke detector.*

She lay on her bed and stared, not at but toward the smoke detector. She went out into the hallway and looked at the other smoke detectors in the hotel. Her smoke detector was different from all the others.

*Ali cannot only hear what I say in my room, he can see it! The smoke detector holds a small camera that has a full view of my room! Ali watches me sleep; he watches me change; he knows what I'm wearing and when I wear it. He knows who I call; he knows who visits me in the middle of the night! He watched Margrite come and heard the words she said. Ali must record everything and watch it later. He has invaded every crevice of my life.*

She lay in bed contemplating what happened.

*Margrite came to my room to talk and Ali watched the whole thing unfold. The same thing happened to the Arabs. Anyone who gets close to me dies!*

*What about Tim? When will Ali kill him? If Ali felt that he was no longer useful to the mission, he would kill him. If the mission requires Tim's help, then he will live. What should I do?*

Liana tried with all her power not to look at the camera.

*Ali suspects nothing and I'll use the camera to my advantage.* Liana picked up her phone.

"Tim, please come over. I need to see you."

"Why?"

"I need you badly," she stated. She undressed and covered herself with her robe. Fifteen minutes later Tim appeared at her door.

"Tim, I wanted to thank you again for all that you taught me."

"What?"

"I knew nothing of America until I met you. I need you to help me again," she said.

"Okay?"

"I am going to be an intern for Senator Wright, and I need your help in Washington. We need to go tomorrow."

"An intern?"

"I didn't think it could possibly happen, but I was accepted onto Senator Wright's staff. That's what I was working on so hard this week. I need you to help find an apartment, to find public transportation routes, to acclimate to the culture in Washington."

"I will be glad to help you, I lo ...." She had put her finger to his lips, and he fell silent.

"Tim, I haven't rewarded you this week for helping me."

"Rewarded me? Liana, have you been drinking?" Liana started to unbutton Tim's shirt and had him undress.

"Are you okay? Are you all right?"

"Don't turn around," she said. Tim lay on his side with a sheet covering him. She walked to the other side of the bed, dropped her robe, and posed for the camera for just a moment. She slid into the bed between the sheets that covered Tim. She pulled the covers over both of their heads and began tickling his neck and side.

"Don't turn over," she whispered. He began laughing and writhing in bed as she tickled him. He was jumping around so much that Liana wondered if she would end up falling out of bed. He finally couldn't take anymore and turned to tickle her. He found it was more difficult than he thought since the sheet separated them.

"That's enough ...." Liana whispered. To her the ruse served its purpose. She was sure Ali had watched and heard everything, and come to his own conclusions about the evening.

## WASHINGTON

Liana wanted to get an early start this morning, as it was her day off. She hoped Tim would still be asleep, as she would have to casually get up and, knowing the camera was rolling, get dressed. She could tell by Tim's breathing that he was asleep, and she quietly slipped out of bed. For a moment she stood for the camera and reached for her robe.

"Liana, you look like an angel." She grabbed for her robe and realized she had made the wrong move, as it wouldn't seem natural. She knew she was blushing but bent over and kissed him good morning.

An hour later they were driving toward Washington on Route 50.

"Liana, about last night?"

"Tim no …."

"I think we're breaking through to another level and … I'm not ready for it. There's a lot you don't know about me, but I've had a hard time getting over some things. If I can deal with these things slowly, I think I can go forward. If things go too fast, then I might not be able to cope." Liana stared at Tim and realized the words he spoke could have come from her own mouth.

"Tim, I feel the same way." They arrived in Washington around 10:00 AM. "How do we do this? How do we find an apartment here?" she asked.

"Since you'll only be here two months, it'll be a real pain in the ass to find something," Tim said. "The two ways are to hire a realtor, which is expensive, or is to search the newspapers and hit the streets." Tim stopped at a McDonalds, and they sat at a booth reading the newspapers.

They drove all over the town looking for rooms. Tim was right; no one wanted to rent her a room for only two months.

"Let's take a break for a while. I wanted to show you Georgetown," Tim said.

"I would like to live here!" she said when they arrived.

"I would too, but we don't have this kind of money."

"Can we stop by the University? I want to get a brochure," she said. On the wall inside the building Liana noticed a three-by-five card, which read that an apartment was available for sublet for the remainder of the summer.

"Tim, could I afford that?" she asked.

"Yeah, the price is right. Let's walk down and take a look. It's probably a college student. During the summer she probably heads home and leaves the place vacant. The apartment is in a nice area near public transportation, jogging trails, and parks. For the Washington area, this is about as safe and convenient as it gets." He called the phone number on the card, and a girl answered.

"It's a studio apartment with a small kitchen, a TV, and a sofa bed. I can meet you there in a few minutes," the voice over the telephone explained.

The girl unlocked the apartment, and they walked in. Liana fell in love with it immediately.

"It's very cozy and has everything I need," she explained.

"I like it, too. This is as good as it gets," Tim said.

"Will both of you be living here?"

"No, just Liana," he replied. The girl smiled and laid the agreement out for them to sign. Tim gave the girl a check, and the apartment was Liana's.

After the girl left, Liana pulled out the sofa bed and sprawled across it. Tim lay down also, and she hugged him.

*I'm finally away from prying eyes!* They both fell into a slumber and didn't arise for several hours.

Tim got up, found some instant coffee in a cupboard, and made a cup. He didn't want to wake her up, but knew he had to.

"Liana, you need to think your day out, how you will get to work, the layout of the city," he explained.

"How long did we sleep? I didn't realize how tired I was," she replied.

"I guess we were out for three hours," he said. "We need to check out the city and then head home."

They found maps of the city that she could follow. For several hours, the two just rode the public transportation around town so she would become familiar with the city.

Late in the day they got back into Tim's car to head to Ocean City. He dropped her off at her hotel.

"Liana," her supervisor called out to her, "Senator Wright explained he chose you as a summer intern. We're so excited!"

"I'm very excited also. Tim and I drove to Washington today to find a room."

"You'll be in Washington, socializing and attending parties with important people."

"It will be different from making beds," she explained.

"How long will you be gone?" she asked.

"I will only be gone for two months, and then I will be back," Liana explained.

"Can we have Tim while you are gone?" a girl teased her.

"Tim will stay close to me while I am gone, and there are boys on the boardwalk for you."

The next morning she walked out to look at the ocean. She looked out across the waves; she was going to miss the ocean and boardwalk.

*If only I could have grown up like this ....*

She looked up to find Ali standing next to her.

*Ali always stuns me by how quickly he shows up and disappears. Maybe I should ask him if he enjoyed the show.*

"The room, you were successful?"

"I found a place."

"I need the address and key. I will copy it and leave it on your dresser."

"Ali, I need to know my role."

"Your role?"

"What am I to do in Washington? Do I kill Senator Wright? Do I blackmail him? What do I do?"

"Your role will be to frighten."

"Frighten?"

"Yes, you will frighten many, but hurt no one."

"And after everyone is frightened, I leave?"

"No."

"Then what?"

"Liana, by the time the Americans are frightened you will already be on a plane to Cyprus and your mother will be there waiting for you."

"When then?"

"Very soon."

"Liana, the Capitol building ...."

"Yes?"

"You need to get in and look for ways to move a small package into the building without being caught."

"A package?"

"Something like this. See if you could sneak this in." Ali held a book.

"Okay."

"The boy?" Ali asked.

"The boy?"

"Tim?" he asked. Liana shook her head not understanding.

"He has been useful so far?"

"Crucial. He allows me to look and think American. He allows me to function."

"He will continue to help you in Washington, or will you need to find another?"

"The boy helps me immensely; he doesn't pry or ask questions. He enjoys what I do for him." When Liana said the words, she saw hurt in Ali's eyes and realized he wanted her for his own.

*He probably became jealous while watching us on his camera.*

"For now the boy is useful then." He gathered his things and left.

Liana sat trying to control her rage.

*Tim's life hangs on a thread and if I screw up, he's dead.* Liana, in her anger, grasped the metal rail of the boardwalk causing her hands to turn red. She looked at her hands.

*Will my hands always be covered in blood? Will this ever end?*

She sat on the bench, and tears began to flow again. Families walked by talking, laughing, and tossing french fries to the gulls. Couples walked on the beach; girls jogged near the ocean. Everyone seemed at peace except her.

*Will I ever have a life, an open honest life where I don't have to hide my name or who I am?*

That evening she returned to her room to pack her clothes, and saw her apartment key sitting on the dresser. She noticed that the original smoke detector, that the hotel installed, was back in her room.

Two hours later Tim drove her toward Washington.

"I'm not going to lose you to another girl over this, am I?"

"Another girl? Liana, there are no other girls." Tim seemed to be torn trying to explain himself and did not know what to say.

"Liana, this is difficult but …."

"Tim, what happened … Tim, please?"

"I've had a really bad stretch these last five years. A drunk driver killed my dad, and my mom went off the deep end. My mom overdosed on sedatives. Now she's in an institution and comes in and out of reality; sometimes she doesn't even recognize me. I've been feeling very alone and empty for a long time. I've tried to keep busy studying and working. I had tried dating, but it didn't work. I almost felt like I didn't know how to function in a relationship. It's just that I always feel so empty and almost helpless, like I can't control my own life." Once again it seemed that her words had come out of his mouth. She undid her seat belt and slid over to hug Tim.

They arrived in Washington that evening. She hung her things up and found places for the rest. All too soon Tim had to leave.

"Call me if you need anything. I can be here in a few hours. I will be back Friday night." Tim kissed her good-bye and Liana watched him walk to his car. Once again, she was alone.

## THE CAPITOL

Senator Wright arrived back in Washington. As a precaution he hired a former KGB officer to investigate Liana and report back to him. They met at a local restaurant.

"Senator Wright, I have the information you requested," he explained.

"You have the documents I requested on Liana?"

"Yes, the package contains medical reports, dental reports, x-rays, college transcripts and even a birth certificate. Many records are missing, but that's not unusual, many were lost when the Soviet Union collapsed."

Liana arrived at work, as asked, on Monday morning.

"Liana, I'm Ellen. I'm supposed to train you. You'll be doing research for the Senator." Ellen, a college intern in her last year of law school, liked Liana immediately.

Liana found the work challenging. She spent long hours in the microfilm section of the library and researched items on the Internet. She prepared reports and backed up the reports with copies of documents, records and newspaper articles.

"I know this kind of work is boring, but what we do is essential," Ellen explained.

"No, I really enjoy this type of work," Liana explained. "It is much better than making beds and vacuuming."

One week later Senator Wright was called to a meeting in the Capitol.

"Who's calling us over?" he asked Ellen.

"Senator Cargill claims he found some information on an Afghan warlord."

"This can't be good; he's probably trying to embarrass us." Senator Wright and his staff including Liana, headed over to the Capitol.

"Whatever you do, say nothing, and for God's sake don't embarrass Senator Wright," Ellen stated. Liana decided to keep her mouth shut at all costs.

When Senator Wright arrived, the press was waiting. He entered and flashes of light shot out as photographers took pictures. He sat down in front of his staff and saw that a large TV screen was setup. Senator Cargill stood in front. He handed a video to Senator Wright.

"We intercepted this a few days ago while you were on vacation.

We have transcribed it, and we want you to view it. The video shows the warlord you selected as being helpful to the United States bragging about the U.S. soldiers he killed. He recorded it in Arabic to send to a sheik in Saudi Arabia." The room exploded with gasps at the Senator's words. Senator Cargill hit a button, the video began showing the warlord talking in Arabic, and a member of his staff read the transcript. Liana listened intently, as it was hard to hear over the noise in the room. The transcript described the warlord as thanking Allah for dropping holy fire upon the enemy and knocking them to the ground. The video showed the Afghan leader talking and smiling. Everyone in the room seemed horrified. Liana slid next to Senator Wright and handed him a note.

"Translation incorrect!" it read. Senator Wright, embarrassed by her move, asked for a momentary recess.

"Afraid to face the truth?" Senator Cargill screamed. "Your man is a terrorist, isn't he?" Senator Wright called everyone outside, and he was as angry as anyone had ever seen him.

"What the hell was that about, and why didn't we know about the video?"

"Senator Wright," Liana said softly, "please listen." He had no choice as he had just had his head handed to him in the meeting.

"The man on the video, he was talking about flowers, you call ah ... poppies?"

"What! Don't tell me you know Arabic?"

"Yes, I have learned many languages."

"Okay, what do you think he's saying?"

"Arabic has many dialects and … the man seems to be thanking Allah for sending a hail storm away from his village's poppy fields and ruining his enemy's fields instead. Breaking his rival's poppy plants in half."

"Are you absolutely sure!"

"Yes," she said. Bob Winslow, an attorney who worked for Senator Wright, came forward.

"Senator, you know my wife, Cathleen? She translates Arabic at the CIA and could confirm what Liana is saying." Senator Wright found his copy of the tape and called her.

"Cathleen, I need to play a tape for you, in Arabic, and I need a quick interpretation."

"Now?"

"Yes, immediately." The Senator played the tape, and she confirmed Liana's interpretation.

"Senator Wright, I understand the confusion, but the man is thanking Allah for saving his poppies."

They all returned to the meeting.

"Senator Wright, what do you have to say? Are you ready to apologize to this committee and the American people for your recommendation?" Cargill arose and seemed agitated.

"Senator Cargill, you're concerned about some flowers while our troops face danger every day?" Senator Cargill had no idea what Wright was talking about but felt the earth beneath him begin to melt.

"The warlord is thanking God for saving his village's poppies, while destroying the poppy crop of our enemies." The room broke into laughter, and camera flashes lit the room as Senator Cargill looked like a deer caught in the headlights. Senator Wright got up, shook his head, and collected his things. He walked toward the door and, just before leaving, waved at the press.

By evening, the word was all over the news about Senator Cargill's embarrassing attack on Senator Wright.

"I don't think badly of Senator Cargill," Senator Wright said to the TV cameras. "He's trying to do his best to guard our country; he just needs to check his facts before accusing." All the networks carried the interview and repeatedly played it. The press labeled the fiasco "Flowergate," and even the late night comedians had a ball with it.

Liana returned from the meeting and resumed work. She hoped Senator Wright would not fire her for the embarrassing scene at the meeting. She began her research and felt at ease. After an hour of work, she saw Ellen's eyes light up. A deliveryman was walking down the hall carrying flowers.

"Are you Liana?" She nodded, and the man placed the flowers on her desk. She looked at Ellen because she had no idea what the flowers meant.

"Have I been fired? Am I supposed to leave now?"

"Red roses," Ellen said, "means someone loves you!"

*Tim sent me flowers at work! How embarrassing!* The flowers included a card, and she opened it.

"Thank you for pulling my chestnuts out of the fire, Norman."

"Who is Norman?" she said aloud. Ellen began giggling again.

"It's Senator Wright. He's Norman!"

"I don't understand. What is he saying to me?" Ellen began laughing hysterically but said she was too embarrassed to explain.

"Tim," Liana said over the phone, "I received this note from Senator Wright, but I don't understand it." Tim tried to explain everything, but she had trouble understanding the exact meaning of it all.

"I guess you could say he believes you saved him," he explained.

The office was going out for a victory celebration after work.

"Liana, we want you to come," Ellen said.

*Now what? Can't I just go home?*

They met at a local bar to celebrate. Every half hour the news would come on and show the clip of "Flowergate" for all to see. When it did, whoops went out from Senator Wright's staff and drinks ordered. He, along with a pretty red-haired girl, was buying drinks for everyone. Liana sipped ginger ale and watched the festivities.

"Liana, I wanted to thank you again," he said.

"Thank you for the beautiful flowers!" she replied.

Liana arrived home late and got ready for bed. She looked up at the smoke detector and wondered if Ali was watching her.

*Is Ali watching me lying in his bed?*

She finally drifted off to sleep. She slept a few hours and woke up to find Ali sitting next to her.

"Liana, you found a way to get a package into the Capitol?" She felt uneasy having Ali sitting next to her bed.

"I believe so."

"How?"

"Senator Wright's daily documents, I prepare them and they are not checked. They are marked confidential."

"The documents?"

"I carry them in an eleven-inch manila envelope." While Ali talked, he rubbed her calf.

"Ali, this is my bedroom. You shouldn't be here." She saw his eyes flash in anger, and she understood.

*Tim had been in her bed, hadn't he?*

"I know it must be hard being away from your loved ones, but devout men don't do this kind of thing. It's the kind of thing I would expect from someone like the Senator or...Tim, men who don't know better," she said. Liana saw the fire go out of his eyes, and she knew she had won, for now. She knew the game she was playing was deadly, but she also knew she must play it.

"Liana, we had a problem today."

"A problem?"

"I heard about the translation issue. It was on the news."

"Tea, Ali?" Liana asked as she heated water in her microwave.

"Bob Winslow's wife is a CIA agent. She is fluent in Arabic and has uncovered several of our operations. You must be extremely cautious of her. She could be on to us already. The knowledge that you translated an Arabic tape just makes everyone suspicious. "

"I had no choice and it made Senator Wright look up to me."

"This went across the wire. An Israeli spy posed as a model and infiltrated our safe house in Saudi Arabia. She made this sketch of you." Liana looked at the drawing and felt her gut tighten.

"Ali, I need to lure Tim here."

"Tim, why?"

"Having Tim here with me would make everyone less suspicious of me. You mentioned this CIA woman. Wouldn't I be less suspicious with an American here?"

"Yes, but where will he sleep?" He blushed as he realized he had just given away his thoughts.

"Don't worry. I will handle the boy." She put tea on the table and sat down. He quickly drank his tea and went to leave. As he left, he turned as if he was going to kiss her.

"Ali, goodnight!" she said and closed the door on him.

*Ali will do whatever he must to have me now. Having Tim here will block his efforts.*

"Tim," she asked over the phone, "can you come and stay with me in Washington? It's more difficult than I imagined."

"I really have nothing going on in Ocean City," Tim explained.

Tim bought a blow-up camping bed that he could lean against a wall. Three days later an incident occurred.

During the night he heard Liana talking to herself in Russian. He did not worry about her dream, as she had them often. She began thrashing around her bed as if digging a hole.

Liana relived the terrible night in Afghanistan in her dream.

*A man parched grain over glowing coals. I lay away from everyone else trying to get to sleep. The man's head suddenly exploded. I heard nothing. A second man stood up and I saw blood spurt from his neck. He moaned and dropped to his knees. A third man lurched and fell screaming. Everyone grabbed their rifles and began firing into the night. The attack made no sense. Men fell from rifle bullets that I could not hear. I squeezed into a crevice.*

*"It's a sniper with a night scope and a silencer," I cried out. "All he can see through his scope is glowing orbs of heat. They're expert marksman, not Afghans or militia." Usef, the boy I had befriended, died next. I knew that at any moment my body heat would bring a bullet to my brain. I only had one chance and I couldn't screw it up. A young man crawled towards me, and I knew what I had to do. He crept up and looked at me. I held the man away for just a moment and felt the impact that the snipers bullet had on his body. I pulled the man's lifeless body, a fellow Chechen, over my own and began sobbing.*

*After waiting forever, the light of dawn finally came. From underneath the dead Chechen's body, I saw a soldier in full combat uniform off to my right.*

*"Twenty-three kills," a man said in English. I could hear muffled sounds and was unsure what I would say, or do, if discovered. A soldier went to kick a body to make sure it was dead.*

*"Don't touch the bodies. These are Chechens, and they often booby-trap their dead. The Russians found that out the hard way. We'll send*

*some engineers down here to look for documents and information. They can dismantle any booby-traps," an officer explained to the men. I felt the dirt and swirling dust kick up from a helicopter's rotary blade.*

*"A silent helicopter for men who shoot silent bullets ... U.S. Special Forces."*

*I waited in the little crevice, still hidden by the dead Chechen fighter. I got up and found I was covered in the dead man's blood. Dead bodies of men I traveled with yesterday lay everywhere ....*

Liana awoke and stared at Tim.

"Tim, I killed him. I killed the man!"

"Liana, you had a nightmare."

"The blood!" she screamed looking over her hands and arms. He saw her hands, and they were clean. She tore her nightshirt from her body and stepped into the shower.

"Liana, it was only a nightmare." He stepped into the shower with her, even though his pajamas were being soaked.

"Liana, it's okay. It's just a dream!" She looked at him, and softness came across her eyes. She hugged him very tightly and broke down sobbing.

"Liana, it's okay." They dried off and changed. He slid into bed next to her. She snuggled next to him and finally fell asleep. The next morning Liana did not know what to say to him.

"Tim, about last night?"

"It's okay. You had a bad dream. I have them, too." She got dressed and went to go to work. On the way up the street, she thought about Ali's last visit. She felt that only she could save Tim's life now, and she also knew that Ali's demands for her would only increase.

*Once again I don't control my own life.*

Liana went to work and began her research. Senator Wright and one of his lawyers stopped by.

"Some people from the United Nations are stopping by today. Would you like to meet them?"

"Of course," she said, dumfounded that he would ask her.

Members of the Senate met with the United Nations in a large hall. Most of the people spoke English, but some did not. She wore her blue dress today because it was hot outside. Senator Wright had mingled with the United Nations ambassadors, and she met several.

Senator Wright met with an Iranian diplomat and explained his displeasure over their nuclear program. Two clerics talked with the diplomat in Pharisaic.

"I'd give a day's pay to know that conversation," he said.

"The Mullah's are saying that since Allah has gifted them with nuclear weapons then he favors them. They also mentioned turning Palestine to dust."

"How many languages do you know?" he asked her.

"Several and smatterings of more." A diplomat from the United Arab Emirates came to talk to Senator Wright.

"Senator, it is so good to see you again. I am happy that our two countries have been able to remain friends and that together we have been able to help those in Africa who were starving."

"I am glad we could work together also," he said.

"It is written, 'Be upright for Allah, bearers of witness and justice …'"

"… and not let hatred of a people incite you," Liana said without thinking. The diplomat looked stunned, as did Senator Wright.

"Yes, yes, that's correct."

*I must control myself, I can't be that stupid!*

The Polish ambassadors came up to Senator Wright.

"Do you know Polish?" Senator Wright asked Liana. She turned to the diplomat and welcomed him to Washington in Polish. She had a short conversation with the diplomat before introducing him to Senator Wright. During the next hour or so Liana talked in Russian, Arabic, German and Czech also. Senator Wright kept her close when any foreign visitors were near.

After work Liana returned to her apartment.

"Liana, I've got to go and meet Mark and Bill in Philadelphia. We need to set-up our courses for the fall, and we need to do it before they leave for their networking session," Tim said.

"Networking?"

"They make a kind of a scavenger hunt that directs them to a secret location where they network their computers together, play games and hack into sites."

"Do they want you to join them?"

"Yeah, but I explained that I have too much going on now …."

*Tim is visiting Mark, and I am again alone. Things are beginning to spin out of control with Ali. The only thing that makes sense is that he wants to have me before I'm gone with my mother. Since he's coming after me now, the time must be near. If my mission is almost over then Tim's life is hanging on a thread. I'm sure Ali will kill Tim, either out of jealousy or to tie up any loose ends. I need to find a way to keep Tim alive and to understand what Ali is thinking. But what should I do…?*

Liana went out shopping, bought a bolt of black cloth, and covered it. She returned home and placed the bag in her closet. She went out jogging every evening and found it was one of the activities she could do without Ali's prying eyes. She felt safe jogging as other young women were always out on the trail also. She returned home, showered, wrapped a towel around herself and sat watching TV. She thought about the camera hidden in the smoke alarm and hoped things might go as she planned. After an hour her phone rang and she heard Ali on the phone.

"Liana, I must stop by."

"Yes, Ali, we must talk about our future."

Liana knew Ali must be on his way. She pulled the bolt of cloth from the closet and began cutting. She was ready and hoped she could go through with this.

Ten minutes later Ali entered her apartment without knocking. He found Liana sitting at her table in full Islamic garb, something she learned in Saudi Arabia. The black robes reached to her ankles and a black scarf covered her head and hair.

Liana arose, walked to Ali and took him to the table.

"Ali, our mission is nearing its end." She poured tea for herself and him. "I did not miss your affection the last time you were here. It surprised me, but I did not miss it. Soon I will be in Cyprus with my mother, and she can contact yours to arrange a formal meeting of our families. We are both, in fact, Sunni." Liana's offer dumbfounded Ali.

"Liana, I …."

"Ali, did I misunderstand your affection?" she asked.

"No, I just didn't …."

"You have been away from your family too long. I hope the culture here hasn't poisoned you?"

"Liana, I …."

"Drink your tea and let your mind rest." She got up, walked behind him, and placed her hands on his shoulders.

"Ali, you have had to do things that you didn't like to do, as have I. The whole episode will be over soon, we will both be free, and perhaps our families could agree on a marriage?"

"Perhaps …."

"Then for now we must be faithful and complete our mission?"

"Yes, but ...." He seemed troubled, and she knew his mind was racing a mile a minute.

"When is the mission complete?" she asked.

"Soon, just a few more days. Liana, I must explain your mission." He was still completely off his game and had trouble coming up with words.

"Ali, the child?"

"The child?" he asked.

"Yes, Tim. Everyone at work likes him. He had a minor traffic accident last week, and everyone stopped by to make sure he was okay. I fear that if anything happens to him, it would bring everyone down on me."

"I understand," Ali said. "Liana put this on for me." It was her turn to be knocked off her game as he handed her a tight dress.

"Ali, do you want a wife or a ...."

"You must put it on," he stated. She put it on as he watched.

"Turn around," he said. She turned around and found herself facing the wall.

"You will carry Senator Wright's package like this ...." Ali lifted the hem and stuffed the package under her clinging dress. "This will work well. You will hide this package, hand Senator Wright his package, and leave. I will pick you up and drive you to the airport; you will board a Turkish airline."

"Ali, the package?"

"A fake bomb. It is a huge flash, a loud boom and smoke. The Senators will all come streaming out of the Capitol terrified and coughing. No one should be hurt, but the Americans will know that we can strike them wherever we wish. I must go to Toronto and bring the device here."

"When will I see you again?" she asked.

"Wednesday morning."

"Ali, the final payment of money to Senator Wright?"

"It is arranged. You will find it on your computer." Liana gave him a hug and a kiss.

"Ali, we will have many children together," she said. He embraced her very tightly.

"Wednesday morning ...," he said, and with that, he was gone.

Liana sank into her chair. The mission was on Wednesday, and only a few days remained. She knew that Ali wasn't stupid and that his family would never agree to a marriage between the two. He knew that and was not deceived, but she felt the dream of such a thing would be enough that he would trust her and keep her in his mind as he flew to Toronto.

*Why Toronto? Ali goes to Toronto to bring back a smoke bomb? I could make one in my kitchen, Potassium Nitrate and sugar ....*

She realized that Ali was not going to Toronto to bring back any smoke bomb but something much deadlier.

*A bomb that I could carry, that would damage a large building couldn't be made. Military-grade explosives wouldn't do it. The only thing small that would damage the Capitol would be a nuclear bomb, but that's impossible ....*

She caught herself as she pondered the words in her mind. Could Walid with all his money and contacts get a tiny nuclear bomb? She knew that the Russians had tiny nuclear bombs. Could Walid get his hands on something similar?

*The blast will go off inside the building. The force does not have to be strong because the radiation will kill everyone eventually. Senator Wright would be sitting at his desk; Ellen and Bob would be advising him. Everyone would be performing their tasks and then a fireball would erupt.*

*Those that died in the blast would be the lucky ones, as the rest would never recover from the radiation. My friends would be in the hospital burnt, sick and awaiting a painful death.*

The attack, Liana realized, would be completely devastating. The very center of the United States, the Capitol, destroyed from the inside? The loss would be incredible, and the United States would reel from the attack.

*Now I understand Ali's advance. He wants to have me before I die. The only thing that had stopped his advance was the story of a marriage and the Islamic garb. I will plant the bomb in the Capitol building; leave and Ali will pick me up. I will never make it to the airport, and I'll join Saleh's team and Margrite in their graves. My mother will be dead, if she isn't already, and Tim, having a jealous Ali after him, will die a horrible death. Again only death, destruction and blood all around and no way to get out.*

Liana headed out to the jogging trail as walking cleared her mind. She had to think a way out of this and to save her mother in the process. She thought again about her friends lying sick and burnt in the hospital.

"Liana, we as Muslim women are the peacemakers. We are a kind and loving people," Sarena had taught her. She thought about her mother's words and realized that she would want her to save her friends.

*Momma, tell me the right thing to do!*

Liana returned home late and knew she was in for a rough night. The thoughts of the war and its aftermath plagued her. It was late, and she finally slid into bed. She soon fell asleep and dreamed.

"Liana, survive!" She felt her mother's arms wrap around her and her mother begin to whisper to her. The whispering and hugging went on all night.

***

Liana woke with a start and found it was daylight. She found her arms wrapped tightly around her and relived last night.

"Momma, thank you!" she said aloud.

She took a bag of clothes with her to work. At lunchtime she left and walked down to a McDonalds. She entered the McDonalds dressed conservatively; she left wearing sunglasses and a mini-skirt. She walked down to a particularly dangerous section of town but hoped everyone would leave her alone. She walked into a second-hand shop that seemed to sell everything.

"I want to buy cell phones, the kind I won't be billed for," she told the man. The man went in back and returned with several stolen phones.

"How many do you want?" She chose two of them and made sure each had a signal. She counted out five hundred dollars and left with the phones.

She went back to the McDonalds and changed before returning to work.

She saw Bob Winslow in the office and went to talk to him.

"How is your wife doing with her pregnancy?" she asked.

"The heat's keeping her near the air conditioner. I'm going to a fundraiser tonight, but she says she can't stand going to another one. She's heading to the movies instead."

Tim returned from Philadelphia and met Liana for dinner.

"Tim, I know you want to stay here with me, but I think it would be best if you went with Bill and Mark to their networking session."

"Why?" Tim asked.

"You've been kind of stressed out, and I think you should just get away for a few days."

"I could use a break …," he said.

"Tell me again about the scavenger hunt they set up?"

"They make a game. You follow clues that lead you to the gathering. We could end up anywhere, in Florida, Las Vegas, or even New York city."

"Just promise me you won't be anywhere near Washington. This town stresses you out," she said.

"I promise it won't be in Washington," Tim said.

"And the room?"

"It won't be in my name," he said. To her what Tim was describing was nearly perfect. He would be away with friends for the week and even he would not know where he would end up.

"I would be very pleased if you went to the networking session because I love you," she said. She gave him a long kiss, and he gathered his things and left.

She took her laptop computer and walked downtown. She found a bookstore with wireless Internet and sat down outside. She brought up the Polish gaming site and hit the clown's eye with her mouse.

"Get package, w borders, 11a, sat." She was to pick up the final bundle of cash on Saturday morning at eleven A.M. The exchange was to take place outside the Borders bookshop. She would pick up Senator Wright's final payment and deliver it to him.

*Allah, allow this to work, and allow Momma and Tim to live through it.*

## THE BOMB

"The bomb is ready," Orman's message to Walid read.

*The bomb's tiny, made with a minuscule amount of nuclear fuel. The brilliance of the bomb is not in what it can do to a large area but in the terror it will cause.*

Walid could imagine the terror.

*The Senate will be in full session, as will the House, and virtually every Senator and Congressman will be there. The press will be there and C-span will be taping. Security in the building is tight and thought to be foolproof. Everything will seem normal for a Wednesday morning and then ... boom! Every state will lose someone known to all. The bomb will destroy the heart of America's democracy in one deadly blast. The panic will spread to every large building and complex in America. Fear will spread across the world as news of a nuclear attack crosses all wires. The Imams in Mecca will rejoice and wait for diplomats from around the world to descend and plead for terms. The Islamic world will consider me a hero.*

Orman and his two workers had been underground in the bunker for two months. Radiation had contaminated them during this time, and they would undergo treatment for it. The treatment would include a painful scrubbing and some medication. He, after spending so much time underground, was anxious to see his wife and family again.

***

Cathleen Hale, nearly due, was having a hard time with the summer's heat. It had been hot lately, and at one point her legs had swollen. She tried as much as possible to stay near an air conditioner, and she wished she'd put in for maternity leave.

*I know something big is up, but I have nothing to prove it. In the past we've been criticized for not "connecting the dots," and I won't let that happen again.*

*It's Friday night and Bob's at a fundraiser. I hate those events, and it seems every fundraiser has a chicken dinner included. I've had enough chicken for a while, thank you. I'm uncomfortable at home, so why not be uncomfortable watching something I enjoy? A new comedy is playing ....*

The theater was only half-full, and Cathleen found a good seat. The movie began and it was funny, as she had hoped. Halfway through the movie she felt fear grip her stomach.

"Cathleen," a voice behind her spoke softly in Arabic, "if you understand me raise your hand."

*Okay, I'll raise my hand, but God get me out of this.*

"Cathleen, you are in no danger, but do not turn around. Together we can avoid a tragedy. Do you understand? I am being watched all the time, and I will be killed if I am found out. If I am killed or captured, many will still die, and neither of us could prevent it. Cathleen, the people watching me seem to know what goes on at the CIA. Do you understand? Do you know someone you can trust, someone who can keep things quiet and not have the alert raised?"

*Jim could help me. I'll raise my hand.*

"Cathleen, I have a favor that must be completed before we can go on." A wadded up piece of paper landed on the seat next to Cathleen.

"Read the note and follow the directions. As soon as this is completed, I will contact you. Cathleen, I want no more blood on my hands. Give me five minutes to leave."

Cathleen waited ten minutes, shivering the entire time. She finally turned around and saw no one suspicious behind her. She cautiously left the theater, walked outside, and called a cab. Arriving home, she found a roll of plastic wrap and laid a sheet out on her kitchen table. She put latex gloves on and carefully pulled the crumpled paper from her pocket. She spread the paper out and read the instructions written in Arabic.

a. Sarena Yastrz is in prison in Russia.

b. Sarena must be declared and certified as having died in prison as Walid Hattab's men are watching her.

c. Sarena must be flown to Johns Hopkins hospital in Baltimore to be checked out and then placed in a safe location.

d. Sarena must be granted political asylum and immunity.

e. Sarena does not know my mission or where I am, so she must be treated well.

f. Time is critical and I will contact you when she is here.

The note was handwritten, not printed. Cathleen knew that computer printers imbedded a code on pages and that the Arab girl knew that also. The writer knew enough not to leave fingerprints on the note.

*I need to contact James Burrett. It's safer to meet Jim in person and explain my predicament than to try to call him on the phone. I'll take a taxi to Jim's house.*

***

"Jim, can we talk outside?" she later asked. They went outside and she described her conversation with the Arab girl.

"The Arab girl believes that Walid Hattab has someone on the inside, in the CIA?" Jim asked.

"That's what she believes. She's very frightened and says she is being watched all the time. The girl believes something awful is about to occur, and she does not want the blood on her hands."

"And the woman in prison in Russia, she wants her declared dead?"

"That's what she wants. Do we have any leverage to do what she asks, immediately?"

"Yes, we can easily arrange to transfer a Russian agent for her."

"How do we keep everything quiet and confidential?"

"We say we have a confidential informant and go from there. Cathleen, we work the problem but ...."

"But?" she asked.

"If some kind of attack occurs while we are fooling with this girl, we're finished. Cathleen, are you sure you trust this girl?"

"Yes, it's more the tone of her voice, like she has seen many die and she wants it to end."

Jim notified a few officials in the agency, and top security was placed on the entire operation. An exchange was set up in which a Russian spy was exchanged for Sarena. The Russians were mystified as to why the Americans would want the woman, but they did as instructed. A coroner pronounced the dead body given him as being Sarena's and had the body cremated.

***

A Russian officer escorted Sarena to the airport and put her on a plane.

*Why are they sending me to the U.S.? I'm flying from Moscow to Baltimore? Did Liana somehow pull some strings to have me sent here?*

Cathleen waited at the airport, expecting an older Arabic woman. The woman before her was young looking for her years but not Arabic. She escorted Sarena, still wearing her filthy prison jumpsuit, from the plane.

"Sarena Yastrz," Cathleen said in Arabic, "I am Cathleen Hale. You have been given political asylum in the United States and immunity of any crimes committed."

"Cathleen, you do not have to speak Arabic. I understand English. What is happening?" Sarena asked.

"An Arab girl negotiated to bring you here," Cathleen said. Sarena, not knowing the circumstances, said nothing.

"I'm supposed to take you to Johns/Hopkins hospital in Baltimore to get you cleaned up and checked out. I will need to keep you handcuffed for now." Cathleen and two agents drove her over.

"I always wanted to see this hospital; I often prayed that one day I would work here," Sarena said.

"Work here?" Cathleen asked.

"I am a nurse. I also teach," Sarena said.

Sarena took a long hot shower and went through delousing. The hospital gave her blue scrubs to wear. Now out of her prison jumpsuit, she had her long brown hair brushed out. Cathleen noticed a grace about her that caught your eye immediately.

"I can get some decent clothes for you later."

"These are fine," Sarena explained. Her initial exam seemed to go well; Sarena was asked to disrobe and that's when the problems began. The physician examining her called several doctors down to confirm his findings. A Pakistani doctor, a Swiss doctor and an Army intelligence officer arrived. Sarena had scars on her unlike anything Cathleen had ever seen before.

After the three doctors finished examining Sarena, the Army intelligence officer called Cathleen.

"The woman has been tortured in ways we've never seen before in a living human being ... we have no idea how she lived through it, and ...."

"And what?" she asked.

"She has a bullet lodged in her skull. My guess is that someone tried to execute her, but the bullet didn't kill her."

"Why would the Russians do that to one of their own?" she asked. Sarena overheard her question.

"Cathleen, I am not Russian. I am Chechen ... a prisoner of war. I was captured while fighting in Chechnya. I am one of the lucky ones. It seemed everyone else died. Only myself and my daughter survived."

"And your daughter?" Cathleen asked.

"I dressed her as a school girl and told her to flee and to survive. I tried to blow myself up. I didn't want to be taken alive. I have no idea how I survived the explosion. Eight Russian soldiers died, but I was only burned."

After the examination, Cathleen talked to the doctors, and they said Sarena was in good physical shape considering all she had gone through. The Army intelligence officer stopped Cathleen and took her aside to talk.

"Cathleen, Sarena, like all prisoners of war, will need time to decompress. It's best just to let her relax and talk. She should have bland food for a while and stay away from anything emotional. Also, there is also something unique about living in Russia, part of the culture. You feel guilty if you ever leave the country."

After the exam Cathleen remained with Sarena.

"You are not a prisoner, and no one will harm you."

"I understand."

"You will remain at a Federal prison for now, and you will be treated well. You will have full access to the yard and its facilities. You can watch TV. Please understand that I have no choice but to keep you in custody until this episode is over."

"Of course, I understand .... Cathleen, do you understand why I am here?"

"No," Cathleen said.

"My daughter was the woman who contacted you to set up my release."

"Your daughter wanted you to be safe?" Cathleen asked.

"I am sure she does want me to be safe, but that is not why I am here. It's not why she contacted you. My daughter, I, we are a loving people, and we were thrust into a war you cannot imagine, and we lost. Cathleen, do you know what we as Muslims in Russia did against the Nazis."

"No."

"We all took in Jewish children as our own and hid them from the Nazis. My uncle was taken by the Nazis and dragged to the village square. The Nazis told us all that they would spare my uncle if we would give up the Jewish children we were hiding. They had my uncle standing on a chair, and no one would give up the Jewish children. My uncle jumped from the chair and hung himself, as he did not want the Nazis to get the Jewish children. The people we saved are alive, and my daughter, Liana, played with their children. She is a grown woman now and understands what I do. We are the peacemakers, and she has been thrust into something she finds horrible and wants no part of it," Sarena explained.

"Why doesn't she just come in, surrender, and tell all."

"Up until today she was probably trying to protect me. She must understand that whatever is happening will happen to someone whether she helps or not. She must know that if she surrenders people will still die, and she wants it to end. We both know how to die; it is an easy thing to do. Living is the hard thing, and we must see that people live. If she has not come forward, then it is because she feels she can be a greater help by staying out," she explained.

"Sarena, the Russians?"

"The Russians?"

"Do you think you can forgive them?" Cathleen asked. Sarena smiled at Cathleen.

"Cathleen, I do not hate the Russians. They have suffered just as much or more than we have. Russian mothers are crying for their loved ones that we have killed just as much as we have for our own. In Russia nurses are caring for soldiers that we injured just as your doctors cared for me," she said. "Cathleen do you know why my daughter chose you?"

"Chose me?" Cathleen said.

"Yes, chose to contact you?"

"No, I don't," Cathleen said.

"It is because you are pregnant. A pregnant woman thinks of the safety of her child, not her ambitions. She trusts you and believes that you will try and end this because it is wrong."

"Sarena, you know I must do everything I can to try and track her down."

"I understand, and she knows that also. The point to remember though is that she is more useful to all while she is out there."

"Could you please show me around the hospital?" Sarena asked the doctors.

"Yes, of course," the Swiss doctor told Sarena. She studied the equipment the hospital had, and it seemed to bring tears to her eyes.

"Cathleen, if only I had this kind of equipment when we did surgery … oxygen, anesthesia, surgical tools, antibiotics ...."

"You've done surgery?" the Army intelligence officer asked her.

"Yes, using the crudest of tools and no anesthesia ... we had nothing, so we used hand drills, axes, pliers, hacksaws, made our own traction equipment, IV's; we used aquarium equipment for blood transfusions. Half of my patients died, but much more importantly half lived, always faced with the choice …."

"The choice?" Cathleen asked.

"Do something that might work, or do nothing …."

Cathleen drove Sarena to a facility not far from Washington. Sarena looked around.

"This is a prison?"

"This is where corrupt politicians and white collar criminals are kept."

"In Russia our political prisoners live out on the ice chopping wood for the railroad, but this ...!" The facility was two years old and looked more like a college dormitory than a prison.

Cathleen wondered if she was doing the right thing. She decided to go to confession and meet with Father Dunzio. She drove over to a Catholic church, not far from her home. She walked halfway up the aisle and sat down. She knelt and prayed for almost half an hour as others quietly sat. She then arose and entered the confession booth.

Cathleen came out of the confessional and walked back down the aisle. She saw Father O'Brien walking toward her carrying his cell phone.

"Cathleen, an emergency call for you!" Cathleen, shocked, took the phone.

"Cathleen," the voice said in Arabic, "I am glad that my mother is safe."

"Why are you calling me here?"

"Because the call would not be traced."

"Your mother says you're her daughter?"

"Yes."

"You can talk in English. Your mother is safe and comfortable now."

"I know, and I am thankful. Cathleen, the man you need to find is named Orman, and he is from Toronto."

"Orman?" she asked.

"Yes, a Pakistani professor. Cathleen, I am very frightened, almost everyone who has come into contact with me has died."

"Died?"

"The Arabs on Assateague and others. Do you understand that if I come forward many will die? The only way to prevent what is about to happen is for me to stay unknown."

"I understand …."

"Thank you for caring for my mother," Liana said.

***

"The girl from the movie theatre called me," Cathleen explained later to Jim. "She gave me a name to check out, and I must get to work."

"Cathleen, you're too far along. You should stay home and rest now. You seem so uncomfortable!"

"I'm uncomfortable standing up, I'm uncomfortable sitting, and I'm uncomfortable lying down. Why shouldn't I be uncomfortable at work?" Cathleen went to work. She had to find the college professor named Orman.

## THE EASTER EGG HUNT

Tim drove to Pennsylvania to meet his hacker friends. Bill designed an Easter egg hunt where each crew used Internet gaming sites to find hidden items. Each crew would search web sites looking for hidden clues that would direct them where to go and what to bring.

The guys regularly used some twenty gaming sites on the net. He gave each a list of three sites where Easter eggs could be found. They would have to use their skills to find the rest.

Ken went on the web and easily found his first six Easter eggs.

*Where did that maniac put those clues?* After two hours of trying, he had all the clues and finally the directions.

*I'm supposed to bring a case of Mountain Dew, six pounds of Skittles and ten microwave meals ....*

He followed the directions to the Harrah's hotel in Washington, D.C.

Mark and Tim searched the gaming sites for items they were to bring to the networking session. Mark had a good idea which sites Bill would use and easily found the first four clues.

"Tim, we're supposed to bring Red Bull and Frito's." He had a lot of trouble finding the last site.

"I bet he used that site that Liana showed us, that Polish gaming site. He'd try something demented like that," Tim said. He searched the site but found nothing.

"Do know what Bill's favorite movie is?" Mark looked at the site and understood.

"Killer Klowns from Outer Space," he said running his mouse over to the clown's eye.

"Get package, w borders, 11a, 25th"

"Tim, we have to pick up a package at Borders at 11 a.m., but which Borders? I mean, they're all over the country."

Mark went to the remaining game sites that he thought Bill might have used. After trying for another two hours he finally found the last clue, the directions to the Harrah's hotel in Washington, D.C.

"That's where I just came from. Liana would be really pissed if I showed up there," Tim said.

"Why?"

"It's a chick thing. I guess I'll be indoors the whole time, so it won't matter, but I know where that Borders bookstore is!"

"Really, where?"

"It's near Georgetown, on the west side."

***

Senator Wright's final payment of fifty thousand dollars was due.

"Hesus, deliver the final payment of money yourself and then fly to Toronto. We have a shipment of diamonds to bring in," Walid said.

*Walid wants me to deliver the package in person. The location is good, and all I should have to do is pop my trunk ....* He had been moving money, jewels, gold and other valuables around the world for Walid Hattab for many years. Many of the packages he moved were sealed, and he asked few questions.

The directions on the money drop came from Walid's own lips when he was in the Sudan. The Egyptian student who transcribed his words transcribed them from Arabic into English. A Philippine student transcribed the message from English into Spanish and sent it on to Hesus. Walid stated:

"A feminine blond will pick up $50,000 at Borders bookstore West D.C. at 11 am on the 25th." When translated into Spanish:

"Boyish blond will pick up $50,000 at 11 am on the 25$^{th}$ at Borders bookstore west Washington D.C." He had the cash in a green duffle bag.

***

Ali flew to Toronto to make sure everything was ready for the attack on Wednesday.

*On Tuesday night I pick up the bomb from Orman. I meet Hesus and we drive to an airfield about ten miles away. We climb into Hesus's Learjet for his scheduled flight to Washington, D.C. Everything is set in Toronto, and I only have to wait out the few days in relative comfort before completing my mission.*

*Perhaps Liana is right, I have been away from girls for too long. In a few days my mission will be over and I will probably be under arrest or dead. Allowances are given at these times ....*

Ali took a rental car downtown and found a bar he liked. He ordered scotch and sat down. The music was good, and he liked to dance. He met a young Filipino girl, and they danced into the night.

*Perhaps there are girls out on the street, maybe someone that looks like Liana ....*

At four in the morning, his cell phone began ringing over and over again. Ali, very hung over, finally answered the call.

"Ali, we have been trying to contact you all night! Where have you been?" He realized he had left his cell phone in the motel room when he had gone out.

"Ali, the girl!"

"Yes?"

"Her mother is dead, and security has broken down completely. The CIA knows something and may be on to Liana."

"Liana?"

"Get back to Washington immediately and plug up the leaks." He staggered around his motel room trying to get his things together. He called and booked a flight.

Ali took the redeye from Toronto to Reagan National Airport in Washington. Still hung over, he felt terrible. He found his car and retrieved his pistol. He decided to check on the girl to see if everything was still in order. He drove over to her apartment and went inside. She was not home. He looked around and everything seemed in order, but where was the girl? His head still hurt from last night, but he decided to head home and view the recording of the surveillance camera. Before leaving he did a *69 on her phone to see who would have called her last. The last incoming call on her phone was his.

Ali arrived home and viewed the surveillance footage. It showed nothing that spiked his interest, but he still had no idea where she was. He remembered the money drop and checked his watch; it was 10:45 A.M. He got into his car to head to Border's bookstore and sat outside waiting for the drop to occur.

Hesus drove up in his car and parked outside the bookstore. Just as stated, a young, blond boy appeared at his car.

"Do you have something for me?" Mark asked. Hesus popped his trunk and pulled out a duffle bag. Mark threw it on his back seat.

"Thanks, man!" he said and drove away. As he went to drive away, Liana walked up to Hesus.

"Do you have my money?" He turned to see Mark's car speeding away and got his license plate number. Ali was watching from his car and saw Tim in the passenger seat.

"The boy!" Ali screamed out.

"The money," Hesus said to Liana, "get in!" She got into the car, and Ali pulled alongside.

"Tim ripped off our money. I'll kill him for this!"

"Tim is away!" she shouted.

"Tim's in that car."

"He can't be!" Liana said, shocked.

"The loss of the money is bad, but if word leaks out that a skinny kid ripped me off, then I'm finished," Hesus said. He retrieved a 9 mm pistol and had the license number tracked.

"Ali drive her home, I'll call you when I know something," Hesus said. She hoped by some miracle to save Tim but had no idea how to do it. Ali pulled up to her apartment.

*I tried to do everything I could, and now Tim will die. He should not have betrayed me, but I want him to live! Tim, why did you do this?*

*Ali is angry enough to kill anyone he comes across. Do I have any control over him at all? I've got to distract Ali long enough to warn Tim. With both Hesus and Ali after him, Tim has no chance.*

"Ali, you look terrible. Come and lay down on my bed." He mumbled and looked very upset. "Ali, are we to be married or not?" As he entered the room she smelled alcohol on him. She looked up and saw a hickey on his neck.

*Ali had a girl last night!*

"Ali, were you drinking last night? I think I smell vodka on you." He looked terrible, and it was obvious that he could not cope.

"I was drinking scotch, not vodka."

"Ali, devout men do not drink alcohol!" He looked very sheepish.

"Let me get you a warm towel."

She sat on her bed and held him close as she put the warm towel on his head. She began massaging Ali's neck as she held him.

"Ali, what's on your neck!" she asked with a look of horror and revulsion.

"I, I must have brushed up against something …."

"Brushed against something? I can see bite marks on your neck! Were you with a girl last night?" she asked in the loudest voice she could muster.

"It wasn't that I picked up a girl. She was just a prostitute"

"A prostitute!" she screamed.

"The girl looked a little like you," he said, catching himself.

"I welcomed you into my home and I find out you chased down a … hooker? Who knows how many diseases she had?" She was waiting for the moment, and now it was here. She stood on her bed as she wound up. Her fist came across as hard as she could and struck Ali on the side of his head. She hoped to knock him out, but instead he fell to the floor, grabbed his head, and fled her apartment. She grabbed one of the stolen cell phones and ran out to the jogging track hoping to phone Tim. She had no idea what she would tell him, but she had to come up with something.

***

Tom Eberly had just returned from a one-week stay in the Bahamas. Relaxed and feeling much better, he returned to his desk at the FBI.

"Tom, I received a note from our Las Vegas office. They want information on some kids from Pennsylvania," Shawn said.

"Do a search on the kids. Find out everything about them, what they do, who they see."

"I'll get right on it," Shawn said. "Also our informant says Hesus is in town."

Tom went to his desk and began going through his telephone recorder.

The last call on his phone was from Cathleen Hale. Tom returned her call first.

"Cathleen, how are you?"

"I'm a really kind of uncomfortable now because I'm expecting almost any time. Tom, I called because Hesus Rodriguez is in town."

"You must be psychic or something. We were just talking about Hesus. Cathleen, I'd love to nail Hesus. I mean, he's been a pain in the ass to me since I began work at the FBI. The problem is building a case against him strong enough that he can't wiggle out of," Tom explained. "I'll call you if anything solid turns up."

Tom returned to his work and began the process of clearing away a week's worth of paperwork. Late in the day, Shawn walked into his office with pictures in his hand.

"I don't want to alarm you, but these kids have turned up in some strange places and have some unusual friends."

"Really, like whom?"

"This kid is named Mark. He's some kind of a math genius that a lot of colleges would love to get their hands on, but the kid doesn't like math. He likes history. The second kid is Ken. He just got back from Israel, and you won't believe who his aunt is."

"Who?" he asked.

"The Israeli woman we were searching for is his aunt."

"Could this kid could be a missing member of the Danite team?" he asked. Shawn put his hands in the air.

"Any others?" he asked.

"Yes, this is Bill and …."

"And what?"

"Well, the Navy confiscated his computer when he was in 11th grade."

"Why?" Tom asked.

"The kid somehow hacked into a classified program the Navy was running. He's some kind of computer whiz. That's what the three do. They get together and play games, hack into sites, develop programs. It's their hobby," Shawn explained. "And, Tom …." He really didn't want to know anymore but looked at him anyway. "All three of these kids were flagged by our people at the Hackers' convention in Las Vegas."

"Flagged why?" Tom asked.

"They spent day after day with some Arab and Pakistani guys." Tom went to get some aspirin for his headache.

"Shawn, find out where these kids are. I'd like to question them." Tom went and called the CIA.

"Cathleen?"

"Yes?"

“There are three kids that popped up, and I need to know if you have anything on them. One of the kids is related to that Israeli woman that fled the country. These kids were also flagged by our guys at the Hackers' convention in Vegas. It may not be anything, but you never know.”

Cathleen asked a technician to input Bill's, Ken's and Mark's names into their system. Half an hour later the technician called back.

“Cathleen, we flagged the three at the Hackers' convention and obtained files on Ken's trip to Israel. You know security companies' track activity in almost all the casinos in Las Vegas. We could ask them for their tapes. They always cooperate with us.”

“Get whatever you can from them,” she said. He made the call.

“When do you need them by?” the Global Security officer asked.

“The sooner the better.”

“We can send the raw data over the ‘net now if you want.” He received the data a few minutes later.

“We can do a facial recognition search on those three kids from their drivers license photos and then search out the relative minutes they were on camera,” the technician said.

“How long would it take?” she asked.

“It's done.”

She now had tapes on the three at the Hackers' convention, and she immediately noted that Bill and Mark spent a lot of time with Arab and Pakistani hackers. One episode interested her not so much in what Mark was doing but in the expression given by the Pakistani man next to him. She called the video specialist back to her office.

“Can you enlarge the kid's computer monitor, the tape is kind of blurry.”

“Yes, we have a program that does that for bank cameras, you know for after a robbery.”

“How long does it take?” she asked.

“It's done!” Cathleen had a blown-up picture of Mark's computer screen, and it showed an equation. She had no idea what the equation meant.

“Jim, can you come down to my office? You know calculus much better than I do.”

He arrived a few moments later.

“Cathleen, what's up?” She pointed to the blown up picture showing an equation.

“Any idea?”

“I have some idea but I'd rather not say anything right now, not until someone with brains can verify this.” They went upstairs to Dr Tikrit.

Dr. Tikrit worked for the agency for twenty-two years specializing in nuclear science. He was a devout Arab Muslim who was born in the U.S.

after his father emigrated from Kuwait. Dr Tikrit felt that radical Islam could destroy all he knew and loved.

"Dr Tikrit, does this make any sense to you?" He laid the print out on his desk.

"Is this some kind of joke?" Dr Tikrit asked.

"It's no joke; it's from a kid's computer at the Hackers' convention."

"Some kid came up with this? Is he some kind of mathematician?

"I don't understand. What is the equation?" Cathleen asked.

"It's nuclear," Dr Tikrit said.

"You mean to make a nuclear bomb?"

"No, it's much worse than that."

"What is it then?" Cathleen asked.

"Getting nuclear material, or like you said, building a bomb is not the hard part. Setting it off is. The equation is a trigger to detonate a nuclear bomb."

Cathleen and Jim ended up back at her office looking at the rest of the data she received.

"Ms. Hale, we have a facial recognition on the Pakistani man at the convention."

"Who is it?" Jim asked.

"A Pakistani professor, Orman Negev," the analyst said.

"Sarena's daughter warned us about a man named Orman. I think she's trying to stop a nuclear attack!" Jim nodded his head in agreement.

"Cathleen, I will inform my superiors, but my guess is that they will use any and all resources to pick her up for interrogation. My guess is that she'll be at Gitmo before the day is out."

Cathleen felt that everything was unraveling so fast that she couldn't keep up with it.

"Cathleen," an analyst called to her, "one of the boys from the video, he checked into a hotel in Washington, D.C." She decided to head downtown and have a chat with the boy.

***

Mark and Tim came to the hotel and met Bill and Ken.

"I have the stuff you asked for. The duffle bag is in my trunk," Mark said.

"Duffle bag?"

"The guy handed me a duffle bag. I put it in Ken's van." Bill was too wrapped up in a computer game to bother about a duffle bag, so he let the matter drop. As they entered the room, Tim's cell phone began ringing.

"Tim, what are you doing here?" He held his phone away from his head.

"It's Liana!" Tim explained.

"Tim, the money, get out of there! You will die!" With that, his cell phone went dead.

"She sounded mad!" Bill said.

"I kinda promised her I would be out of town. I guess she thought it would be too expensive staying here. She was worried about the money."

While challenging the next level on the game, Bill heard a knock on their door. When Ken answered the door he found two men waiting outside dressed in suits.

"Tom Eberly--FBI. Are you Bill?" Ken pointed to Bill.

"Bill, the three of you were flagged by our people at the Hackers' convention. We have a few questions about it." At the mention of "Hackers' convention," everyone sank into their chairs. Tom questioned Bill extensively before leaving.

"What a great idea. Hey let's go to the Hackers' convention!" Bill said. A few moments later, there was another knock on the door. This time Mark answered the door.

"Fred Barger--Homeland Security. Is Ken here?" Mark pointed at Ken. "We have a few questions about your recent trip to Israel. Did you meet with your Aunt Sarah in Israel?" He explained that he had never met his Aunt Sarah.

"We really don't talk with that side of the family." They talked for half an hour, and he described his trip to Israel.

"Ken, weren't you at the Hackers' convention?" the man asked just before leaving.

"This place is turning into a circus with everyone coming and going. I'm heading into the other room for some peace and quiet," Ken said. He had just set his computer up when there was a knock on the door.

"We don't want any!" Bill screamed at the door. The knocking continued. He opened the door to find a very pregnant-looking woman standing out in the hallway.

"Are you Mark?" the woman asked.

"No! Who are you?"

"Cathleen Hale—CIA," the woman said. Bill pointed at Mark.

"Let me guess. You're here about the Hackers' convention?" Mark asked. Cathleen nodded yes.

"We need you to come down to the agency; we have some questions to ask you."

"Do I have any choice?"

"No," she explained. Mark left with Cathleen. Bill looked at Ken and Tim.

"What the hell's going on? Homeland Security, the FBI, the CIA, everyone wants to know about Vegas and the Hackers' convention." Ken returned to the adjoining room. Bill sat down at his computer and tried to calm down. Then there was another knock at the door.

"I'm not getting it! The hell with it!"

Tim got up and walked toward the door. Ken had already opened the other door to look out and saw an Arab guy at Bill's door.

"Can I help you?" Ken asked. The guy responded by pulling a gun and firing at Ken. He shut and locked the door.

"Arabs! Guns!" Tim had opened Bill's door but had not removed the chain. A hand holding a pistol appeared next to his head and fired, shattering the window in their ninth-floor room.

"Grab our computers. Don't let them get 'em. Let's get the hell out of here!" Bill screamed. The hand holding the pistol fired at the door chain.

Bill, Ken, and Tim shuffled along a ledge, nine floors above the concrete pavement.

"Let's go to the Hackers' convention. It's time to embrace the horror!" Bill said.

"I thought it would be fun," Ken said.

"Shut up and move on!" Tim screamed.

***

Tom and Shawn sat talking in their car after leaving the hotel.

"Shawn, do you know who that is? If I'm not mistaken that's Hesus Rodriguez, but its been a long time since I've seen him," Tom explained.

"What's Cathleen Hale doing here?" Shawn asked. They watched a very pregnant Cathleen walk into the hotel. Tom decided it would be better to just wait and see what happened. A few minutes later she reappeared and had the smallest guy, Mark, with her.

"What the hell!" Tom screamed as he saw Bill, Ken and Tim shuffling along the side of the hotel, nine stories above his car.

"Who's the guy firing at them?" Shawn screamed.

"Call it in!" Tom screamed, pulling his pistol. The guys on the ledge smashed a window and disappeared back into the hotel.

"Take cover behind the car," Tom screamed at Shawn.

"Stop! FBI! Put the gun down! You're under arrest!" Tom screamed at the gunman on the ledge. The gunman fired at them before disappearing into the hotel.

"Did you call it in?" Tom asked.

***

Cathleen dragged Mark behind a car and hit the dirt when the shooting started. Now lying in mud, she called the shooting in on her cell phone. Hesus, seeing the boy in front of him who had stolen his money, got out of his car brandishing a pistol.

"Where's my money!" Hesus said as he fired at Mark. Tom and Shawn saw Hesus firing and ran toward him.

"FBI, stop! FBI!" Bill, Ken and Tim ran out of the hotel with Ali right behind them.

Mark had enough; he ran toward Ken's car screaming for the other guys to join him. They all piled into his car.

"I'll kill you!" Ali screamed at the guys. Now both Ali and Hesus began firing at Ken's car as they sped away. Ali and Hesus jumped into Hesus's car and sped after Ken. Cathleen lay in a fetal position on the ground.

"Cathleen, are you all right?" Tom asked.

She got up and showed she was fine. "What the hell happened? One minute everything was quiet, and the next moment all hell broke loose."

"I don't know, but I think the cavalry's coming and it'll be too late!" The sound of sirens filled the air.

"What do we do now?" Shawn asked.

"We find those hackers before Hesus and his friend do," Cathleen said

***

Ali and Hesus lost Ken almost as soon as they left the hotel.

"What the hell happened? I get out of the car and the FBI is waiting for me. Ali, we've got to get out of here," Hesus said.

"Hesus, we have to get to Toronto and get the package."

***

"What the hell are we going to do? Where are we going to go?" Ken asked as he sped out of town.

"Let's head to my house," Mark said.

"Oh like the CIA doesn't know where you live. They'll be waiting in your driveway when we pull up."

"What happened? What did you guys get into?" Tim asked.

"Look," Bill said, "everything was fine until you and Mark showed up, and then it was Homeland Security, FBI, CIA …, and then some Arab guy shows up and starts shooting at us."

"Arab? You mean the Cuban guy. I had the Cuban guy who gave me the duffle bag shooting at me in the parking lot," Mark said.

"Pull over here," Bill said. Ken pulled into a crowded parking lot at a grocery store.

"Let's just sit and think a minute," Bill said.

"I'm going in and getting some food," Mark said. "I'm starved."

"Get me some Red Bull," Bill said.

"There's a case of it in the trunk," Ken said. Bill went to the back and opened up the trunk. The case of Red Bull lay in back, as did the duffle bag Mark had brought.

"What's in the duffle bag?" he asked. He opened the duffle bag and stared at bundles of money.

"Do you guys want to come back here?" Everyone walked to the back of the van.

"Take a look!"

"I guess all we have to do is call the Cuban guy and say, 'Hey, we have your drug money. Come take it back,'" Mark said.

"Look," Tim said, "everyone knows who you guys are, but no one knows me. Why not head to my apartment and just chill out for a few days?"

"Nobody came to question him because he was smart enough not to go down to the Hacker's convention," Bill said.

Ken turned down Route 50 heading east.

***

Liana returned home and turned on the evening news. The news showed an amateur video taken at a Washington hotel. She watched as Tim, Bill and Ken slid along the ninth floor ledge of a hotel as Ali shot at them. The video showed them running from the building as Hesus fired at them.

Liana spent a lot of time in thought, as she was unsure of what to do. Tim was now on the run with Ali and Hesus after him. It was time for her to do something radical. She knew where her mother was and decided to take a cab to the prison.

*I'm taking a terrible risk, but everything is spinning out of control so quickly that I can't keep up with it.* She entered the prison and gave her name as indicated on her identification, Liana Yeglov. She entered a large room, and Sarena was brought out.

"Liana!" Sarena screamed and ran forward. Liana ran forward also, and the two women hugged very tightly.

"Liana, you look so pretty, not a mark on you! You shouldn't have come. You'll be caught!"

"Momma, I need to tell you everything." Liana told of the plot, where she was working and what was going on. Sarena thought about what she said, and both women got on the floor and prayed, facing east.

"Call Cathleen Hale and tell her everything," Sarena said as she arose. Liana made the phone call.

Cathleen had returned home and changed her clothes.

*Shots start firing and I, pregnant, jump into mud puddle! I'm not feeling well. I'd better lie down.* She had just fallen asleep when her cell phone went off.

"You asked us to contact you if anyone visited Sarena?" the prison ward said. "A young blond woman is here with Sarena now." Cathleen's phone beeped indicating another incoming call. She switched to it.

"Cathleen, I'm with my mother. Could you come to the prison?"

"I'll need to bring a man from work with me, James Burrett."

"Bring whoever you need."

Cathleen and Jim hurried to the prison. They walked in and found the two women sitting together.

"Cathleen, my name is Liana." Cathleen and Jim stared at the tiny woman before them, as at first the situation seemed unreal.

"Don't I know you?" Cathleen asked.

"I've seen you before also," Jim said.

"I work with your husband in Senator Wright's office. I've seen both of you at the Kennedy center."

"How did you ever get onto Senator Wright's staff?" Jim asked.

"Well, duh, she's beautiful, that's how. Senator Wright has always chased …."

"Liana," Sarena said, "tell them everything."

Liana described meeting Walid Hattab in Pakistan and assuming the alias of a Russian girl. She described what she knew of her mission and the bomb that Ali wanted her to carry into the Capitol. She described that somehow her boyfriend had become involved in all this.

"I believe that the bomb they want me to carry into the Capitol is really a nuclear bomb. Do you understand my fears? If anyone suspects that I won't complete my mission, then some other target might be hit, another building, a shopping mall, wherever will cause the most carnage."

"Liana, we are going to have to take you, under cover, back to the agency until we can decide what to do," Jim said.

"Mr. Burrett, Ali has ears inside the agency, and everyone I love is at risk. Please be careful. He has killed my friends and will not hesitate to kill anyone who gets in his way. My boyfriend and his friends are about to be killed by him, and I don't know how to stop it. My mother is no longer safe here either."

Jim drove everyone back to the agency.

"You mentioned your boyfriend," Cathleen said. "Was he the fourth man in the hotel room?"

"Yes," she said, "but I have no idea how he found out about the money."

"Money?" Cathleen asked. She described about using the ruse that she was in contact with some wealthy Russian mobsters to convince Senator Wright to take her on.

"I thought it was a great idea, I mean how many politicians would turn down cash … to Walid, the money I gave to Senator Wright was a drop in the bucket. I went to pick up the cash from Hesus, and Tim beat me to it. Hesus had to scramble to replace the money he lost," Liana explained.

"Liana, there's a ten-million-dollar bounty on Walid Hattab's head if you help us." When Cathleen said the words, Liana broke down sobbing and even Sarena could not console her.

"Is she that attached to Walid?"

"It was the words you used. A Chechen militia officer forced Liana to kill a Russian Colonel and bring his head back as proof, or I would be killed. She suffered terribly during the encounter."

"I'm sorry. I had no idea."

"Liana, what did you do during the war?" Jim asked.

"I killed … I was a sniper with hunter/killer teams. Each team consisted of a man with an AK-47, a man carrying RPG's and a sniper. We acted as an independent unit and could fight alone or in groups with other teams."

"And the others?" Cathleen asked.

"Dead … I believe I was in at least sixty hunter/killer teams. All those who fought with me died. We would go out and set up in a good location, and when the time was right I would shoot seven times, hitting as many of my friends as I could; then I would flee."

"Your friends, you mean the enemy?"

"I mean the Russian boys I grew up with. I may have even played with them in school. I really don't want to talk about it anymore. I still have terrible nightmares."

"Will you call Tim and his friends?" Cathleen asked. "We could have someone pick them up and bring them here?"

"You won't hurt them?"

"No, we won't hurt them." Liana looked at Sarena who nodded yes. Liana asked for a cell phone and Tim answered on the second ring.

"Tim, you're okay?" Tim described the shoot-out and escaping to his apartment.

"Stay there and don't leave."

"Sarena," Jim asked, "what was your thought on the war? Did you consider the war in Chechnya to be a holy war, a jihad?" he asked.

"Jihad does not mean holy war. It means struggle. If you're asking if we were fighting a holy war, then I would have to say the opposite. We were fighting an unholy war. My father-in-law knew our only chance in the war was to make a peace agreement with the Russians and to do so quickly. When Grozny fell, we knew all was lost. After Grozny fell we were on the run and fighting for our lives, but it was hopeless. As far as a holy war is concerned, we did what we are taught not to do. We killed. Our role as Chechen women was to be the peacemakers, to settle issues, and we failed and it's something Allah will hold us accountable for," Sarena explained.

"Do you plan at some point to return to Chechnya to fight?" Jim asked.

"No, I did all I could, and now we must attempt to salvage what is left of our lives and live again," Sarena answered.

"I will never pick up another rifle," Liana said, "even if it means my life."

"Perhaps my grandchildren will return to Chechnya when things are safe, but I will not. Chechnya," Sarena explained, "is now ruled to the extreme. Criminal drug gangs, you call them mafia, rule many areas. There are extreme Muslims, extreme nationalists, extreme socialists, extreme everything. There is no place for Liana or me in it."

***

Tim unpacked the food they bought. Bill sat down and tried to relax. Ken heard helicopters approaching and saw one land on the street.

"They're here!" he screamed and ran for his computer. He did not make it in time, and they found themselves surrounded by armed men in black jumpsuits. They handcuffed everyone, took their computers, and flew off.

"Do you think we'll end up at Gitmo?" Bill asked.

"We're heading west, not south; probably take us to Area 51."

"Oh great, we'll spend the rest of our lives decoding alien transmissions."

"Oh, let's go to the Hackers' convention. It's time to embrace the horror!"

"I can just imagine these guys sifting through all our computers," Ken said. "Pirated programs, homemade sniffer programs, code breaking programs -- we'll probably get life."

"I know what will happen if they try to go into Mr. Self Destruct," Bill said. "I hope I get a chance to warn the guys before they try and goof with it." Washington appeared ahead.

"Where do you think we're going?" Tim asked.

"I think were gonna end up at Langley, at least for now," Ken said.

"Langley?" Bill asked.

"CIA headquarters," Mark stated.

The helicopter landed on the roof of a building. Guards took them to separate rooms.

"If you know what's good for you, don't touch my computer," Bill screamed.

"What's in your computer, son, that you don't want anyone to see?" an agent asked.

Mark found himself waiting in a room. After a very long wait, the door opened and Cathleen and Jim entered.

"Do you want to tell us about Las Vegas?" Jim asked.

"You mean about the Hackers' convention ...?" Mark started to explain.

"We don't want to know about the Hackers' convention. We want to know about the equation."

"The equation?" Mark asked. Jim laid a blown-up picture taken from the surveillance camera in Las Vegas.

"This equation!" he screamed. Mark looked at the equation and seemed dumbfounded.

"What about it?" he asked.

"Why did you give the equation to Orman and where did you find out about it?"

"Orman … who's he?"

"The man standing next to you?" Jim played the videotape.

"Oh, that guy. He had an equation on his computer, and I explained to 'em that the equation was wrong."

"And?" Cathleen asked.

"I corrected the equation …."

"Do you know what the equation was?" Jim asked.

"It looked like nuclear theory to me, but I've never gotten into that." Jim and Cathleen seemed disgusted but decided to leave the room for now.

Steve Nayer was the man in charge of sifting through computer records and recovering deleted files at the CIA.

"That kid Bill," an agent said, "was worried in the worst way that we not look at his computer." The agent placed Bill's homemade computer on his desktop.

"That kid must have made this thing himself. What a pile of junk!" Steve walked over and looked at the computer.

"That computer is about as powerful as anything I've ever seen. The ram, the system board, even the video card are all prototypes." The agent plugged the computer in and a strange-looking screen came up asking for a password.

"Let me try the kid's birthday," the agent said.

"No!" Steve screamed as he ran across the room. At the first keystroke, a flaming skull appeared on the screen, and the skull began disintegrating. Smoke began pouring out of Mr. Self destruct, and the agent was convinced that the computer was really a bomb. Bill was sitting in a room when he heard the alarm go off.

*I guess they didn't believe me about Mr. Self Destruct!* The CIA evacuated the area, and bomb technicians studied "Mr. Self Destruct."

"It's not a bomb. The kid simply rigged the thing to destroy the hard drive if the wrong password was used. The program shut down the system fan. The chip and ram overheated, frying the board."

"And the hard drive?" the agent asked.

"It's totally cleansed," Steve explained. "An incorrect password started a program that completely erases and destroys the hard drive to DOD standards. It runs over and over again until the ram and system boards burn out. If I'm right, the hard drive will be as clean as fallen snow. Please, don't even look at the other computers, okay?"

Steve and Jim entered Ken's room and began firing questions back and forth at him.

"Can I get some Skittles?" Ken asked.

"Skittles, what are those? What did you have on your computer?" Jim asked.

"I don't know, some games ...."

Steve dumped a bag of hard drives on the desk.

"And these? Why have so many blank drives?"

"People are always trying to steal our stuff, so if we think someone might steal our stuff we switch hard drives and place a clean one in our computer." Jim and Steve left the room to talk.

Bill waited in a room for six hours, but no one entered. Late that evening Steve, the agent who destroyed his computer, and Jim entered the room.

"Do you want to tell us what you had on your computer before it burnt up?"

"You idiot, you goofed around with my computer after I warned you not to?"

"What was on the computer?" Jim screamed.

"I guess we'll never know now that your idiot fooled with it!"

"I want you to tell us everything," the agent told Bill.

"Everything?"

"Yes, all about how you met the other three and all that you've done." The agent got a tape recorder.

"I had gone to a park to meet Sarah, a girl I knew, and found Ken sitting at a picnic table ...," Bill explained.

"In Washington?"

"No, in Pennsylvania!"

"So you met in Pennsylvania and then traveled to Washington. Was this girl, this Sarah, at the meeting?"

"Yes."

"And Mark, how did he fit into this?"

"He was sitting at another table."

"And you three got together, why?" the agent asked.

"To play a game."

"And this game, what was it and why?" the agent asked.

"The game?"

"Yes, the game, the game...," the agent prompted.

"It's called the game of Life."

"This life game, you played it, why?"

"Because we didn't want to play softball ...."

"When did all this take place?" Steve asked grinning.

"Park program in second grade," Bill said. Steve began laughing hysterically; Jim could not keep from grinning either. The agent who had destroyed Bill's computer looked ill.

"That's all for now," Jim said and escorted everyone out of the room.

"Look," Jim said, "these kids are just a couple of hackers that get together and network. They have no idea what's going on, and they're convinced we're sending them to Area 51 to transcribe alien transmissions."

"Area 51," Cathleen asked, "where's that?"

"In the Nevada desert, but we don't send people there," Jim said.

"And Hesus's money?"

"A coincidence. Liana had showed them the Polish gaming site, and they thought it was interesting."

"Ali and Hesus?" she asked.

"They're out there, and we have to find them quickly," Jim said.

***

Orman finished constructing the bomb and now awaited the arrival of Ali.

*In a few days the attack at the Capitol will take place and the U.S. will be begging for peace ... just a few short days.*

Ali knew that their mission was really in Toronto and the money, and the kids who stole it, secondary. They flew into town on Hesus's Learjet and would fly out tomorrow morning. They checked into a small motel, as each needed a few hours to rest. The situation had not gone well in Washington.

At three in the morning Ali drove over to the bunker that Orman had refitted to create the bomb. He called Orman's phone.

"Orman, we are ready." He heard a small cheer go up, as the men were anxious to get above ground also. Orman unsealed the bunker, and Ali climbed down into the bunker with them. Orman showed Ali a small box.

"It is detonated by cell phone. With the red switch on, it is armed and awaiting your call."

"The destruction?"

"All in the building will die, some by the initial blast, the remainder by the radiation."

"We all need to pray," he said. Everyone knelt as they had every day since going underground; Ali was quick and shot all before they could arise. All three would have needed treatment for radiation and traced back to the bunker. He sealed the bunker shut with the bodies inside.

Ali drove to meet Hesus as the plan had to move forward like clockwork. Ali sat outside the motel, took his cell phone out and called.

"Walid, we have the package and I am in route."

"Ali, there may be a change of plans."

"What? A change?"

"Liana may have become too dangerous. I will contact you in route if I decide to go with plan B, but for now the mission goes on as planned."

Ali was not happy with the news but followed Walid's orders.

***

Liana felt Tim was now safe. The CIA supplied computers for the four and placed them in a small room.

"Look," Shawn said, "you have games; just don't try to contact anyone, okay? Hopefully this will all be cleared up soon." Shawn wasn't happy with guarding them, but it wasn't the worst duty either.

With the plot now understood, the CIA released Liana so as not to alert Ali. The CIA would intercept the bomb as it came into the United States. The CIA could not track Ali, but could track Hesus. They knew about his planned flight into Dulles Airport.

Liana returned to her apartment to await Ali. Very early in the morning she decided to go jogging and ran down the path she always took. Liana knew the CIA was watching her and saw a woman jogging behind her. Today she ran along the river and ended up at a coffee shop.

She ordered a cup of coffee and began reading a newspaper. She heard a voice that sounded familiar, looked and saw a very pretty girl walking with an older man. Liana sat shaking like a leaf. Margrite and Congressman Stevens stood on the street corner. Ali had explained to her that he had killed Margrite and dumped her body in the ocean; she looked alive enough to Liana.

Liana sat in the coffee shop desperately trying to decide what to do.

*Had Walid sent a second girl to deliver a bomb, in case I didn't? Is Walid going to set off two separate bombs? I'd better call Cathleen. The problem is time! Where is the woman who was tailing me?*

Liana dialed her phone, but Cathleen did not pick it up. She tried Jim's phone and got no response either. In desperation, she called Bob Winslow.

"Hello?"

"Bob, I need to get Cathleen immediately!"

"She's showering I'll get her."

"Liana, what's wrong!" Cathleen screamed over the phone.

"Margrite, a Russian girl I worked with at the hotel, is on the street with Congressman Stevens. Ali told me he had killed her, but she's here and alive."

"And you think she might be someone Walid planted here also? Liana head straight to the agency, this is moving so fast that I can't keep track of it." Liana found a cab and headed over to Langley.

***

Hesus got dressed to fly to Dulles Airport. He had a strange premonition of danger this morning, and felt very uneasy. Hesus tried to choke the feeling down, but today it would not go away.

*Something is very wrong, but I must complete the task at hand ... I have never feared smuggling diamonds before ....* Ali stopped to pick up

Hesus.

"Hesus, are you ready?"

"A change of plans. We take my hidden Cessna or we don't go." Ali was furious and called Walid.

"Walid, we have the package and we are ready to leave, but Hesus says we must take his Cessna instead of his Learjet, and the Cessna will take longer. He says he has a bad feeling. We change our plans based on his feelings?"

"Hesus has met death and survived more times than anyone I know. Take the Cessna and deliver the package to Margrite. If we cannot work with Margrite, then kill her and give it to Liana." They boarded the Cessna for the trip.

"Ali, I usually don't need to know, but it is diamonds we're hauling, right?" Hesus asked.

"Yes, of course," Ali said.

***

At CIA headquarters Cathleen, Sarena and Liana sat in a room trying to follow the morning's events. Tom Eberly hoped to catch Hesus and Ali when they boarded his Learjet. Cathleen's team found Congressman Stevens, and he admitted Margrite was his secret lover. They searched her apartment downtown but didn't find her.

Bill, Ken, Mark and Tim seemed happy enough to be using the computers the CIA had lent them and were getting along with Shawn. The guys nearly drove Shawn insane at first, but he had warmed up to them. Cathleen and Liana waited to hear news of Hesus's capture at his Learjet.

"Cathleen, I do not mind if Hesus and Ali are imprisoned, but you must promise they won't be killed. I have enough blood on my hands."

"I can only promise that we will try our best."

"Walid Hattab?" Liana asked.

"As planned, we have a team ready to capture him in Somalia when you contact him."

Liana nervously sat.

*If this fails thousands will die and I can do nothing to stop it. If things go bad, Momma and I will be in great danger.*

Liana looked over and saw Cathleen praying using prayer beads.

"Cathleen, are you Muslim?"

"I'm Catholic. This is a Rosary, but it would help if we all prayed."

The three women, two Muslim and one Catholic, knelt on the floor praying and asking for God's help, as everything was beyond their control. They waited, hoping to hear something as the time ticked away. Finally, after one of the longest waits Cathleen had ever encountered, James Burrett came downstairs.

"I think we have a lead on them. We have men waiting at Hesus's

Learjet." A few moments later Jim received a phone call and felt his knees buckle under him.

"Cathleen, Hesus and Ali never arrived at the Learjet."

***

"What is that up ahead?" Ali asked as they flew.

"Lake Erie," Hesus said.

"Is that a parachute under your seat?" Ali asked.

"It's a low level stunt parachute. I've been forced to use them many times to avoid capture."

"It won't do you any good over the water," Ali said.

"The water frightens you?"

"I can't swim," Ali admitted.

"We cross the lake and then New York State and Pennsylvania," Hesus explained. He had flown missions like this for some thirty years now and had spent countless hours in planes. He remembered when he first started flying planes, as those were similar to this one.

Hesus saw Niagara Falls under him and Buffalo, New York, to his left. He turned to grab a drink out of the cooler behind him and saw two jets flying very quickly straight at him. He recognized the jets immediately as F-22 A Raptors, and he saw they were armed.

"Diamonds, hell," he screamed at Ali. "What do you have in that box?" The jets were now whizzing back and forth around the Cessna. Hesus had no choice but to follow the instructions given.

"Cessna," the F-22 pilot called over the radio, "turn immediately and follow us down!" He looked down and saw a military base almost below him.

Ali produced a pistol from his coat and held it to Hesus's head.

"Hesus, do not land!" Hesus had no intention of landing, but he wasn't an idiot either. He quickly dove low over Buffalo, New York. He knew he had a few seconds, as the pilots would not fire over a large city without receiving orders.

"What now?" Ali asked. Hesus's move was so sudden and so unexpected that it caught him off guard. Hesus pointed his plane back toward the lake and set the plane on autopilot. In one smooth move, he slid into the parachute and bailed out of the plane.

The chute opened immediately. He saw the Cessna gliding toward the lake. In seconds he was on the ground in Buffalo, New York.

***

"They found them. They're in a Cessna at the border," Jim told Cathleen as he listened to unfiltered radio communications. "Someone bailed out of the plane into Buffalo, New York … the plane crashed into Lake Erie …."

Sarena, Liana, Cathleen and Jim awaited word on the plane and the incident.

"If the press gets hold of this ...," Jim said shaking his head. "The Navy dispatched divers at the crash site .... someone is dead inside the plane."

"Who did they find in the plane?" Cathleen screamed.

"A dark-skinned man ...."

"Cuban, Arab, Pakistani ... what?" Cathleen asked.

"They're searching the sunken plane now."

"Who was on the plane?" Cathleen asked.

"They found the bomb!" Jim stated. "The body on the plane ... I.D says it's Ali."

Liana felt the world lifted off her shoulders. The fact that Hesus had escaped did not worry her, as he was in this for the money, not some fanatical cause.

"More blood on my hands ...," Liana said.

"Liana, Ali could have surrendered. He chose not to," Sarena said.

"I know, but the blood is still on my hands," Liana said. "Cathleen has this hit the press yet?"

"The press knows that a small plane went down in Lake Erie, but they know little else."

"Then Walid does not know about the plane crash yet? Cathleen, you said you have a team waiting in the Somalia? Walid will not be harmed?"

"You're concerned about harming a man who has killed countless?" Jim asked.

"She doesn't want any more blood on her hands," Sarena said, "and neither do I."

"Liana, we have a team, and if possible we will capture Walid, but I cannot guarantee he will not be harmed," Cathleen explained. Liana looked at her mother, and Sarena nodded yes.

"And if Walid calls me back you can pinpoint where he is?" Liana asked.

"Yes, to within one yard," Cathleen said, pointing to video screens on the wall.

Liana picked up her cell phone and called a long distance number. She got a recording.

"Walid," she screamed in Arabic, "I have the package. Ali was captured. I do not have final instructions. Please call in person so I know my mother will be safe." Liana laid the phone down. A few moments later Liana's phone rang, and she picked it up.

"Liana, proceed immediately as instructed. Once the package is delivered and switched on, dial 555-3125."

"Walid," she said trying to keep him on the phone as long as possible, "what about my mother?"

"Your mother is on her way to Cyprus. The Russians freed her this morning. Now do exactly as instructed."

"Walid, I will fly to Cyprus tonight?"

"Yes, I will have someone waiting for you at the airport, but you must complete your mission now!"

"I will hang up now and proceed on my mission, but you must be available if I need further instructions." She hung up the phone and stared at Cathleen.

"Cathleen, do you have him or not?" Liana asked. Cathleen was on the phone, and people were frantically running around the office. The video screen showed nothing.

"Liana," Jim said a few moments later, "I am sorry, but we pinpointed Walid in the Sudan, not in Somalia as thought. Liana, in ten minutes we need you to call Walid one more time."

"Will Walid be harmed?"

"I won't lie to you. He will not survive," Jim said as the video screen came alive.

"If I allow Walid to die, then I have blood on my hands. If I allow him to live, then I will have even more blood on my hands. It's never over, is it?" After waiting, she picked up her cell phone and called the number.

"Walid, I am in the Capitol but something is up. They have guards everywhere and are searching everyone. I need to know what to do before I am caught."

"Liana, turn the switch on, and I will take things from there. Do it now!"

"I am no fool. Tell me my mother will be cared for, and I will turn on the switch."

"Liana, I prom ...." Walid's phone went dead, and Liana could see a white flash on the video screen. Everyone in the room cheered after seeing the flash and hearing the phone go dead. Sarena and Liana did not cheer.

"Tell me that wasn't a vacuum bomb?" Liana asked. "Momma and I saw those with our own eyes. I wouldn't want that on a rat."

"A cruise missile."

"It's done?" Liana asked. Cathleen sadly nodded.

"Liana, we have Margrite in custody. She's downstairs."

"And?"

"She does not seem to know anything about Walid or the plot. She did know Ali but said he was threatening her family. He found out that Congressman Stevens had a thing for her and felt she would be useful. Ali felt that Margrite would be an insurance policy in case things did not work in the future. He told her that if she kept Congressman Stevens happy, her family would not be harmed, and she did as he asked. Margrite's role was evidently to keep in close contact with Congressman Stevens and if possible to get into the Capitol with him, and that was it. As of now we are not going to charge her with any crimes," Cathleen explained.

"Can I see her?" Liana asked.

"Not now, perhaps when everything settles down."

"And Tim?"

"I think you can see Tim." Sarena walked up to Cathleen.

"Cathleen, your water broke, your baby …." Cathleen looked horrified because somewhere in all the excitement she had not noticed.

"Cathleen, you need to lie down." An ambulance sped her to the hospital where Bob met her. She delivered a baby girl that evening, and they named their little girl Megan.

***

"What now?" Liana asked Jim.

"For now, until things completely settle down, we need you to remain here." Over the next few days, Jim and two other agents questioned Liana and Sarena about their activities in Russia, Chechnya and Afghanistan. Jim wanted to know specifically how Walid found Liana in Pakistan and about his safe house in Saudi Arabia. She explained about the cash payments to Senator Wright and her apartment. The questioning was neither heated nor stressful for Liana or Sarena, and they answered each question.

On their third day at the agency, Margrite joined them in their room. Margrite was very happy that everything was over but seemed very frightened of returning to Russia.

"The government in Russia will not understand," she explained.

"Margrite, do not fret. I think things will work out. They usually do," Sarena explained. "In the meantime we have books to read, a small gym to use and …."

"And nice, good-looking young men to flirt with," Margrite joked.

"I just hope Tim is okay," Liana said.

***

Tom Eberly walked downstairs where Shawn and the guys were holed up.

"The agency has decided against charging any of you, but I have no idea why," Tom explained. "Somehow you managed to involve yourself with known terrorists, drug smugglers, renegade nuclear scientists and God knows who else, but they say it's all innocent. The money you picked up was drug money, so we confiscated it." They nodded, as they wanted out as quickly as they could. "You're free to go, but whatever you do, don't do something this stupid again on my watch, okay?" The four drove away in a rental car, unsure as to who they would tell their tale to or who would believe them if they did.

***

After being off for seven days, Cathleen stopped by the agency to check on Liana, Sarena and Margrite.

"Liana, I'm sorry, but Tim is no longer here. They released him yesterday," Cathleen explained. "We need to talk and discuss the situation." James Burrett joined them in the room.

"Due to national security," Jim described, "we have decided that the entire episode of the last three weeks never occurred. There was no bomb, there was no crisis at the Capitol, and there was no incident. We released the story that a plane carrying drugs was intercepted crossing the border from Canada into the United States and that the pilot of the plane bailed out and was never found. Margrite has asked for political asylum and has been granted it due to the unstable political climate of the region. We are putting her into the witness protection program so she can start a new life."

"I won't have to go back to Russia?" Margrite asked.

"No, you won't have to go back," Cathleen said.

"What about Liana and I?"

"Sarena, you already have been granted political asylum and a general amnesty, and Liana has been granted the same." Liana, unsure of what to do and not wanting the others to understand, talked to Sarena in Latin.

"Momma, can we trust them?" Liana saw Jim and Cathleen's eyes brighten up when she asked the question. It had never occurred to her that the two might understand Latin.

"You know Latin?" Sarena asked.

"We're both Catholic, and Latin was required in high school," Jim said. Sarena shook her head in disbelief.

"Liana," Cathleen said, "you can trust me, and I want you two to be at church with me when Megan is baptized, if your faith will allow it." Liana relaxed and felt that she could trust her.

"What you need to realize is the panic that would have occurred if news that a nuclear bomb, even a tiny one, had ever entered the United States," Jim said.

"That's why we had to keep this quiet," Cathleen added. "No one in the agency, or the government, had ever thought of the possibility of a pretty, blond-haired blue-eyed Muslim terrorist. I mean, we expected middle-aged Arab men. Liana, we want you and your mother to go into witness protection also. We will provide you with new names, a good job, housing, money and cars, and you will be safe."

"Can my mother and I talk alone for a few moments?" Liana asked. They went out of the room for a few minutes and talked before returning.

"Cathleen, my mother and I thank you for your concern about us and we understand your thoughts, but we must reject your offer. Ever since I was little I have had to be someone I am not and have had to call myself names that are not my own. My mother and I have had to hide in basements, been under siege in crumbling cities, in huts, in the forest, and in caves in the mountains. We have had to be everything that we hated and yet endured, which is what Chechen women do," she explained.

"What Liana is saying," Sarena said, "is that we want to live openly and be who we are, not what others tell us to be. We have endured everything, and we are still here. Cathleen, Liana and I survived many years of attacks by the Russian army. We survived being attacked by fellow Chechens. We survived the Wahabbi militia, the CDF, hit squads, Cossack guerillas, the Dagestanies, the Afghan Eastern alliance, the Taliban .... Liana even survived an attack by your special forces. We will survive here."

"You survived all that?" Cathleen asked, stunned

"We only wish to live our lives quietly in peace," Liana said.

"When you make a knife out of steel," Sarena said, "you take something steel that you have and you heat it very hot and you hammer the hot steel until it forms the shape you want it to be." Cathleen did not understand Sarena's words and stared blankly.

"When you are done, you have a knife that's harder, sharper and more beautiful than the one you started with," Liana explained. "Chechen women are made of this steel."

"Where will you live then?" Cathleen asked.

"In Ocean City, Maryland," Liana explained. "We can find a small house, and my mother will find meaningful work in the area, hopefully as a nurse or at least a nurse's aide. I hope to return to school and become a teacher someday."

"We can grow a garden, and in time the horrors of the war will be softened in our minds," Sarena explained. "If things go well, I may try to go to medical school also. On the evenings, we can drive to the beach and watch the waves, allow our minds to rest and forget all we have known ...."

"And Tim?" Cathleen asked.

"Tim?" Sarena asked.

"I have a boyfriend."

"A Muslim?" Sarena asked. Liana shook her head no. She pointed to her neck where she still wore the tiny cross Sarena had given her to try and prove she was Russian.

"He thinks I'm Russian," she said. Sarena rolled her eyes.

## HOME

"Momma, I rented a tiny home just outside town. It has two bedrooms; the back yard has a tire swing and a large vegetable garden. The garden's weedy but has red tomatoes hanging on the vines. Cantaloupes and small watermelons are growing, and some are ripe and some green. We can take the bus to it, it's just off the highway."

They rode the bus over. Sarena walked inside and loved it immediately.

"Is it expensive?" Sarena asked.

"No, it's cheap and, Momma, I want to take you food shopping!"

"What day is the market open here?" Sarena asked. Liana just giggled. They took the bus east to a Food Lion.

"It's open today?" Sarena asked.

"Momma, it never closes."

Sarena followed Liana into the store, and her jaw dropped as she saw the amount of food the store stocked. Liana took Sarena through displays of fruits and vegetables that defied her imagination.

"This is a real papaya, and coconuts too, all the fruit you're ever heard of," Liana said. They decided to spend as little as possible for now, as it would be a while until money began to flow in. The women bought tea, rice, dried beans, dried peas, flour and salt. Sarena thought it extravagant but bought bananas, lettuce and cucumbers. They found a display of cheap vegetable seeds and bought leaf lettuce, cabbage, green beans, beets, cucumbers, and radish seeds.

"Liana," Sarena asked, "did I dress strange?"

"Momma, you look fine, why?"

"Because all the men keep staring at me."

"They're staring at you because you're pretty. Men do that here," Liana said. "Momma, I bought one other thing." She held up a small tube of brown hair dye. "I want you to wash the gray out of your hair; you're too young for that."

They returned home and decided to tackle the garden. The garden soil was sandy and easy to work. They carefully hoed away as much of the weeds as possible, since they didn't want to hurt the tomatoes or other vegetables already growing.

"Momma, I invited Tim over for dinner, to celebrate moving in."

"Tim is coming over?" Sarena said, frantically looking around the house. Liana took her mother by the hand.

"Momma, it's okay. Just relax. The house is fine."

"Liana, can we afford all of this, the house, the food, the bus passes ...?"

"Money will be tight, but we will manage. Momma, I saved almost two thousand dollars working this summer; we have that to fall back on. I have much to explain to Tim, and I don't know if he will stay with me or not after I have explained things to him."

Tim came by, and Liana introduced him to Sarena.

"Liana, I was worried when I got arrested that I might not see you again."

"Tim, I survived years of combat. I killed many men. I am not Russian ...."

***

Liana began work at the hotel again, and Sarena took a job at a local nursing home. For now she worked as a nurse's aide and was happy to be helping people again. On the third week at work she heard a woman trying to talk to her nurse in Chechen.

"She does this sometimes, and no one can understand what she is saying."

"She's talking in Chechen and she's concerned that no one is caring for her puppy," Sarena explained.

"The nursing home has a dog, and the residents feed it treats from time to time," the nurse explained.

"We fed the puppy this morning. She is fine," Sarena explained to the woman. The woman seemed relieved and went to sleep. That afternoon the woman's daughter stopped by to see her, and the nurses referred her to Sarena.

"You know Chechen?"

"Yes."

"You're Muslim?"

"Yes, I'm Muslim." As it turned out, a small community of Muslims had left Chechnya before the war and had settled in the area. The group was not only Muslim but also Sufists like herself.

"We would like you to come and visit us." Sarena promised that she would.

Cathleen Hale stopped to visit six weeks after her baby was born.

"This is Megan; I want you to come to her baptism this Sunday, if it doesn't conflict with your beliefs."

"We do not believe in baptism, but there isn't anything that says we can't come and witness it," Liana said.

"Liana, I have a much larger issue to discuss with you, and I didn't know if it was a good time or not." Liana and Sarena tensed up, as they didn't know what she might have to say.

"Have you two been able to manage on your own so far? I mean, are you keeping your heads above water financially?"

"Yes, we've been able to even save a little; I was hoping to start classes at community college this spring."

"Liana, remember there was a reward for Walid, dead or alive?"

"Yes."

"The money is to go to you!" Liana did not seem impressed with the knowledge.

"Momma and I need to talk." Liana and Sarena went into the bedroom for a few moments and then reappeared.

"Cathleen, thank you for the consideration of the money, but to Liana and I it's blood money, and we think it should be given away."

"Given away?"

"Yes, give it to the Crescent."

"The Crescent?" Cathleen asked.

"The Red Crescent, you call it the Red Cross. Let the blood spilled be used to give aid to someone else."

"Sarena, I was able to get your certification from Russia, and the Maryland authorities say that if you pass the nursing exam you can work as a nurse."

"I will have to study hard to pass the exam."

"Liana, you mentioned going to community college this spring? Sarena, you talked of going on to medical school? The agency has a scholarship program, and I could put both of you in, if you would accept it." Liana and Sarena disappeared back into the bedroom for a moment and reappeared.

"We'd love to," Sarena said.

On a warm October morning Liana, Tim and Sarena were standing outside a Catholic church in Washington. Cathleen, her husband Bob, Tom Eberly, Shawn and James Burrett arrived. Sarena and Liana covered their heads with light scarves and followed Cathleen inside the church. They listened first to the message the priest gave and then watched Megan's baptism. Cathleen had everyone over for a light meal afterwards at her Georgetown home.

***

As promised Sarena and Liana took the bus to Snow Hill, Maryland, to meet with other Chechen women, as Sarena understood that several lived there. She had no idea what to expect but was shocked to find a group of almost thirty women waiting for her and Liana. In the yard nearby a group of twenty Chechen men had gathered to talk.

"Please," the women asked Sarena, "tell us everything that is happening in Chechnya." Sarena, Liana and the group sat drinking Chia tea, eating small cookies and talking. One woman stood in back and just stared.

"Sarena?" Sarena turned but had no idea who she was looking at.

"Sarena, I'm Amanta Katsa, Elisa's sister. My husband and I live here now." Sarena and Liana remembered meeting her in the mountains of Chechnya.

"I'm sorry to be staring, Aunt Sarena, but everyone thought you and Liana were dead."

"Everyone?" Sarena asked.

"My mother said that you were killed in an explosion."

"Zara is alive?" Liana asked.

"Yes! Zara's living with Elisha and Valid on their farm."

"And your father?" Sarena asked. She shook her head no.

"Sarena," Amanta said, "we made Chechen food for all to enjoy." Sarena was thrilled to see Chechen dishes she had as a child.

"Puluu," Sarena said taking a scoop of rice and raisins.

"Momma, what is this?"

"It's zhilzhig-gala, like meat, dumplings and garlic"

"And this?"

"This is xingal'a," Amanta said. "It is scone with sweet pumpkin jelly. Didn't your mother remember to feed you?"

"We ate Russian food," Liana said, "when we could get it." Amanta, Sarena, Liana and the other women talked until late in the afternoon.

"We must go soon," Liana said, "or miss our bus."

"Sarena, will you come for prayers on Friday?"

"Yes, of course."

"Aminia is our Imam, and she lectures to us on Friday afternoons, just before prayers."

## EPILOGUE

Hesus Rodriguez had settled into his villa on the Cayman Islands. As a measure of goodwill he and his lawyer agreed to talk with the CIA at his home.

"About the incident, we would like to hear your version of the events, off the record," the agent asked.

"I understood we were carrying conflict diamonds into Washington, or I wouldn't have agreed to fly Ali in. How is Ali?"

"He died in the wreck, drowned."

"And Ali's package?"

"Well, let's just say it wasn't diamonds."

"My contacts tell me that Walid Hattab is dead also, a guided missile attack?" The agents stared at him and said nothing.

"And me?" Hesus asked.

"Hesus, live a long life. Just don't ever enter the United States again." Hesus nodded that he understood.

"And the girl and the money?" he asked.

"The girl and the money never existed."

***

Tom Eberly retired as he said he would. He found a home he liked in northern Wisconsin, where he fished. With Tom retired, Shawn took over his position.

***

Cathleen Hale and James Burnett remained at the CIA and went about their normal duties.

"Cathleen," Jim said, "Liana was correct about Walid Hattab having a contact in the agency."

"He did?"

"We were able to decode a series of transmissions to Walid and traced it back to an agent."

"An agent, who?"

"Mark Haskings."

"The man I replaced? Why would he help Walid?"

"He had gambling debts that he had to pay off or else …." Cathleen just shook her head in disbelief.

***

Bill, Mark and Ken all returned to school that fall. The CIA had offered Mark a position decoding transmissions when he graduated; Mark declined the offer as he hoped to teach history someday. Ken returned to California as he hoped to find a career editing movies, and Bill returned to Penn State. The three decided that, for safety's sake, they would meet at Bill's apartment this winter to network their computers. If Tim wished he could come and join them.

***

With the beach vacant of summer guests, Liana's work as a maid ended, so she went to work at Wal-Mart. Sarena worked as a nurse, and the pay was better. Sarena would begin studying medicine at the University of Delaware in the spring.

Tim had asked Liana for some time to reflect on all she had told him. It made no difference to him that Liana was a Chechen Muslim, rather than Russian, but her stories of combat disturbed him. He finally decided that his past, and hers, were something they would both have to deal with. They remained very close. At his insistence Liana enrolled at the University of Delaware and he transferred his credits to the same school.

"Liana, it would make much more sense if we all drove back and forth together," he said. The University was about a fifty-minute drive from Liana's home. She liked the idea.

On warm autumn evenings, Liana and Sarena would sometimes ride the bus to the beach and walk on the boardwalk together. Sometimes the two would kick off their shoes and run on the warm sand.

They loved sitting on the benches overlooking the ocean and just staring out over the waves. Looking out over the water helped them to forget the horrors of the war they had fought in and that had cost them so many friends on both sides. Liana had been sleeping well since Sarena had arrived, and if Sarena held anger toward anyone, Russian or Chechen, she never expressed it.

They would sometimes sit side by side for three or four hours just staring out across the open ocean and not saying anything. The waves helped to heal both of their minds, and it seemed the salt water acted as a tonic on their souls. Tonight after sitting for the longest time, Liana reached down and squeezed Sarena's hand.

"Momma, thank you for being here with me. I love you."

"I love you too, Liana." Both Liana and Sarena sat staring out into the Blue Ocean's Peace.

**About the Author**

Walt is an avid hunter, fisherman and gatherer who has journeyed to the remotest regions of the country. He began traveling around the country at the age of fourteen, often hitchhiking to his destination.

Walt's travels, encounters, and memories are often the inspiration for his writing. His novels THE BEACHCOMBER AND THE CABIN relate to portions of his life and the people he interacted with. His novel THE BLUE OCEAN'S PEACE describes a Muslim Chechen girl who grew up fighting the Russians before being sent on an assignment in the United States. Tiny, blond haired and blue eyed she will raise no suspicions. Walt lives in Lancaster, Pa. with his wife and two children. He still loves to travel and spends his free time hunting, fishing and writing.

Breinigsville, PA USA
11 April 2010

235909BV00001B/8/P